IMPOSSIBLE LOVE?

Ginny came out of the living room. "Oh, there you are! I was getting worried. We're all invited to dinner and I didn't know where to reach you. Have you a nice evening dress?"

Elinor laughed softly. "Are you plotting to introduce me to another perfectly *mar*-velous man?"

"Oh, you couldn't marry him, I'm sorry to say. Mr. Sewell married a girl named Mary and they have a son."

Turning her back on her sister-in-law, Elinor blinked away dimness. Why, they were tears! She brushed them away hastily. How ridiculous. There was nothing to cry for.

He married a girl named Mary and they have a little boy.

Queer that no one had mentioned Mrs. Stephen Sewell or the child. What difference does it make? Elinor asked herself sternly. She did not try to find the answer.

D1416198

Bantam Books by Emile Loring
Ask your bookseller for the books you have missed

EMILIE LORING

THROW WIDE
THE DOOR

BANTAM BOOKS · TORONTO · NEW YORK · LONDON

*This low-priced Bantam Book
has been completely reset in a type face
designed for easy reading, and was printed
from new plates. It contains the complete
text of the original hard-cover edition.*
NOT ONE WORD HAS BEEN OMITTED.

THROW WIDE THE DOOR

*A Bantam Book / published by arrangement with
Little, Brown and Company*

PRINTING HISTORY

Little, Brown edition published January 1962
Grosset & Dunlap edition published February 1963
Bantam edition / March 1965

2nd printing	July 1965	6th printing	August 1967
3rd printing	September 1965	7th printing	June 1968
4th printing	September 1966	8th printing	November 1968
5th printing	November 1966	9th printing	May 1969
	10th printing	May 1970	

New Bantam edition / July 1975

Published simultaneously in the United States and Canada

*Bantam Books are published by Bantam Books, Inc. Its trade-
mark, consisting of the words "Bantam Books" and the por-
trayal of a bantam, is registered in the United States Patent
Office and in other countries. Marca Registrada. Bantam
Books, Inc., 666 Fifth Avenue, New York, New York 10019.*

PRINTED IN THE UNITED STATES OF AMERICA

I

The girl in the paint-stained smock stood back to look at the woman whose portrait she was to finish this morning. Pale wintry sunshine filtered through the skylight and the big north window and fell on the face of the woman who sat in a high-backed chair raised on a slight platform at one end of the studio.

The light picked out mercilessly the lines of discontent around the mouth, of querulous annoyance around the eyes. Heavily ringed hands rested on the carved arms of the chair. Her head was tilted back to display the heavy string of pearls around her sagging throat. A low-cut green satin evening dress revealed the overweight body and the thick bare arms, weighted down with bracelets. Expensive as the evening dress was, it looked tawdry in the light of day. The bare arms had gooseflesh.

Elinor Parks smothered a grin of amusement. Mrs. Halstead had insisted on wearing evening dress for her portrait, though Elinor had warned her that the Greenwich Village studio was heated only by a fireplace.

"But I can't," Mrs. Halstead had drawled, "wear enough jewelry with day clothes to be really impressive."

Certainly the woman had plenty of jewelry: pearls at her throat, diamonds on her fingers, rubies and aquamarines on her wrists. A lavish display but a tasteless one.

Elinor, mixing colors on her palette, reminded herself sharply that she was lucky to have this commission.

If she could do a few portraits that sold—and Mrs. Halstead had promised to show her work to a circle of friends—she would be able to justify to herself the money her brother Clay had so generously spent on her art education and on rent for the studio.

"Though why," he had said, puzzled, "you want to live in a place like this when you could be in Hastings, I simply don't know."

Seeing the studio through Clay's fastidious eyes, she could understand his viewpoint. Except for the big north window, there was little light in the room. A fireplace provided all the warmth, even on a winter day, but Elinor had refused an electric heater. Clay had done so much for her already.

"It's not cold at all," she had assured him, her larkspur eyes shining with her earnestness. "And a fireplace is so much more cozy. I like it."

She had done her best to conquer the bleakness of the studio, to transform it into a home. The couch, on which she slept at night, was covered with bright chintz and piled high with pillows. An old bridge table had been painted a gay blue and held pumpkin-colored pottery dishes. She had bought them in a bargain basement, but they made her lonely meals seem more festive. In a tall vase she had bronze chrysanthemums. An extravagance, she knew, but she would rather spend less money for food and have this beauty in the room with her.

She looked at the woman on the raised model stand; the brush followed her bidding in a long bold stroke, and then she stepped back.

"It's finished, Mrs. Halstead."

Her voice shook with a combined sense of achievement and doubt. Would Mrs. Halstead like it? It was so desperately important.

Mrs. Halstead got stiffly out of her chair. She moved, Elinor thought mischievously, as though she were launching a battleship. She gathered up her long rustling skirt and came to look at the canvas.

A minute passed that seemed as long as a year. Another minute. Elinor stole a look at the woman's face. It was like a thundercloud. Her heart sank in dismay. What was wrong? It was a good portrait—the best she had ever done. She stood looking from the woman to the canvas and back again.

"Don't you like it?" she asked, unable to control a slight quaver in her voice.

Slowly Mrs. Halstead turned around, her face congested with fury. She looked at the slim girl who was so lovely, so vivid. At the larkspur eyes with their long lashes that swept her cheeks. At the dark hair that framed the eager face with its soft lips and brilliant eyes.

"Do you expect me, for one single instant to pay for that—that caricature?" Mrs. Halstead's voice was shrill with fury.

"But what's wrong?" Elinor faltered, while her world fell to pieces around her. There was going to be no check, no money for all the work she had done.

"Anyone would think I was forty!" Mrs. Halstead stormed.

But you're fifty, at least, Elinor thought.

"You've given me a—fretful sort of expression, and all my friends talk about my disposition."

Elinor bit her lips. I'll bet they do, she thought, and for a moment she was so near laughing that some of the disappointment faded away.

"It isn't what I want. That's all there is to it."

"Perhaps I could make changes, improve it," Elinor said quickly. "Please let me try, Mrs. Halstead."

"Do you think I'd like my friends to see that kind of picture of me? Never. I don't want it, Miss Parks, and I refuse to pay for it. And, what's more, I shall certainly tell my friends that your work is totally unsatisfactory."

She put on a long mink coat, pulled elbow-length white gloves over her ringed hands and went out of the studio, banging the door behind her.

Elinor put down the palette and began to clean her brushes, working automatically.

"When your thoughts are in a turmoil," her Aunt Maggie had once told her, "keep your hands busy and work it out. But don't feel sorry for yourself and don't let yourself be panicked."

She put away the painting paraphernalia, stood the canvas against the wall and folded the easel, face set, grimly absorbed in her task. Then she began to shiver as reaction set in.

She dropped a shovel of coal into the fireplace and sat down in her only easy chair, bought at a secondhand shop on Third Avenue. She had repaired the broken springs herself and done the upholstery. It looked almost as good as new, if she remembered not to sit on the arms, which had a tendency to fall off.

For a long time she stared into the fire, oppressed by a sense of failure. But, she told herself, it was a good portrait. I know it was good. I didn't fail at that. Only —only—what was a painter to do if the subject was ugly and wanted to appear beautiful?

She got up and walked restlessly around the room. She had counted on the five hundred dollars from Mrs. Halstead. There were only two hundred dollars left in the bank and she didn't want to call on her brother again for help. Even with self-denial, two hundred dollars wouldn't last long. Not that Clay would mind. But there was Ginny, Clay's wife, who minded a great deal and made no secret of it.

The day Elinor had left her brother's house in Hastings, the house that had been her home, the house in which she had been born, to take a studio in Greenwich Village, Ginny had come to help her pack. This had been unexpected enough. Ginny usually demanded that people help *her;* she did not offer her services. She stood beside Elinor as the latter folded dresses and sweaters and hose, stacking them on her bed.

"I'm glad you've seen the light," she said in the little-girl voice that made her seem so helpless, so endearing. "I began to wonder whether you'd ever make the move. Of course, I know, in a way it's your home, too, but that old saying about no house being big enough for two women is certainly true." Her big hazel eyes swept over Elinor's flushed face.

It would have been easy for Elinor to say: *But the house and the money were left to me as well as to Clay. I turned everything over to him so he could start his own law firm because I knew how much it mattered to him to be independent, because I wanted him to be happy.*

It had been difficult to persuade her brother to accept the offer. Eventually, he had done so only on the tacit understanding that the house would be her home always and that he would be responsible for her support.

It did not occur to the stunned girl to justify herself. She was conscious only of the fact that, unwittingly, she had caused difficulty for Clay, that she had been unwanted.

"I didn't know," she said huskily. "I didn't realize I was in the way."

"Of course not, dear," Ginny said sweetly. "How could you? So immersed in your—career. When Clay and I were first married I thought you'd be getting married yourself before long. Goodness knows I've introduced some of the most *mar*velous men to you. But no one seems to suit you, or . . ." This time the malice in the hazel eyes was clear to read.

"Or I don't suit anyone," Elinor finished for her. "Well, I'm moving out now, Ginny, and I'll stay in New York."

"New York," Ginny echoed wistfully. "All the lights and the excitement, the theaters and the wonderful shops, the restaurants and the night clubs. You don't know how lucky you are to be getting out of this sleepy dump and having New York instead! If only Clay would see the light and move to the city. What heaven! Well, I suppose if you marry a small-town boy you have to expect to live in a small-town way."

Small town? Clay? A Yale graduate, with a year of foreign travel behind him. A cultivated mind, the perfect but unstressed manners of all the Parks men, an honorable man who loved his wife profoundly. What on earth did Ginny want of life? Excitement, apparently. Empty, meaningless excitement.

"You're so used to Hastings you don't know what you've been missing," Ginny said. "When you come back here from New York—"

"I won't be coming back," Elinor said shortly.

And she hadn't meant to. Not ever. Not even her love for the gracious old white-pillared Colonial house set in its lovely grounds in the New England village of Hastings had drawn her back. Not even her devotion to her older brother Clay, who had tried to take the place of the parents who had died while she was still a child. Not even her deep love for the peace and quiet and beauty of the country as opposed to the noise and clutter and nervous excitement of the city.

She had thought that Greenwich Village was a romantic place where painters and sculptors, poets and playwrights gathered, where there would be other young people like herself with whom she could share her interests. Instead, she had found it half slum, half shoddy night clubs and noisy bars. This was not her world. The months she had spent in New York City had, consequently, been lonely ones, for she had little in common with the people she had met there.

She walked to the small window that opened on the street. Here and there were still traces of the winter storm, blackened snow in ugly heaps. She thought of wide fields of pure white, sparkling in the sunlight, of a place where the air was clear and tangy, where there was no sound but the scrunch of frozen snow under the feet of some solitary walker through the woods.

Below her there was a sudden uproar. Two little boys were pummeling each other, rolling in the gutter almost under an oncoming truck, while their mothers shrieked belligerently at each other and made no attempt to control their children. Elinor shivered with disgust. Why was she here? She didn't belong here.

She saw a familiar figure walk out of her building and go into the next one. The mailman. She ran down the rickety, uncarpeted stairs and unlocked her box. There was only one letter, an official-looking notice from her bank. She tore it open, read it, reread it in stunned surprise. Her account was overdrawn. Would she kindly deposit one hundred and thirty dollars immediately?

Overdrawn. Overdrawn by a hundred and thirty dollars! But it wasn't possible. It simply couldn't be possible. Someone had made a mistake. She still had . . . she stopped midway up the stairs, her hand on the railing. Thirty dollars! She had given Ginny her check for thirty dollars only two days earlier, when her sister-in-law had come to New York to do some shopping and had run out of money. Was it possible—surely Ginny wouldn't have raised the check . . . surely . . .

Elinor went quickly upstairs and called long distance. In a few minutes she heard the phone ringing, and pictured the big comfortable living room with its open fire and the oil painting of her mother smiling down from the mantel.

Then Ginny was speaking. She caught her breath when she heard Elinor's voice.

"I know what you want," she said, before Elinor had an opportunity to ask her question. There was a moment's confusion, as though other people were talking in the background. Then she said, quickly, softly, into the telephone, "I can explain it to you, Nell. Honestly I can. And I'll return it as soon as possible. Only please don't let Clay know. Please."

"Of course I won't, Ginny. The only trouble is—"

"Well?" The girlish voice was sharper now.

"You see, you took all I had—more than I had— My account is overdrawn. And," she steadied her voice, "the woman who gave me a commission for a portrait doesn't like it. She won't pay for it."

"I see." There was a thoughtful pause. Then Ginny said briskly, "Well, I guess you'll have to give up the studio and come here for a while, Nell. There's just no help for it. We'll expect you on the 4:10. I'll meet you myself. See you then."

She hung up before Elinor could make any reply.

Dressed in a trim black suit and white blouse with a tiny ruff tied under her chin, and a small pillbox on her dark hair, Elinor slipped into the fur coat that Clay had given her for Christmas. She paused for a moment to study herself critically in the mirror.

"All right," she told her image, "you don't look like a failure who has been driven back to the old homestead. You look as though you were on top of the world. Now try to act that way."

The small chin came up proudly and she smiled at herself, blinking back the tears that starred her long lashes.

"You'll do," she said in approval, and turned for a last look at the studio.

Now that her own things had been packed—the bravely gay pumpkin-colored dishes, the big vase that had held the chrysanthemums, the slipcover from the couch—it looked bleak and drab and almost sordid. The fire had died down in the blackened grate.

Impulsively she caught up the chrysanthemums she had taken out of the vase, holding the dripping stems away from her coat. She tapped at a door on the floor below.

The elderly woman who lived there alone peered suspiciously at the girl, and then her tired face broke into a smile.

"Miss Parks! Do come in."

"Sorry, I can't," Elinor said. "I'm giving up the studio. I'm going—home, this afternoon. I thought perhaps—" She held out the flowers.

"For me!"

The look of incredulous delight on the old woman's face made Elinor say huskily, "I hope you'll like them."

"Like them!" The gnarled old hand touched a blossom gently. "How lovely," she said softly. "I'll miss you, Miss Parks, and your nice and thoughtful ways. You've made these old halls seem bright while you were here."

"Thank you." Elinor waved to her and went back for her two suitcases.

By the time she had checked them in a locker at the station it was only 1:10. She still had three hours to fill in. When she had drawn from her savings account—which she had sworn never to touch—enough money to cover the overdraft, she walked over to Madison Avenue and got on a bus. At Fifty-ninth Street she turned west to Central Park, past the cabby waiting patiently beside his open carriage, then into the park along a snow-covered path. Here the snow was fresh and clean and she walked more quickly, taking deep breaths, feeling the air cold and stinging against her cheeks.

When she came to a frozen pond where children were skating, she paused to watch them. Sinking down on a bench, she pulled out of her large shoulder bag the sketching pad and pencils she always carried with her. With swift, economical strokes she caught the movements of a boy's body, bent over, as he skated furiously past, the line of an arm and shoulder as a little girl leaned to fasten her skates, the long swing as a boy threw a snowball.

She had removed her fur-lined gloves to work and her hands were icy, but she did not notice it, engrossed in the endless changing motions of the children as they played and skated and threw snowballs.

A snowball crashed and spattered on the back of the bench on which she was sitting and she looked up to laugh at the little boy who had thrown it. Then she noticed the women who sat beside her; a girl, really, not much older than herself, but slumped in discouragement, mouth drooping, helpless and hopeless.

That's the way I felt an hour ago, Elinor thought. Now you see what it's like. Never be sorry for yourself. Never. Keep your hands busy.

She sketched the gloomy figure beside her, labeled it "Dreadful Warning," and then looked for another subject. The children were milling around now and it was difficult to catch one of them in isolated movement.

She saw the man then. He was standing beside the pond, watching the children. It was his stillness that attracted her first. So few people are able to stand without fidgeting or shifting from foot to foot. He stood quite easily, a tall thin man with a narrow face and deep-set dark eyes, sternly intent over the two little boys who struck out across the pond in a wild inept race, staggering, sliding, falling down. Then the smaller one lost his balance, flailed wildly, caught his skate on that of another boy, and pitched forward.

"Oops!" The man moved like—like a whirlwind, Elinor thought. He caught the boy, swung him up, set him on his feet. He brushed him off, saying lightly, "All right?"

"Okay." The little boy grinned, revealing a mouth with three teeth missing, and the babyishness of the smile caught at Elinor's heart. It did at the man's, too.

"Fine," he said in a deep quiet voice, and he smiled back at the boy. A smile that illuminated his face and took every bit of sternness from it.

Elinor, intent on the man, was only dimly aware that small boys were skirmishing around her bench until a snowball aimed with deadly accuracy struck her sketchbook and sent it flying. It landed at the man's feet and he picked it up, laughing.

"This yours?" he asked, coming toward her. He looked at her, stopped smiling. It seemed to Elinor that they looked at each other for hours.

Then the man wrenched his eyes away and glanced at the sketchbook, at his own face, caught in a few vivid strokes, his stern face without the smile, watching the little boys with brooding intensity.

He looked at her again, differently this time, and returned the sketchbook.

Elinor's face burned with embarrassment. What would he think of her? Why had she been stupid enough to draw the man's face?

"You're—" He hesitated. "That's exceptionally good work."

"Thank you, sir," Elinor said lightly.

"You shouldn't joke about it, you know," he told her. "One should never joke about the thing that is most important. And this," he tapped the sketchbook, "must be very important to you."

"It is," she said, answering the simplicity in his tone with an equal simplicity in her own. "Only—I'm not really very good."

The deep-set eyes swept her face. "May I see?" He took her hesitant nod for consent and turned the pages. There were a few hasty sketches she had made in Hastings, some people she had seen walking through Washington Square, a man's shoe which had caught her attention on the street because it was scuffed and worn and somehow tired-looking. What else there was she could not recall.

He glanced from the sketch labeled "Dreadful Warning" to the apathetic woman beside her and smiled slightly. Over the pictures of the children he lingered.

"I hope you're not going to waste this—exceptional talent."

"At the moment I need that encouragement," she confessed. "This morning I finished my first commissioned portrait and Mrs.—that is, she refused to take it."

"Not flattering enough?"

She looked her surprise. "How did you guess?"

He smiled, and once again she was startled by the change it made in his face, warming it, softening its sternness.

"The one you did of me," he said. "You draw what you see. Not flattering, perhaps, but—salutary."

Elinor's soft gurgle of laughter roused the lethargic woman beside her, who frowned as though she disapproved of laughter on principle.

"Well, after all, you can't expect her to pay me for being salutary."

"Sometimes it's not a bad idea." He touched his hat and walked swiftly away.

Elinor thrust her cold hands into the lined gloves and noticed the time. Heavens, where had the hours gone? She got up in a hurry and dropped the sketchbook into her big shoulder bag.

She set off almost at a run for the Fifth Avenue exit, where she should be able to get a taxi. Darn, what had made her so late? Ginny would be furious if she failed to catch the 4:10, and she would have to wait in the station for an hour and a half until the next train was due.

Because she was in a hurry she was careless. Her bag slapped against her side as she ran. Out on Fifth Avenue she looked up the street, saw a taxi, ran forward to hail it, slipped, and her feet went out from under her. She fell on her back, skidded across the icy sidewalk, over the curb, under—

She was caught by both arms and jerked up on the sidewalk. The driver of a passing truck was standing on his brake, which screamed with the strain.

"Careful, lady," he yelled. "Watch where you're going. Nearly got yourself killed."

"All right?" said a man's deep voice and she turned her head. His face was drained of color, his mouth grimly set. It seemed quite natural that he should be the one who held her in strong arms.

"It seems to be your day to be a rescuer," she said, trying to laugh because she was still so shaken by her fall and the moment of terror when she had thought the truck would crush her.

"It seems to be my day."

Elinor released herself gently. She was surprised to find how reluctant she was to free herself from those strong, sustaining, gentle hands.

"Thank you again." She waved to a passing taxi, which drew in to the curb. She climbed inside. "Grand Central," she directed and turned to wave to the waiting man. "Good-by!"

"I'll find you again," he said, as the taxi moved away from the curb.

II

As the train rumbled out of Grand Central Station through the long tunnel, Elinor saw her reflection in the window. Her eyes were sparkling, her mouth softly curved, the tilt of the tiny hat over her dark hair was just right. She smiled at her shadowy self and wondered what had raised her spirits so much since the disasters of the morning.

She handed the conductor her ticket, humming to herself, "I'll see you again." Where had she dug up that old waltz tune? Oh, it was the Noel Coward song, of course. It was because of a man's deep voice saying with grave certainty, "I'll find you again."

Not in Hastings, she thought. Not in a little Connecticut village seventy-five miles from New York. But he had sounded so sure. For a moment she summoned up the stern narrow face that was so unexpectedly altered and warmed by his smile. Then she firmly put him out of her mind. A passing stranger, that's all he was. Someone whom it would have been nice to know. But out of her life permanently. He would never find her, not even if he really wanted to. And that wasn't likely.

How white he had been when he pulled her away from the truck. She remembered that curious feeling of security, of being at home, she had experienced for a fleeting moment while he held her. She had never felt like that before. She had always been popular, she had been receiving proposals of marriage since she was eighteen, but she had never taken them seriously. She had been gay and friendly and lighthearted in her dealings with the boys and young men who had fallen in love with her. But never serious. Love and marriage were so important that she could not settle for second-best. And the best? Well, she would recognize it when it came her way. Meantime, she was content to wait.

The train crawled out of the tunnel into gray twilight, the early darkness of a winter day, past lighted rooms so near the tracks one seemed to be in them, past long bleak rows of brownstone fronts and dingy brick houses, looking slovenly and discouraged. Like the girl on the park bench. Past Bronx Park and the beginning of open space.

Then they were riding through fields of snow, clean snow, and even in the stuffy car it seemed to Elinor that the air was fresher and more invigorating. She was going home.

At Hastings, the conductor came for her suitcases and helped her off the train. For a moment the icy air stung her cheeks and shut off her breath.

"Nell!"

At that high, sweet, girlish voice she turned around, her heart sinking. Ginny had come to meet her. It wasn't, after all, home she was coming to, it was Ginny's house. The house Ginny hadn't wanted her in.

Ginny came running up to her, looking no more than eighteen. The hazel eyes were shaded by dark, gold-tipped lashes, her hair was pure gold under a smart blue hat. She wore a stunning new sable coat. There were pearls in her ears, a small pearl necklace around her throat.

"Hello, Ginny."

Ginny looked down helplessly at the suitcases, "How on earth are we going to get them to the station wagon? I keep telling Clay we need a chauffeur but he's going through this 'We've got to retrench' stage. That's why—" She bit her lips.

"I'll carry the bags." Elinor watched her footing carefully down the icy steps from the station platform to the parking lot, with Ginny trotting beside her on three-inch heels. Trust Giny to wear spike heels in the country.

When Elinor had lifted the heavy suitcases into the back of the wagon, Ginny took the wheel. Elinor looked from the luxurious upholstery to the dashboard, which resembled the instrument panel of a jet plane.

"This is new, isn't it?"

"No, we've had it at least a year. Clay doesn't see the sense of turning a car in every year, but I try to make him understand you really save money in the long run."

She backed the car and turned it competently. It was always a surprise to Elinor to discover how efficient Ginny could be when she wanted to. As a rule, she made a potent tool of her helplessness.

Elinor looked eagerly around her as Ginny drove through Hastings. It was still the same, with its old houses and its small business center: a supermarket, a bank, a three-story office building, a small dress shop, electric supply shop, hardware store, and beauty salon.

Ginny turned carefully onto the Green, got the car out of a skid on loose snow. This, Elinor thought, taking a long breath, is the way I always remember it. The branches of the trees were etched in snow; snow lay in long gleaming blankets over the tree-lined Green, over the deep lawns, over the white houses set far back from the street. Welcoming lights shone through windows where draperies had not yet been drawn. They passed the ivy-covered library and the circular driveway that led to the Hastings Inn, cheerful with light spilling from the windows.

"It's just the same," she said happily.

"Nothing changes here," Ginny said in a discontented voice. "Where else would a forty-year-old doctor be called 'young Doctor Dick' because his father is still regarded as the doctor and the son as a mere boy?"

Elinor laughed. "Most of the people in this town remember his father taking care of them. To the older ones, Doctor Dick seems like a newcomer, a young man without experience. I suppose he's still working himself to death."

Ginny shrugged. "He seems to like it that way. He was offered a magnificent consultant's job in Chicago and he turned it down. Said he was needed here." She laughed impatiently. "No, everything in Hastings is just the same. Just as deadly. Oh, there have been a few changes, of course. The Rivers estate has been sold."

The bitterness in Ginny's voice made Elinor uneasy. Her sister-in-law was more discontented than she had ever been. Poor Clay! What must it be like to face this sullen unrest every day? Elinor warned herself that under no circumstances must she interfere.

"The Rivers estate!" she exclaimed with exaggerated interest. "It must have been bought by Rockefeller. Unless they finally agreed to sell it in separate parcels."

"No, the new owners bought that huge tract of land as well, nine hundred acres, and the house. They're going to make quite a development of it. In fact, they have built three houses already. And who," Ginny demanded in an odd voice, "do you think is the architect?"

"I haven't the slightest idea. Oh, Ginny! Not Jed!"

Ginny nodded, her lips tight.

"I'm so glad, so terribly glad!"

"Nell at her maddest. I never could see what you found to like in Jed Gordon."

"He's my oldest friend in the world," Elinor said quietly. "We played together when we were little, we've known each other all our lives."

"That doesn't alter the fact that he's nothing less than a criminal."

"Don't say that again, Ginny." Something in Elinor's voice made her sister-in-law give her a startled look. "Never say that again. Jed did get into trouble when he was sixteen; he took the blame for all the things that gang of his had done. And he paid for it. A whole year in that school for difficult boys. But no one could find anything against him now. That's the real trouble with a village; too many people remember. I used to think he was wrong to stay here; I believed he ought to go away to make a fresh start. But Jed always said that here was where he had made his mistake and here was where he had to re-establish himself. It was like him to do it the hard way."

"It was darned silly, if you ask me."

"But," Elinor pointed out gently, "if he's been given a real chance by these new people, he's been proved to be right. And I say more power to him!"

"Have it your own way, Nell. You never did have any judgment about men. I hope you aren't going to cold-shoulder Harold Brown now that you're back. He's still as crazy about you as ever. If you would just play your cards right—"

Elinor shied away from the subject of Harold Brown. Ginny was determined that she should marry him. There was no point in starting a useless argument.

"Who are these new people who have bought the Rivers estate?" she inquired hastily.

"A brother and sister. She's Mrs. John Campbell, a widow with one little girl. The brother is Stephen Sewell, simply rolling in money, though no one seems to know where it comes from."

Elinor giggled. "Are you going to dangle him before these eyes as another *mar*-velous catch? Poor Ginny!"

Ginny drew a long breath. "That reminds me, Nell —about the check. I'm poor Ginny, all right. Clay has cut my allowance almost in half and then I met Mrs. Campbell and went to the Rivers house—the Sewell house now—to play bridge. I lost my shirt, and I simply didn't dare tell Clay. You know how he feels about gambling."

"I feel the same way. But I can't imagine being afraid of Clay. He adores you, Ginny."

"Just the same, I can't tell him. But I'll try to pay back that money I—borrowed—from you as soon as I can. Anyhow, you won't need any while you are staying here. Clay is pretty crazy about his kid sister, too."

Elinor ignored the jealousy in Ginny's voice. As an only child, her sister-in-law could not really be expected

to understand the bond between brother and sister or realize that it didn't impinge on her own relationship with
her husband.

"I don't think I could be satisfied to be dependent
on Clay for long."

Ginny brightened. "That's what I thought. You can
get a job of some sort. Maybe, as you're not too good at
portrait painting"—Elinor winced but made no comment; sometimes Ginny did not even know when she
was being cruel—"you might use some of your training
in color and design and all that—for it certainly cost
Clay enough to send you to art school—and set up a little decorating shop."

"That's an idea," Elinor admitted. "But, of course,
it would require some capital."

Ginny had the grace to blush. She stopped the car
before the big white Colonial house with its six pillars.

"Clay can bring in your suitcases."

In the wide entrance hall she tossed her coat care-
lessly over a chair. From the big living room on the right
—two rooms originally, but made into one—came the
sound of voices.

"Ginny?" Clay called. "Is Elinor with you?"

"I'm here."

Elinor ran into the big room. One side was almost
all windows, opening in summer on a rose garden. For a
moment she stood still in shocked surprise. The room
had been furnished in the Sheraton and French Empire
designs as they had been adapted by Duncan Phyfe,
with satinwood and mahogany. The effect had been one
of gracious dignity without extreme formality. Now it
was a bewildering blend of Art Nouveau with the fussy
elegance of the first part of the twentieth century. Tubu-
lar chairs warred with Victorian tables. The result repre-
sented a prodigious expense and was unharmonious and
jarring.

Now gold-brocaded draperies shut out the winter
night. They didn't, Elinor felt, belong to this New England house, but Ginny had preferred them to the soft
muted tones of the chintz that had been there before.

On the opposite wall a big fireplace held the center spot, and above it—still unchanged—smiled down the portrait of Elinor's mother, looking very much like her daughter, with the same bright eagerness in her eyes, the same tenderness in the mouth, the same bone-deep beauty in her face.

The two young men who had been sitting before the cracking fire jumped to their feet.

"Elinor!" Her brother caught her in his arms and then held her off to look at her. "But you look just fine! After what Ginny said, I thought you were half dead or something. Oh, it's grand to see you!"

Ginny caught her sister-in-law's eyes in an alarmed warning.

"I just thought I'd like to have a change," Elinor said, and Ginny relaxed in relief.

Clay Parks was a taller version of his sister, with the same dark hair, the same eyes; but his face was graver. There were new lines in it which Elinor had never seen before. Something was worrying him.

Then the other young man protested, "Hey! When do I get my chance?" and Clay released her, laughing. "Jed!"

"Elinor!" He gave her a hug. "You look like a million dollars, gal. How's the feminine Rembrandt?"

Jed Gordon was shorter and slighter than Clay, with sandy hair that just escaped being red. He had a plain face with a likable quirk to his lips and direct gray eyes.

"Honey, you've turned into a knockout. I hope you haven't grown too uptown for us country yokels."

She laughed. "I've come back prepared to be terribly impressed by Hastings's own Frank Lloyd Wright. Do tell me about it, Jed! I'm so thrilled."

"At least, give Nell time to take off her wraps and freshen up," Ginny said tartly. "You'll have plenty of time to tell her about your great success."

Elinor's face burned with anger. Then she caught sight of Clay, watching his adored wife in distress, hat-ing her rudeness to an old friend but unwilling to criticize her, even in his own mind.

"Coming, Ginny," she said lightly. "And I want to see Mrs. Groom. I suppose she's still running the house."

"She's still running everything, including Clay and me. The day I get rid of that woman will be the happiest day of my life."

Elinor was aghast. "You wouldn't fire her, would you? She's been here years and years, as long as I can remember."

"Too many years."

"Mrs. Groom isn't leaving," Clay said evenly. "She has a job and a home here as long as she wants one. She just about brought Elinor and me up, and we owe her a lot."

There was an uncomfortable little pause. Ginny started to protest, looked at her husband and changed her mind.

"Clay, bring in Nell's suitcases, will you?"

Elinor waved at Jed, who sent her a mocking salute and winked at her as she followed Ginny up the beautiful staircase.

"I've given you your old room," Ginny said as she opened the door.

Elinor stood looking at the four-poster bed, the rag rugs on the gleaming wide floorboards, the old-fashioned rocker, the tallboy and the familiar pictures. She was home at last. Then she belatedly heard what her sister-in-law had said: "I've given you your old room." It was Ginny's house now, and Ginny intended that she should not forget it.

There were voices in the lower hall.

"Of course," Clay said. "Glad to see you, Harold. Come in by the fire."

Another man spoke and Clay said, "No, no one here but Jed Gordon."

"Oh." Harold was checked for a moment and then he laughed. "Oh, well, what difference does it make?"

Elinor stood listening. She and Jed Gordon and

Harold Brown had known each other all their lives, and, from the beginning, Jed and Harold had treated each other with bare politeness. They had never liked each other. They probably never would.

Ginny closed the bedroom door and leaned against it, her color heightened.

"Look here, Nell, don't be a fool. Harold has come to take you out to dinner. Don't spoil everything by hanging onto Jed, just because he was a childhood friend. I know you don't care for my advice, but just the same you could do a lot worse than marry Harold Brown. He's in line for a vice-presidency, and he'll end by being president of the bank. And that's a nice spot for any woman to have her husband in."

"How did Harold know I was coming?"

"Why—I just happened to run into him on the street on the way to the station. He asked about you, as he always does. I said you were coming on the 4:10."

Her eyes fell under Elinor's steady gaze. "It was just one of those chance meetings," she said vaguely. She slipped out of the room, as though anxious to escape, and Elinor slowly took off her coat and hat, wondering at her sister-in-law's manner. Something seemed to be very wrong in the big Colonial house.

The table at the inn held a vase of tiny chrysanthemums and Harold Brown moved it to one side.

"Now that's better," he said in relief. "I can really look at you. I suppose other men have told you that you are beautiful, Nell. And that dress exactly matches your eyes."

Elinor brushed aside the compliment, trying to ignore the fervor in his voice. She was still bemused over the ruthless way Ginny had arranged matters. Almost before she knew it, Ginny had said that, as long as Nell was dining at the inn with Harold, she and Clay would have to put up with an old-fashioned clam chowder supper at home, as that had been Mrs. Groom's suggestion.

Jed had flushed darkly and then Clay had intervened. "No clam chowder on a night like this. Darling, you and Jed and I are also going to dine at the inn. I am in a mood for a thicky juicy steak. We'll sit across the room and leer at Elinor."

There had been a burst of laughter and the situation had eased. Now Jed sat across the room at the inn with Clay and Ginny, looking wistfully at Elinor, while she faced a triumphant Harold Brown.

"How long are you going to be here, Nell?" he asked eagerly.

"I don't know. I haven't any plans. Sooner or later, of course, I want to get a job of some sort."

"I can suggest a job that is waiting for you, a permanent one."

She shook her head. "Don't, Harold."

He leaned forward, speaking earestly. He had a broad face, earnest expression and round solemn eyes. It was a nice face, on the whole, except for the lips that were too thick, the eyes too close together.

"I want you to marry me, Nell. I've been in love with you for three years. Never looked at another woman. I'm doing well. I could give you a comfortable home, and I think I could make you happy. Heaven knows that I would try."

"I'm sorry," she said gently. "Truly sorry. But I—can't, Harold."

"Is there anyone else?"

Unexpectedly she heard a man saying, "I'll find you again." But he couldn't, of course.

Her hesitation worried Harold. "It's not Jed, is it?" he demanded.

"Jed is my oldest friend, but that's all."

Harold chuckled with amusement. "Is that all you know about it? The guy is nuts about you."

"Jed? That's ridiculous."

"That suits me fine. But look here, Nell—"

"Please don't call me Nell. I've never liked that nickname."

"But Ginny always—Oh, I see, she does it because she knows you don't like it." Harold grinned. "That's just like our little Ginny."

"You're speaking of Clay's wife," Elinor reminded him.

"And you're the loyal kind, aren't you? Loyal and steadfast in everything you do, everything you think. What a magnificent wife you'll make! Elinor, please think it over. Don't give me a final answer now."

Elinor wanted to insist that she had given her final answer, that Harold must not continue to nourish a hope that was without foundation. But he spoke first.

"Maybe I'm a fool to go on hoping, but I have to, or there wouldn't be anything left for me. You're so lovely, Elinor! And Ginny tells me you aren't interested in any other man."

"This hardly concerns Ginny, does it, Harold?" In spite of herself Elinor betrayed her anger in her voice.

For a moment there was a flicker of amusement in Harold's round eyes. Elinor had an uncomfortable impression that he was laughing at her.

"She takes a lot of interest in you," he said. "She wants what is best for you."

"I'll have to decide that," Elinor said crisply. "And it surprises me that you and Ginny should have discussed me in this way."

"Does it?" After an uncomfortable pause he added, "Sometimes I suspect you don't know your sister-in-law as well as you think."

From the next table a voice spoke clearly in a sudden silence. "Clay Parks and his wife. Not Hastings's richest citizens, but the oldest and most respected family around here. The chap with them is Jed Gordon, a young architect. On his way up. And fast. I understand there is unlimited money behind him."

"Really?" drawled a woman's voice.

Elinor, turning slightly, saw the young woman who sat at the next table. She was what movie publicists call a curvaceous blonde, with hair an even deeper gold than Ginny's—though there was a suggestion of darker hair at the roots. She had a small upturned nose and she revealed dimples when she smiled. Her eyes were china-blue and just about as hard.

"Really?" she repeated. "Jed Gordon. How do you pick up all this fascinating information?"

"Asking around." Her escort was a heavy man with thick shoulders, blunt pudgy fingers and blue jowls. He repeated, with a chuckle, "Just asking around."

"Who on earth are they?" Elinor asked in a whisper.

Harold shook his head. "No idea. Newcomers, probably. I haven't seen them around Hastings before."

The couple at the next table had risen and the girl dropped the handbag that she had been holding on her lap. Her escort, leading the way out of the restaurant, paid no attention. Harold bent over and returned it to her.

Eyes shielded by preposterously long artificial lashes blinked at him softly.

"Oh, thanks a lot," she gushed. "How terribly sweet of you."

She followed slowly in the wake of her big companion, her eyes fixed on the table where Clay and Ginny and Jed were talking.

As the blond woman went through the doorway into the inn parlor, Elinor noticed a man talking to the manager. She looked again, unbelievingly. It was the man from Central Park. Then he stepped back to let a vivacious young woman precede him into the dining room. As they passed the table where Elinor sat, the man asked, "Is this all right, dear?"

The woman turned to smile up at him. "Just perfect."

He laughed, but without any humor in the sound. "Don't try to beguile me, Julie!"

"Don't be angry," she pleaded.

"You know how I feel about it," the man told her.

"Sometimes you act like an old fuddy-duddy. You're years behind the times."

"I don't want to quarrel with you, Julie, but in my opinion you've done an unjustifiable thing."

"Oh, that's ridiculous."

"I wonder if you realize just how much harm it could do? What unhappy—what criminal results there could be?"

"Criminal! If you're going to be melodramatic about it," the woman exclaimed, "I'm going home."

"Stay where you are and eat your dinner, Julie," he said, in the tone of authority of a man who is accustomed to being obeyed. "But you aren't going to run away from your responsibility."

"But I told you—no one could possibly have been hurt."

"I know you did, but how did you know?"

"Why—" The woman's voice faded out uncertainly.

"Promise me you won't do a fool thing like that again," he said urgently.

"Oh, all right, I promise," she said reluctantly, "but I still think you're crazy."

Elinor wrenched her attention away from the conversation at the next table. She was eavesdropping and there was no excuse for her.

"You haven't been listening to me," Harold was saying accusingly.

"I haven't missed a word. Every jeweled syllable has been admired."

He chuckled. "Let's go skating tomorrow afternoon. The ice at Green Pond is wonderful now, hard as steel and smooth as glass."

"I'd love it. You sound like a singing commercial for Green Pond."

"Three o'clock?"

"Grand."

A spot of white on the floor between the two tables caught her eye and Elinor bent over, thinking she had dropped her handkerchief. It was a slip of paper bearing the words: *Tomorrow. Four o'clock. Usual place.*

She dropped it back on the floor. Someone at the next table must have lost that furtive-looking message. And yet they weren't furtive-looking people.

As Harold came around the table to pull out her

chair, Elinor looked swiftly at the couple beside her.
The woman called Julie was studying the menu. The
man from Central Park was fumbling in his pockets, a
worried frown between his brows.

III

"Breakfast in bed! What luxury," Elinor exclaimed as
Mrs. Groom set the tray across her knees and brought
her a fluffy bedjacket.

The housekeeper—tall, angular, with a face like a
box, all angles and sharp edges—looked down at the
girl, her grim face softening.

"From the little peek I got at you last night," she
said in her flat Maine voice, "I figured some solid food
wouldn't hurt you any. Looks to me like you haven't
been eating much since you left home. You never did
have any sense about taking care of yourself." The se-
verity of the words was canceled out by the look of genuine concern on the woman's face.

Elinor felt ashamed that she had done no more
than call a gay "Hello, there!" when passing Mrs.
Groom the night before. Ginny had swept her along
without giving her an opportunity to speak, but this
woman had taken care of Elinor as though she were her
own child, nursed her when she was ill, supervised her
play, watched over her acquaintances, stayed up to see
she returned home safely from parties, and dried her
tears with rough but real comfort during the emotional
stresses of growing up.

"I'll get fat on your cooking," she said gaily.
"Please sit down and talk to me while I eat breakfast."

"Young Mrs. Parks won't like it."

"Oh, Ginny won't mind. What time is it? Ten o'clock! Good heavens, why didn't someone wake me?"

"I told Clay you needed the rest and he left orders." Mrs. Groom sat bolt upright on a straight chair. "I want to see you eat every bite. Those blueberry muffins are fresh out of the oven. Baked them specially for you. Eat 'em while they are hot, with lots of butter. You sure need fattening up."

While Elinor ate under Mrs. Groom's watchful eyes, the latter said casually. "Wouldn't hurt Clay to put on some weight either. He's beginning to look puny."

"There's nothing wrong with him, is there?" Elinor asked. "I thought he looked tired, worried perhaps."

"He's worried plenty, if you ask me. The law business is all right when you make your clients pay their just debts, but you know Clay. He won't press anyone, though he pays his bills right on the dot. And with young Mrs. Parks running them up right and left and saying he ought to move to the city in a law firm that would pay him a lot—"

"But Clay would never be happy away from Hastings!" Elinor exclaimed in consternation. "He loves every foot of this village, and he wants to be a real part of it and help it maintain its traditions."

"What does that wife of his care if he's happy or not? It's all just money with her."

"Mrs. Groom!"

"All right, I'll keep my thoughts to myself. But if you hold your eyes wide open, you'll see for yourself. And maybe with you living here where you belong—"

"But I'm not going to live here. Not permanently, that is. I've been a burden to Clay for too long as it is."

"And who called you a burden, I'd like to know. Not Clay. And the money and the house were left jointly to the two of you. And you turned your share all over to him, as I remember."

"Anyhow," Elinor said hastily, "I want to be independent. People who don't work at something never have any real meaning as human beings. I'm going to look for a job as soon as—before long."

"You and me both," Mrs. Groom told her.

"You! But you can't leave Clay. What on earth would he do without you?"

"It's not Clay. He's like you. I could call this my home until I die and he'd make me feel it was."

"But it is!" Elinor assured her.

"Not any longer. Young Mrs. Parks doesn't like me and my ways. She wants someone who'll do half the work for twice the money but will look nice in a black dress and a lacy bit of apron for show. And a cap. With ribbons!"

Elinor gurgled with laughter at the older woman's outrage.

"Well." Mrs. Groom got up stiffly. "I've got to plan my menus. I had a nice roast of beef cooking for dinner last night and then they went to the inn without notice. Maybe I can heat it so it won't be too well cooked. Clay likes his meat rare. I guess I know what he likes to eat better than any French chef young Mrs. Parks would get in here."

Elinor was silent. Clay disliked clam chowder and Ginny had told him they were to have it for dinner— Mrs. Groom's idea. A little thing, of course, but if there were a number of tiny pinpricks of annoyance Clay might eventually agree with Ginny that this stanch and faithful woman must go. It was not only the injustice that troubled Elinor. It was Ginny's dishonesty. And yet Clay loved her with blind devotion. He would be more irrevocably hurt by disillusionment in his wife than by the loss of this faithful housekeeper.

When Elinor had dressed in a coral wool skirt and matching sweaters she pulled on arctics and a short quilted car coat with a hood, which she drew down over her hair. In the small morning room where her mother had written her letters and made out menus, she found Ginny sitting before a stack of bills, biting her pen.

When she saw Elinor in the doorway she made an instinctive movement to sweep the bills into an open drawer, and then checked herself with a helpless gesture.

"The way these things mount up!" she said lightly. "It's absolutely terrifying."

Elinor's eyes fell on the top bill. It was for ninety dollars for four pairs of shoes. No wonder Clay was worried! For his sake she made no comment.

"That's a good color for you," Ginny said. "But not as good as the blue you wore last night." She added casually, only the fixed intentness in her eyes betraying her interest, "Have a nice evening?"

Elinor thought of Jed's wistful face while she talked to Harold, of Harold's insistence that she marry him, of the man from Central Park devoting his attention to the vivacious young woman who was probably his wife. He had talked to her about something criminal. Criminal! A queer word to be spoken by those two. His wife? Was she the one who had dropped that odd-sounding note? No, it hadn't been a pleasant evening. It had been sheer disappointment.

"I had a headache," she said.

Ginny's frown gave her a petulant look. "Harold seemed rather depressed. Your headache must have put him off. I had a kind of suspicion that he planned to propose to you."

"He did."

Ginny pushed her chair back from the desk. "Nell! You didn't refuse him!"

A surge of anger swept through Elinor. In the past, Ginny's efforts to marry her off had only amused her. Now the look of outraged fury on her sister-in-law's face was more serious. Nothing could excuse her interference.

"After all, Ginny, that concerns me, doesn't it? Just me." She tried to speak as lightly as she could.

"Does it?"

The brightness was gone from Ginny's face. It was almost haggard. For the first time Elinor caught a glimpse of how she would look when she was old.

"I'm sorry if I upset you." Elinor's voice was gentle in the face of that strange despair. "But marriage is something that each person has to decide for himself.

It's so terribly important. I'm not in love with Harold.
I've never really even liked him very much. I don't
know why. And nothing—nobody in the world could
persuade me to marry him."

She went swiftly out of the room, and in a moment
the front door closed behind her. Ginny sank into her
chair and dropped her bright head on her folded arms.

"What am I going to do?" she whispered. "What
am I going to do?"

Elinor walked swiftly, hands thrust deep into the
pockets of her coat, the icy air cooling her flushed
cheeks. Only one thing had emerged clearly from that
brief talk with Ginny. Somewhere, somehow, Elinor had
to find a job that would support her and a place where
she could live. If Ginny intended to force her into marriage, she could no longer stay under her roof.

The Parks house was on the edge of the village and
Elinor turned down a narrow road that led into the
country. Like most Connecticut roads it wound way-
wardly up and down hill. On one side was a snow-covered slope, on the other a rocky ravine, the water looking black where it showed between patches of ice.

There was no sound but her own steps on the fro-
zen snow, no human being in sight. Little by little, the stillness and the beauty of the winter scene wrought their customary magic and quieted Elinor's spirits. Here and
there she saw the narrow tracks of deer; once a pair of
pheasants walked daintily across the road, ignoring her
presence.

She passed a fingerpost reading: SEWELL PROPER-
TIES. OFFICE. Around the next curve in the road she
came upon a small white saltbox. Blue smoke coiled up-
ward from the chimney. On impulse, she opened the
door and went in. Jed Gordon stood with his back to her
at a long, high drafting table, hard at work on a blue-
print. He turned quickly when he felt the cold draft
from the open door.

"Elinor!" His face lighted up. "This is wonderful.
Let me take your coat, and come sit by the fire." He

knelt to remove her arctics and drew her toward the fireplace where two chairs had been drawn up invitingly.

"Sure I'm not interrupting?"

"There's no hurry about what I'm doing now. Just
designing another house."

"*Just* designing another house!" Elinor laughed
delightedly. "How blazé you've grown."

Jed laughed with her. "Not I. Every morning I
pinch myself to see if it's real. I always expect to wake
up and find I'm just another young architect looking for
someone who will trust him to build a chicken coop or a
garage, and that I never met Steve Sewell."

"Tell me about it," Elinor said quietly.

Sewell, Jed said, was a wonderful guy. Distant and
cold on the surface, a withdrawn sort of man, not the
kind you could be intimate with. He knew exactly what
he wanted and he expected to get it. Jed had met him
shortly after the sale of the Rivers estate. Actually, he'd
been taking a walk, met the guy who was prowling
around the place, and they got to talking. Jed had described what he'd do with the land if it was his and the
other man had seemed interested and then had asked
him about his training.

"That was all. Not a clue as to who he was. Then,
a couple of weeks later, I got a letter reminding me of
our conversation and asking me to go to New York to
call on him. And the letter was signed Stephen Sewell."

Elinor smiled at Jed's excited expression. There
was nothing blasé about him now.

"So then?" she prodded him.

"Well, he gave me this chance to build some houses.
I told him he could get a hundred better guys, that I was
just out of school. And he looked at me, his eyes half
closed, and all he said was, 'Afraid to try it?' "

"No wonder you still think you are dreaming! And
now everything's perfect."

The wide, delighted grin faded from Jed's face.
"Well, not perfect," he said slowly. "It's one thing to
build a house, but it's another to sell it. Particularly in
winter. And Sewell doesn't want to handle the sale

through a real estate agent. That's part of my job, too."

"What's worrying you, Jed?"

He grinned at her. "Well, you see, it's rather an unusual setup. What Sewell had in mind was that these first three houses were to be kind of an experiment. Model homes, in a way. He's a queer duck. I've been working with him for months and I don't know him any better than I did in the first place. I don't even have the slightest idea where all his money comes from. He doesn't like the ranch houses that are cropping up all over the place. He doesn't think they belong in a New England landscape—that they are too streamlined, too impersonal. So I've built a saltbox and a Cape Cod and a conventional cottage. But now he wants me to furnish them so people can see the way what he calls a 'real home' should look. And that's out of my line."

Jed ran a hand through his sandy hair and gave her a perplexed look.

Elinor leaned forward, clutching his arm in her eagerness. "Jed! Would you give me a chance to do the decorating and the furnishing? Would you, Jed?"

"Would I! Would I accept manna from heaven? Are you serious?"

"I couldn't be more serious. I need a job and that's just made to order, not only because I have the training but because I love making empty rooms inviting and livable."

"But how about your painting?"

"I can still do that in my spare time. But I must earn enough money to support myself."

"You—but you have half the Parks—oh, I forgot. You turned it all over to Clay, didn't you?"

"He needed it at the time to establish his own law firm," Elinor said quickly.

"Then it's a deal. I'll talk to Sewell about it right away. If he's not pleased as Punch to get you I'll eat that set of blueprints."

Elinor drew a long breath of relief. Then she sniffed.

"Jed! You're scorching your jacket."

He jumped back from the fire, twisted around to view the damage and gave a rueful laugh.

"Darn! And that's my new suit, too."

"Well, if you have to crawl into the fireplace to keep warm," Elinor retorted heartlessly.

Jed laughed. "Do you remember . . . ?" he began.

"Do you remember . . . ?" Elinor was saying at the same time, and they both laughed.

"What a lot we have to remember," Jed said more soberly. "All our childhood. All the years of growing up. All the fun we've had." He grinned. "And all the times Mrs. Groom spanked me. She certainly didn't believe in sparing the rod. Even now, every time I see her I half expect her to tell me to hold out my hands so she can see for herself that I've washed them properly."

"She mothered all of us," Elinor said softly. "You and Clay and me."

"I'll say she did," Jed replied fervently. "I can remember now how she kept cold towels on my head all night when I had a fever and brought me special soups and custards while I was sick. Nothing I could ever do, repeat nothing, would pay my debt to her."

"Or mine," Elinor said. For a moment her heart seemed to be pinched by the pain of knowing that Ginny was determined to cast Mrs. Groom out into the world to fend for herself, after twenty-five years of faithful and loving service for the Parks family.

"What's wrong, Elinor?" Jed asked. "Something is worrying you."

She laughed and shook off her depression. "Could we look at the houses now, Jed? I'm so excited I can't wait. Anyhow, I might be able to get some ideas so I could talk to Mr. Sewell."

Jed laughed. "Come on, then." He pulled on her arctics for her and shrugged into an overcoat. As he helped her into a ramshackle jeep he said anxiously, "I hope you won't be too cold."

"Nice ventilation. I like it," she assured him gaily.

"Next year I'll get a better car; but right now I'm

still paying back my college loans, so money is as scarce as hen's teeth."

As the jeep backed onto the road, he commented, "In a way, I'm glad you're looking for a job, Elinor."

"Why?" she asked in surprise.

"Well—last night I got the idea—that is, I thought maybe you were planning to get married."

"To Harold Brown?"

"Yes. Ginny was sure of it, and she seemed to be delighted. She kept talking about the way he's forging ahead at the bank and how he's investing money and all that. First time I've ever thought I'd like to rob a bank just to have enough money to make me a good prospect. Clay didn't say anything—but *he* wasn't pleased. You could tell that."

"I'm not going to marry Harold. Not ever," Elinor said crisply. "Ginny was mistaken about that."

"Thank God!" Jed said fervently.

"You've never liked Harold, have you?"

Jed seemed to concentrate on maneuvering the jeep over some deep frozen ruts. "Oh," he said at length, "Harold's all right. We just never hit it off. But he doesn't deserve you. I guess no one does."

There was a wistful tone in his voice that Elinor had never heard before. Was it possible that Harold had been right—that Jed was in love with her? Was that why he had betrayed so much eagerness to get money? Rob a bank just to have enough money! The idea that Jed might care for her was strange and new. Jed had always been like a younger Clay, a brother with whom she had played and laughed and fought.

Jed cleared his throat. "Only trouble about these houses," he said in an impersonal, businesslike tone, as though aware that he had betrayed his feelings, "is that they're rather isolated. The roads are kept open, but there's not much traffic. A lot of people won't like that —too lonely for them. And most women don't like being so far from neighbors. They don't feel safe."

"But nothing ever happens in Hastings!" Elinor exclaimed. "What in the world is there to be afraid of?"

"There's always a first time."

She laughed. "You sound like Mrs. Groom. Always expecting the worst. Though what could happen in a peaceful village like this?"

"Well, look at Lynchburg, with the fire that destroyed all those beautiful old houses. And the flood at Sealey that swept away the business district. And the bank robbery at Newcomb. Three hundred thousand dollars taken and not a trace of it since."

"Br-r-r." Elinor shivered in mock terror.

"Just the same, laugh if you want to, but remember that old saying, 'It can happen here.' "

Jed stopped the jeep. "Well," he tried to conceal his bursting pride in the guise of indifference, "here's my first house. Why, that's funny. Someone is here. Hey, hurry up. Maybe we've got a customer!"

He helped her down and they started through the snow to the house. Ahead of them was a single set of footprints. The front door opened and a woman in a green ski suit came to meet them. Under the green wool cap Elinor caught a glimpse of brassy gold hair. It was the blond woman who had sat at the next table at the Hastings Inn the night before.

"I am Mrs. Alice Grant." The words were for both of them, but the smile was for Jed. "I do hope I'm not intruding, but the house seemed to be unoccupied and it was *so enchanting* I couldn't resist it."

"We're delighted to know that you like it," Jed told her, beaming. "My name is Jed Gordon, and this is Miss Parks, who is going to furnish the house. I'm the architect."

"Mr. Gordon! How delightful to meet you." The china-blue eyes turned for a moment to make a swift survey of Elinor and she nodded casually to the girl. Then she turned back to Jed. "You really deserve the highest praise. I'm simply *in love* with this cottage."

The artificial lashes fluttered like a hummingbird's wings. "From the moment I saw this dear little village I knew it was going to be my fate." She held Jed's eyes and then her own dropped with a fair imitation of shyness.

Elinor, looking at Jed to share her amusement, was astonished to see the dark blush over his cheekbones. He was completely bemused.

"Well," he stammered, "that's mighty nice. It would be fine if you decided to stay in Hastings. Perhaps —may I show you over the house?"

"I'm ashamed to say I've been all through it. Exploring." Mrs. Grant hesitated for a moment.

"Would you—that is, there are two other houses I've built. Maybe—"

"Wonderful! Do show them to me, Mr. Gordon."

Jed turned to Elinor. "Is that all right with you? We won't be gone long. Give you a chance to look the place over at leisure."

"Of course," Elinor agreed.

"Then shall we go?"

At the dulcet question Jed looked at the blond woman, still with that dazzled expression on his face. She tucked her hand possessively under his arm and nodded coolly to Elinor. "We won't keep you any longer from your labors," she said, and the touch of amused patronage in her tone set the blood humming in Elinor's ears. With difficulty she kept her voice cool.

"Fine. I can hardly wait to start my own voyage of exploration."

With a ripple of laughter Mrs. Grant led Jed firmly away to the jeep. Elinor swallowed a giggle. It might have been a Rolls-Royce by the way Mrs. Grant swept up to it. Then the laughter died in Elinor's throat. She hadn't supposed that it would hurt so to see Jed fall, all of a heap, for a strange girl. Swept off his feet. She certainly was attractive, Elinor admitted reluctantly to herself. Different from the home-town girls. Glamorous.

The jeep started off and she turned back to the house. Jed's first house. She stood looking at it with a glow of pride. It was attractive, almost wistfully appealing. With her eyes half-closed she pictured it in the summertime, its windows clear and gleaming, its door inviting. The location seemed made to fit its Early American plan; the great maple divinely designed as a background for its red brick chimney.

Elinor stopped in the middle of the flagstone path. It was perfect. All it needed now was a woman to live in it and love it. But not Mrs. Alice Grant, she thought. She doesn't belong in his house, she wouldn't understand it. Elinor had an odd feeling that the house would be unhappy with such a tenant and tried to laugh at herself.

"Nell at her maddest," she quoted Ginny, but the feeling of discomfort, of distrust, remained.

IV

Elinor opened the front door of Jed's first house. Next time she came she must remember to bring soap for those antique hinges. They squeaked like a stuck pig.

Slowly she looked around her, studying the general layout, the proportions of the rooms. She pictured the empty grate with a blazing fire, she curtained the windows and furnished the rooms. In this bleak season of the year they cried out for color. Next time she came she would bring some ivy and cut flowers with her. Or perhaps some salmon-pink geraniums. It was astonishing what a vivid effect of occupancy they could give even unfurnished rooms.

When she had finished her tour of inspection she sat on the broad window seat and pulled out her sketch book. Idly she flipped over the pages, noticing with approval a sketch that caught Jed's youthful gaiety as he stood beside the old cannon on the Green, seeing once more the children in swift movement at Central Park, pausing to study the stern face of the man who watched the children with such a bleak expression.

She became aware that she had lingered over the man's face for minutes and hastily chose a blank page. Busily she made a note of dimensions and then she began to sketch the rooms as she visualized them, planning furniture, lamps and curtains, making suggestions for color.

A blue corner cupboard in the dining room, a dropleaf table against a wall, a flip-top chest with brass handles, a reproduction of a handwoven bedspread in some deep rich color for the master bedroom, a hooked rug.

She made a mental note to start looking into local handcrafts. There might be things that would help give these old houses charm and a feeling for the traditional and at the same time interest local people in devoting more time to handcrafts, so adding to their incomes. The faster she worked the more excited she became.

The work was so absorbing that time passed unnoticed. What roused her at last was the realization that her hand was too cold to control the pencil, that she was chilled through from sitting motionless in the unheated house. She looked at her watch. Jeepers, no wonder she was shaking with a chill! She had been sitting there for two hours. What could have happened to Jed? Had he been so infatuated with his cooing blonde that he had completely forgotten her?

Unable to sit still any longer, she went outside. Walking would warm her and restore her circulation. She set off at a brisk pace in the direction in which the jeep had gone. There was a flash of color, and a red fox dashed across the road and into the bushes, pursued by a boxer. Crows rising from the road with a flapping of wings startled the big dog. They startled Elinor, too, and she lost her precarious footing and went down in the snow.

She was unhurt by the fall, because the snow was deep and soft, and she lay for a moment looking up at the gray sky. As she looked, a cloud slid away from the sun and the world suddenly blinded her with color. Something wet and soft touched her cheek. The boxer was nuzzling her face.

"Hello, there," she said and held out her hand. Gravely he put his paw in it. Then he nuzzled her again, trying to prod her into getting up.

She laughed. "I'm quite all right," she assured him and scrambled to her feet.

She brushed off the snow and looked down the road. There was no sign of the jeep and she didn't know how far away Jed's other houses might be. A trifle disconsolately, she turned back, the boxer leading the way to show he was in charge of the expedition, and looking back at her from time to time.

"Go home," she told him.

He hesitated and looked at her so imploringly that she laughed.

"Home, sir."

He trotted back in the direction from which he had come. Elinor, with her hands thrust deep in her pockets and the hood pulled far over her face, started the long tramp home. Indignation at Jed seethed in her. However fascinating Mrs. Grant might be, he had no right to forget her, to leave her for hours in that freezing house, to make her walk home.

She trudged along, the road seeming endless in her irritation. Then she remembered the Dreadful Warning on the park bench and laughed at herself. Suppose Jed had forgotten her temporarily. At least, he had given her a job, three houses to make warm and beautiful for someone to live in.

I have a job, she thought, and her heart began to sing.

Half a dozen young people were already on the ice, circling to a Strauss waltz coming from a big loudspeaker, by the time Elinor and Harold Brown reached Green Pond that afternoon. When they had put on their skates Harold took her mittened hands and they moved out across the smooth ice in time to the music, calling greetings to the other skaters.

"Elinor! When did you get back?" . . . "Call me tomorrow!" . . . "Come to dinner Monday!" . . . "Have you time to work with the Girl Scouts again?" . . . "How long can you stay?" . . . "When's the first one-man show to be?"

Elinor called back gay replies, heart warm at her welcome. Ginny or no Ginny, this was home. This was where she belonged. At her side Harold beamed. Other people noticed, as well as Elinor, his proprietary manner and turned to give the couple a look of surprised speculation as they swooped and dipped across the ice.

A tall sturdy girl, skating alone, began to whirl and leap, and the other skaters cleared a space for her while they watched. The beauty of the motion was like the soaring flight of a bird.

"I hear she's going in for the Olympics again," Harold said. "She got third place last time, didn't she?"

"Yes. Betty's really wonderful. I'm so proud of her I could burst," Elinor said, her face glowing.

"Betty Martin. Another old friend. You're certainly loyal, Elinor. Why, she's only a beauty parlor operator."

"We went to school together, and I like her. She has supported her ailing mother and a young sister for four years. I think she's a fine person."

Something in her firm tone made Harold say with an easy laugh, "Okay. Calm down. She's fine if you say so. Did you know she's engaged to be married?"

"No. Who is he?"

"Bert Jackson, a state trooper."

"Oh, grand! I must see her and hear all about it."

"Not this afternoon," Harold said. "This belongs to me. Remember?"

He caught her hand and led her, in long swift strokes, toward the lower end of the pond where they could be by themselves.

"Elinor, have you been thinking about what I said last night? About that job I want you to take?"

"Please, Harold, don't. It's no use. I'm grateful and I'm flattered and I'm proud to think you want me to be your wife, but—"

"But the answer is no?"

"The answer is no."

They skated side by side without words. Stealing a quick look at his face, Elinor felt a pang of sympathy. All the assurance had faded. He looked profoundly depressed.

"Harold—" she began impulsively.

He summoned up a wry smile. "I've just been trying to figure out what to do next. When you've based all your plans and your ambition and your dreams on one girl—" He broke off. "Well, that's that. What are your plans, Nell—Elinor?"

"I've found a job. That is—I think I have."

"You've got a job already? What?"

"Jed found it for me, furnishing the houses he designed and built."

"Jed," Harold said thoughtfully. "But Jed's stonybroke. He had to borrow money at the bank last month. He can't support himself, let alone pay you a salary."

"Oh, I wouldn't be working for him. For Mr. Sewell. It depends, of course, on what he thinks about it, whether he approves of my qualifications."

"He'll approve of you if he's normal. Any man—"

"Oh, Harold, please!"

"Okay." He was thoughtful again. "Sewell the mystery man. Well, well. Ginny will be pleased."

"Why?"

"Oh, she's already become thick as thieves," he chuckled, "with Sewell's sister, Mrs. Campbell."

Elinor disliked his words but she was more troubled by what he implied. At length she asked lightly, "But why mystery man? What's so mysterious about my prospective boss?"

Harold shrugged. "People don't just step out of a vacuum with what seems to be a fortune. I don't want you to get mixed up with these people, that's all."

"But why?" Elinor asked, suddenly worried about

Jed. If all his bright hopes were to be dashed now it would be a bitter disappointment to him.

"The rumors around town are that the guy is a big gambler. I can't prove it. Nobody knows anything. But you don't belong in that kind of circle, you belong— well, in a garden," Harold said.

"That's one of the nicest things anyone ever said to me."

He smiled at her. "Remember it, will you?"

"I'll bear it in mind."

As the early twilight dimmed the sky and the landscape, he took her back to his car. They were silent on the drive to Hastings. He helped her out in front of the house.

"Thank you, Elinor, for a happy time."

He was gone before she could answer him. As she entered she felt more kindly toward Harold than she ever had before.

Ginny came out of the living room. "Oh, there you are! I was getting worried. We're all invited to dinner and I didn't know where to reach you. Have you a nice evening dress?"

"Only that old yellow one. I haven't needed evening clothes in New York."

"I suppose it will have to do. I'll tell Mrs. Groom to press it. Mrs. Campbell telephoned. Her brother is here and she wants us to know him."

Elinor laughed softly. "Ginny, you *are* plotting to introduce another perfectly *mar*-velous man!"

"Oh, you couldn't marry him, I'm sorry to say. Mr. Sewell married a girl named Mary Todd and they have a son. That's all I know. I don't think his wife is with him. Mrs. Campbell hasn't said much about them. I know there was another brother but something happened."

Ginny looked at her tiny jeweled watch. "You'd better see about your dress. I do hope Clay gets home on time for once. He usually stays at the office until after six, seeing people who claim they can't get there earlier. If he'd only take a job in a New York firm—" She sighed and led the way upstairs.

While Elinor bathed and dressed she thought about her disturbing conversation with Harold. Something seemed to be wrong with the man Stephen Sewell. Ginny and Mrs. Campbell were "thick as thieves." At least she would see the man for herself. It would be better to have some idea of what he was like before she told Ginny and Clay about her job. If Mr. Sewell was willing to give her the job, of course.

She brushed her dark hair until it was burnished and slipped over her head the yellow evening dress. With her coat on her arm she went downstairs. Clay and Ginny were waiting for her, the former gravely handsome in his dinner jacket, Ginny enchanting in a short white evening dress that made her look about sixteen. Clay looked from one to the other, smiling.

"I'm proud of my two girls," he said. "You're both very lovely."

"We'd better start," Ginny said nervously. "The roads are slippery and I don't want to be late. You're so crazy about houses. Nell—wait until you see the Rivers house—the Sewell house. It's magnificent."

The word wasn't too extravagant, Elinor thought, when Clay maneuvered the station wagon into the big circular driveway before a fieldstone house that seemed to stretch two city blocks. The door opened and a butler admitted them to a round entrance lobby out of which rose a graceful stairway. There were men's and women's cloakrooms, beautifully appointed, on either side.

"Mr. and Mrs. Parks, Miss Parks," the butler announced.

The big drawing room on the left took up half the length of the house, a spacious room, formal in design but warmed by a blazing fire, by glowing color and by massed flowers on low tables.

The woman in the flame-colored dress who came to meet them had a narrow face and an eager vivacious manner.

"Mrs. Parks! How kind of you to come out on this brutal night. Mr. Parks! At last I have a chance to know you. Steve and I have been looking forward to becoming acquainted with our neighbors. Miss Parks! This is good of you. Steve, come here and meet these charming people."

The warmth was real. Her eager hospitality seemed genuine. But Elinor was staggered. This was the woman called Julie whom she had seen the night before, who had been warned about something criminal. Behind her she heard a deep, quiet voice and braced herself.

"My brother, Stephen Sewell," Mrs. Campbell said.

Elinor turned to face the man from Central Park.

Afterwards, Elinor had the most confused impression of that evening. Stephen Sewell had been a flawless host, though his manner had the sternness, the remoteness she had first seen in his face. He was watchful of his guests' comfort, unobtrusive in his attentions, but he remained a stranger. They might never have exchanged those few simple friendly words in the park, he might never have saved her from an ugly, perhaps a fatal, accident.

If it had not been for Jed's unexpected presence Elinor would have felt completely lost, a new sensation to a girl who, though unspoiled, was accustomed to an unusual degree of popularity. Jed seemed to be at home in this house.

"Elinor!" he called eagerly. He stepped back with his hands up in a gesture of surrender. "Will you forgive me? That was really awful. How did you get home?"

"I walked." She laughed at his expression of dismay. "So long as you confess your sins, you are forgiven."

Jed flushed. "Well, you see, we got talking and—"

"I see." Her face was grave but her eyes sparkled with amusement. "Did she decide on one of the houses?"

"Not exactly. That is, by the time we had finished lunch—"

"Oh, you went to lunch, too?"

"*Kamerad!*" He turned, laughing, to the tall, thin man, who was watching them soberly. "Mr. Sewell, I hope you and Elinor will have a chance to talk later. No one could handle the job we were discussing better than she could."

Sewell arched his brows. "Are you really interested in furnishing my houses?"

"I'd love to try it," she assured him, the larkspur eyes wide with earnestness. "When I was in the cottage this morning I had all kinds of ideas. There are Early American reproductions that aren't terribly expensive but would be perfect there."

Julie Campbell caught her words. "Steve has this thing about Early American. I call it a fixation. Just because Rod—" She caught her breath and looked at her brother in dismay. When the butler announced dinner she sighed in relief.

At the long table with its polished damask cloth Elinor was seated between Stephen Sewell and Jed. Ginny, on her host's right, was monopolizing his attention, and Mrs. Campbell was talking to Jed, speaking almost in a whisper. Elinor, sipping the clear soup, looked at the paintings on the wall, the conventional and the abstract elbowing each other in a friendly harmony. A glowing Turner next to a Toulouse-Lautrec. And surely —surely that was a Manet seascape? A man in a high collar and stock, of the period of 1820, looked down sternly at her from eyes deep-set in a narrow face.

Unconsciously Elinor turned from the painting to the man beside her. She was confused to find him watching her. He nodded.

"My great-great-grandfather. The family type hangs on, doesn't it?"

"I see you're looking at our grim ancestor, Miss Parks," Julie said. "Isn't his resemblance to Steve amazing? It might be his own portrait, except for the clothes."

"It's the work of a very fine painter," Elinor said. "I don't recognize the style. Who was he?"

"No one knows. Are you interested in painting. Miss Parks?"

"I've studied a bit," Elinor said lightly.

"Speaking as an entirely prejudiced brother." Clay put in, "I think Elinor is darned good. The portrait she did of my wife is much the best I have of her."

"But it makes me look so—immature, Clay," Ginny said fretfully, and for a moment there was a shadow of a smile in Steve Sewell's eyes, though it did not reach his lips.

"Have you ever tried to paint children?" Mrs. Campbell asked.

"I've done some sketches."

Elinor half expected that Steve would speak, would say he had seen them and liked them, but he was silent. Had he forgotten their earlier meeting? Didn't he recognize her? There was nothing in his manner to indicate that he had ever seen her before. Severely handsome in dinner clothes, he was a stranger, a cold but polite stranger.

"Do you think you could tackle my little girl?" Mrs. Campbell said eagerly. "Merry is only seven and she simply can't keep still, but I have my heart set on a picture of her while she's still so—so new and dewy. Could you?"

Elinor smiled at the eager face of her hostess. "It would be fun to try."

"You're an angel! If it works out, Steve, that will be your birthday present from me."

"Then, for once, I shall look forward to my birthday," he said.

Cornish game hen and wild rice were followed by crisp salad with cheese straws that melted in the mouth and then by a lime ice and tiny cakes.

Coffee was served in the library, a smaller room than the big drawing room, with deep comfortable chairs.

"It's cozier in here," Julie Campbell said as she poured coffee. "Now tell us about Hastings. My brother and I want to know our community and be part of it."

"Good," Clay approved. "That's the spirit. We can use people like you who want to be good citizens. It's a nice village. Law-abiding. Some poverty, but not much and not too bad, though we could do with a new industry to employ more people. A rewarding place to live in."

"But there's nothing in Hastings!" Ginny exclaimed. "Just a village. A backwash. Stagnation. The PTA and the Girl Scouts and the hospital committee. It's a desert island. When I think of New York and all the life going on there I could scream."

Clay gave her a startled look as he became aware of the extent of her dissatisfaction.

"But life goes on everywhere," Steve said quietly. "Personally I think one gets closer to it, closer to people, closer to reality in a village than in a great city. I intend to put down roots here so deeply that I can't be dislodged. Don't you, Julie?"

His sister nodded emphatically. "Yes, I do. I think it is the perfect place for both of us to start over." She caught her breath. "Bridge?" She glanced at her brother and added, hastily, "No stakes. Just for fun."

She, Ginny, Clay, and Jed settled down at a bridge table, while Steve, at Julie's suggestion, showed Elinor some of the *objets d'art* which a seafaring ancestor had collected on his voyages around the world. Before a Ming vase she stood for a long time in wordless delight.

"Tell me why you want to furnish the houses," Steve asked, when they had finished their inspection and had drawn up chairs before the fire.

"Well, first," Elinor began, telling herself that it was absurd to feel shy with this man, "because I must have a job; second, because I love transforming an empty room into a warm and livable place; third, because it would be such fun to work with Jed. He's my oldest and dearest friend."

"So I understand," he said evenly. "Gordon was telling us before you came."

"Mr. Sewell"—she swallowed nervously—"do you think I'd do?"

He smiled then, and his face was warm and alight. "You'll do."

"When do I start?"

At her eager expression he suddenly laughed. Hearing the unexpectedly joyous sound, his sister looked up, and turned from him to Elinor. There was something very like gratitude in her expression.

"Tomorrow, if you like."

"I do like."

"Suppose we go over them together," he suggested. "We'll make the Grand Tour. I'll pick you up—would ten be too early?—and we can get a general idea of our problem."

"That will be fine," Elinor agreed.

"Sorry to break up a nice evening," Clay said, "but I have some papers to go over tonight before I see a client at 9:30 in the morning."

"Oh, must you?" wailed Ginny.

"Sorry, darling, I really must."

As they left the library Jed said in a half-whisper, "Well?"

Elinor nodded. "I think it's going to be all right."

He gave her an exuberant hug. "I knew it would be! Couldn't fail. Honey, you look like a daffodil in that yellow thing. As though spring had walked into the room."

She laughed at him and turned to see Steve's eyes on her. Hard to believe that stern face could ever warm in a laugh.

"Have lunch with me day after tomorrow and meet my little girl," Julie said. Impulsively she leaned forward and kissed Elinor's cheek.

Steve took her hand in a warm, firm clasp and then stood back. "Good night, Miss Parks."

In the back of the station wagon Elinor blinked away dimness. Why, they were tears! She brushed them away hastily. How ridiculous. There was nothing to cry for. She had a job, hadn't she? And a pleasant boss.

He married a girl named Mary Todd and they have a little boy.

Queer that no one had mentioned Mrs. Stephen Sewell or the child. What difference does it make? Elinor asked herself sternly. She did not try to find the answer.

V

Next morning, Elinor was the first in the house to be awake. Outside her window the crows seemed to be holding a convention, their caw-caw-caw rising stridently in the silence. In another few months, she thought with a surge of joy, there would be thrushes singing their hearts out, cardinals and bluebirds splashing the air with color.

She chose a leaf-green knitted dress, tied a yellow scarf under her chin, and nodded saucily at her reflection. The light of battle was in her eyes. Apparently Stephen Sewell had forgotten their meeting, forgotten the sketches he had seemed to admire so much. Never before had any man treated her as though she had failed to make the slightest impression on him, in spite of Ginny's implication that though she was given every chance, she didn't please men. There was an impish expression on her face. So he hadn't remembered her! Before this day was done she would see that he did.

By the time Mrs. Groom came into the kitchen Elinor had already finished breakfast.

"What got you up at the crack of dawn?" the house keeper demanded, trying to frown but smiling in spite of herself at the radiant girl. "I declare you look better already. And that dress is mighty becoming to you."

"All this bouncing energy is a sign of the working

woman," Elinor told her gaily. "I've got a job and I'm starting this morning."

"Does Clay know it?" Mrs. Groom asked as she bustled around the spotless kitchen starting her preparations for breakfast.

"Not yet. I'll tell him after I'm sure it's all settled."

"You mean you're supposed to be on the job at 7:30?"

"No, but I have some preparations to make."

While Mrs. Groom stirred muffins and put on coffee and set out eggs to boil and grapefruit to cut, Elinor told her about the job. It was her way of showing the housekeeper that their relationship had not changed, that she could still pour out her confidences as she had as a child, knowing they would meet with understanding.

"Don't you worry," the older woman said, putting her hand for a moment on the girl's slim shoulder, "it's going to work out fine. Only thing I don't like—"

"Well?"

"It should be your own home you're planning to make beautiful and livable. You'll be the kind of wife and mother that your mother was. And with the same loving heart and the same sunshine about you. All I hope is"—and she blinked away tears—"you'll have a long life to gladden the hearts of those about you. I always kinda hoped you and Jed—"

"Jed's like a brother," Elinor assured her. "Anyhow," she added more soberly, "I wouldn't be a bit surprised if Jed had found someone of his own."

"That would surprise *me*," Mrs. Groom retorted. "He's always thought the sun rose and set in you."

Elinor laughed and told her about Mrs. Alice Grant, the glamorous blonde who had swept Jed off his feet and made him forget all about her.

"Hmm. If he falls for a girl who simply snaps her fingers and expects him to follow, he's not as bright as I think he is. And Jed's sound all the way through. Remember that time Clay broke the window and Jed took the spanking for it?"

Elinor laughed. "Then Clay found out and he was furious because he should have been the one to be punished and so they fought about it. Aren't boys crazy?"

"No crazier than girls. Those two never ran away from trouble in their lives. That's always a good sign."

"A good sign of what?"

"Of a good husband. And if I were you, young lady—"

Elinor smiled to cover her annoyance. "Between you and Ginny, you'll marry me off yet."

"Well, not to the same man. That's for sure."

"Good heavens!" Elinor's peal of laughter forced Mrs. Groom to smile in spite of herself.

"Now you know what I mean." She looked up as the gray mist rolled away, showing the deep blue of the sky. Icicles hanging from the eaves began to drip under the sun, sending bright drops down into the snow. "Sometimes it seems to me you bring the sunshine into this house, Elinor. And one thing sure—you bring laughter. Not much laughter here since you've been away. I wish, for Clay's sake, young Mrs. Parks knew how to be happy by giving instead of getting."

It was always young Mrs. Parks. Never Ginny. Not even the more formal Virginia.

"Give her time," Elinor said. "She's awfully young."

"She's a year older than you are," Mrs. Groom retorted. "And looks it, too, for all her baby ways."

"But she loves Clay. In the long run, she wouldn't hurt him. Not if she knew it."

"I'll hope you are right." Mrs. Groom slid a pan of muffins into the oven. "What do you want with that laundry soap?"

"Squeaky hinges," Elinor explained. "I've got things to do. I'll tell you all about it when I get back."

She hugged the housekeeper and went through the swinging door waving the bar of yellow soap like a trophy and singing "I'll see you again."

When the long sleek car drew up before the house, Elinor was ready and waiting. The proper tone, she thought, would be a pleasant but impersonally business-like manner. She opened the door, filled her arms and started down the steps. With that lack of a sense of the timely so characteristic of inanimate things, the flower pots in her arms began to slide.

"Hurry!" she wailed. "These things are s-slip-ping!"

Stephen Sewell opened the car door and ran up the steps to meet her. He took the flower pots and the large bar of soap out of her arms and then had to stand help-lessly while she opened the back door of the car. Care-fully she deposited the flower pots on the floor.

"There!" she said with a sigh of relief.

"Where do you want these delivered?"

"They are for the new houses. Wait and see what a difference they make."

"And the soap? Were you planning to scour the houses today, Miss Parks?"

At his grave tone she looked up quickly and saw in relief that his eyes were laughing at her. He was ob-viously delighted and amused by her novel approach to house furnishing.

"That's for the hinges. They squeak."

"That would never do, would it?"

He took the same road Jed had taken the day be-fore. This time the trip seemed to be much shorter.

"I thought at first this was going to be another bleak winter day," he said.

" 'The sun that bleak December day rose cheerless over fields of gray,' " she declaimed.

"And then," he said with a glance at her, "the sun came out."

His manner was impersonal but something in his voice gave the words a personal meaning.

"So," she said hastily, "we won't be snowbound, after all."

"Pity, isn't it?" Sewell passed without stopping the office where Jed was at work.

"Mr. Sewell," she said abruptly, "I wonder if you

know—Jed was telling me yesterday how you came to give him this opportunity. He's terribly grateful."

"I was lucky to find him. Most young architects today want to go all out in new designs—not that I blame them, of course—and they're not happy when they are asked to go back to old conventional building."

"If all your houses are as charming as the saltbox I should think anyone would love to live in them."

"You don't object to old-fashioned houses then? You don't think, as Julie does, I have a bee in my bonnet?"

"After all, they're your houses. You have a right to build them as you choose."

"True, but that's not quite the point, is it?"

"Well," Elinor said carefully, "I think they're both good, the old ways and the new. I don't see why we should discard what is good about the old. But I don't see either why we should close our eyes to new things. But what really matters with a house is how you live in it."

He gave her a quick smile. "You're right, of course. This idea I have—building old houses—it's a kind of debt I am paying." His hands rested lightly on the wheel, his eyes were watching the road with brooding intentness.

He did not speak again until they reached the little saltbox.

"What do we do first?"

"If you'll help me with the flower pots—"

He carried them inside and set them on the broad window seat.

"Br-r-r, it's cold in here!"

"Wait until you've been in it for two hours as I was yesterday," she said feelingly.

"I have an idea." He went outside while she set the geraniums and the ivy on the windowsills and mantel. In a few minutes he returned with some dry brush and loose boards from which he had beaten the snow, and a newspaper from the car. He knelt and laid a fire. He struck a match and the paper caught. In a few minutes the wood was snapping cheerfully.

"Now what?"

"Now we'll soap those hinges on the door so it will open invitingly and not seem to protest when people come in. So inhospitable."

He laughed.

"It's important, I think, to throw wide the door when people come, as though the house opened its arms to welcome them. It's—well, a kind of symbol of welcoming life itself."

"What ideas you do have." He spoke gaily but a light had been kindled behind his yes. "No, let me. You are the director of this enterprise and I'm the handyman."

"And very handy, too," she conceded, when he had proudly opened and shut the silent door half a dozen times.

They sat side by side on the broad window seat, with the fire making the room bright, and Elinor showed him the rough sketches she had made of the rooms.

"I don't want them to look like those impersonal decorated rooms in department stores," she explained, "where you can't move a chair or lay down a magazine without spoiling the whole effect. I want them simple and bright and warm, so they're lovely to look at but not too fine to live in. A place where children can run around without spoiling things but still learn about beauty."

"I see," he said quietly.

"Do you like the idea?" She looked up and caught the expression on his face. Color flooded her cheeks.

He did not seem to notice. "Yes, I like it very much." Unexpectedly he got up. "Perhaps," he said, his manner brusque, "we'd better get on and see the other houses. I'll douse that fire first."

When every spark had been extinguished he paused for a moment at the door.

"The geraniums do make a difference, don't

they?" Elinor said, breaking a silence that was beginning to disturb her. "I do love leautiful things!"

"So do I," he said unsteadily. "Shall we go?"

The Cape Cod house was a quarter of a mile down the road. As Steve's long black car negotiated the icy driveway, there was a deep growl and a boxer ran toward the car.

"Wait a minute," Steve warned the girl, "until I take care of that dog."

She laughed. "We're old friends," she declared. She opened the door and held out her hand. The boxer came forward slowly, paused, and then gravely held out its paw.

"Well, I'll be doggoned!" From behind the house came a man wearing overalls on top of a heavy sweater and slacks. "Ho! Ho! I never saw him make friends as fast as that before. Down, Ho!"

"What a funny name," Elinor said.

"I had two of them, Ho and Hum. Hum was too trusting and got himself killed. Ho is more cautious about getting acquainted, as a rule."

"We got acquainted yesterday," Elinor told him, "and he practically adopted me."

"I wish you could adopt him," the carpenter said, bending over to pat the dog's head. "I haven't got a place to keep him any more. Itinerant worker. Footloose and fancy-free. I just move from job to job. Trouble is the next one is going to be in a place where the workers have a kind of boardinghouse to themselves. Living paid for, which is good; but no dogs allowed, which is not so good."

"You must hate to give him up," she said sympathetically.

"Yeah." His hand rested on the dog's head for a moment. "Yeah. He's kind of companionable and I wouldn't want anyone to have him who doesn't understand his good points. I don't suppose you—"

Elinor shook her head. "I'd love to have him, but I'm staying with my sister-in-law. She doesn't like animals much."

The carpenter leaned against the side of the car while he and Elinor discussed the dog, and Steve watched them both, smiling. How simple and friendly she was! And how unconscious of her loveliness. Jed had been right. She was like the spring itself. He scowled. Confound Jed! Why should he have all the luck?

Elinor, seeing the frown, got hastily out of the car. She had been keeping her boss waiting.

"Just finishing the garage," the carpenter said. "Everything else is shipshape. I suppose you've got a right to see the house?"

"I own it."

"Oh, then you'd be Mr. Sewell. Seen you around town. The architect was here yesterday, showing the place to a lady." He whistled appreciatively and strolled around the house. Ho followed a few steps and then returned, his rear end wagging in ecstasy, and stood looking at Elinor with pleading eyes.

"No walk," she told him.

He pressed his nose into her hand, imploring her.

"You're just a con man," Elinor said, "trying to beguile me."

Steve laughed. "You've made a conquest."

"So has Ho. I wish I could keep him. He's a darling."

An hour and a half later they had completed their tour of the houses. Steve looked at his watch.

"Twelve-thirty. Is it too early for you or will you lunch with me at the inn? We could sort out our impressions and plan the next step. All right?"

Thinking of the 6:30 breakfast, Elinor grinned. "I'm starving," she declared.

There were only a few people in the dining room at the Hastings Inn when the headwaiter led them to a table. When they had ordered, they decided on the pieces that Elinor would buy, how her drawing account was to be arranged, and what was to be done about draperies, slipcovers and lamps.

"I'd like to have the slipcovers made in Hastings. I know a woman who could do them as well as they'd be done in the city and much cheaper. And she does need the money."

"The decision is up to you."

"For that blue kitchen I'd love to have copper pans, gleaming and bright on the walls. But I suppose it's too extravagant."

"Let's splurge."

"And in the dining room, which is a little dark, I'd like to put a blue vase filled with forsythia. It would be like bottled sunlight and might give ideas to the future owner. And the house with that rather stiff-looking lawn and driveway—couldn't we set out crocuses and plant some flowering bushes along the drive and maybe set out a cherry tree or a Japanese maple on—"

She glanced up and broke off. Across the room, their heads together, completely absorbed in each other, were Jed Gordon and the brassy blonde.

Later that afternoon Elinor lay back in a chair in the Hastings Beauty Salon while Betty Martin shampooed her hair.

"We saw you at Green Pond yesterday," Elinor said. "Your skating gets better and better. You gave a spectacular performance."

"Saw you, too, with Harold Brown. From the way he acted I expected the loud-speaker would start blaring 'Here Comes the Bride.' "

"It won't. Not for me. But how about you? I hear—"

The big sturdy girl wrapped a towel around Elinor's hair, tilted up the chair and turned it so they could see each other in the mirror.

"Bert Jackson. He's a state trooper stationed at Newcomb."

"I'm so terribly glad for you, Betty. You deserve a lot of happiness."

"I don't know about the deserving, but I'll be getting it."

"When is the great day going to be?"

"I don't know. Right now Bert is on a special assignment and his hours are simply awful. We hardly get to see each other at all."

"That's a shame."

"No, it isn't, really, because he loves his job. Did you ever know a trooper who wasn't proud of his uniform and his job? Hard work and long hours and danger and low pay. But he couldn't be anything else and I wouldn't have him change. If he's happy in it then I'm satisfied."

Thinking of Ginny, Elinor was silent. This plain girl whose life had been one of self-denial had learned more about happiness than Ginny had even guessed.

Looking into the mirror Elinor watched Betty as her deft fingers made pin curls. Plain? No, the glow in Betty's face made her almost pretty. Who was it who said that all brides are beautiful?

"Tell me about your Bert."

"Well, he's good-looking and he's kind and he's hardworking. I don't know how to put him into words. I wish," Betty said shyly, "you could meet him someday."

"Of course, I've got to meet him. How long do you think he'll be on that special assignment?"

Betty shrugged her shoulders. "There's no telling. It's that big bank robbery at Newcomb. They got away without a trace and the money never turned up. Bert said there was a roadblock within twenty minutes, but somehow they slipped through."

"But that was months ago—last year. How can they expect to catch the robbers now?"

"Well, it's Bert's idea that the Newcomb robbery was part of a pattern. There's been one just like it every year, one big *coup* and then the men probably live on the proceeds until the next time. They've put Bert onto it."

"But it might be months before the case is solved."

"I know. But Bert and I can wait. Anyhow, we have to wait. He's willing to look after my mother and Sue, my kid sister, but it isn't fair to bring him more burdens. Maybe Sue will find a job one of these days and when my mother is stronger she'll be able to get back to her sewing. We've just got to be patient."

"How is your mother now?"

"She doesn't seem to pick up. I just don't know why."

"What does the doctor say?"

"I can't afford a doctor," Betty said.

There was the *ping* of a warning bell as the door opened. Betty looked out of her booth.

"That darned woman again," she muttered. "Wants a touchup for those blonde locks. I told her the only time I could give her was late yesterday afternoon, but she had an engagement she couldn't break. Now she's back again."

In the mirror Elinor saw Mrs. Alice Grant, wearing a magnificent mink coat.

"You've simply got to take me," she said. "My hair is a mess."

Her voice, when she talked to the beauty operator, was so different from the dulcet tones with which she addressed men that Elinor smothered a giggle.

"I'm sorry," Betty said. "The only free time I had this week for a touch-up was yesterday afternoon."

"I might as well have come. My friend never showed up." She was furiously angry. "Well, if you can't, I suppose you can't. I'll have to run over to New Haven. That's one of the many reasons why I loathe small towns." She flounced out, leaving a wave of sickening perfume in the air, and the door banged behind her.

"Well," Betty exclaimed, "what a nice addition *she's* going to be to our little circle. You know what I think?"

Elinor, who had a strong distaste for gossip, said hastily, "Do tell me about the skating. Are you planning to try out for the Olympics?"

VI

When she came out of the beauty parlor, Elinor hesitated for a moment. She was reluctant to go home and face Ginny's questions about where she had been. Better wait until Clay was home and tell them both at once about the new job.

On impulse she left the shopping center and walked swiftly toward the little back street where the Martin house, shabby and unpainted, stood beside a busy garage, the front door only a couple of feet back from the sidewalk. She stood looking at it, hands thrust deep in her pockets. If it were painted a barn red it would be most attractive, present a gay front to the world.

She knocked on the door and waited. After some delay a young girl opened it and peered out at her.

"Miss Parks!" she exclaimed. "Oh, swell. Come in, won't you?"

"Thank you, Sue."

The living room was shabby and untidy. It hadn't been dusted for a long time. Sue looked around in discontent. She would have been a pretty girl if it had not been for her sulky expression.

"The place is a mess," she said. "I've been giving myself a manicure," she exhibited blood-red nails with exaggerated points, "and I haven't had time to do anything to the house. Mom rides me about it all the time. She seems to think a girl has nothing to do but be a slave."

"How is your mother?"

"Just the same. Want to see her?"

She led the way upstairs to the room where Mrs. Martin lay on the bed. Her worn face lighted when she saw Elinor.

"Miss Parks! How very nice of you. Betty told me you were back in Hastings."

"How are you?"

Mrs. Martin made an impatient gesture. "Just the same. It enrages me, lying here helpless while Betty carries all the load. And yet I'm sure I could get enough sewing to do to help out if I could just get off this bed."

"Can't Sue help?"

Mrs. Martin sighed. "I'm afraid we've spoiled Sue, Betty and I. You see, we were both born plain as a plate but she was the pretty one. She thinks no job is good enough for her. Now and then she'll take one but she never stays more than a month. She thinks the work is dull."

Elinor leaned forward and said, in a conspiratorial whisper, "I'll bet I can find a job she'll stick to. Leave it to me!"

"I wish you could. It's so unfair to Betty. Not that she grumbles."

"Just wait and see. You know, I've had the most marvelous idea." Elinor described the work she was going to do for Stephen Sewell. "And," she concluded, "I want you to do the draperies and slipcovers. As I came up here I was thinking what a perfect location this is for a shop, selling materials for curtains and all that. And painted a bright red it would be so attractive."

Mrs. Martin looked at her with wistful eyes. "It would be perfect—if only I could get off this bed."

"Wait and see," Elinor promised her. She leaned over to kiss the worn cheek. "Wait and see."

As she went downstairs she saw Susan turning the dials of the television set and she let herself out of the house without calling a greeting. Something was going to be done about Sue Martin.

Her next stop was at a white Colonial house on the Green, which had a small plaque: DR. RICHARD MALLI-

SON. A smiling nurse in a crisp uniform admitted her.

"Miss Parks? I heard you were back. But you certainly don't look as though you needed a doctor."

"Not for myself," Elinor said. "Is Doctor Dick busy?"

The nurse laughed. "He's always busy. But right now he's stolen an hour to try to catch up on the medical journals. They're stacked as high as his head. But I know he'll see you."

In a moment she came back to lead Elinor into the familiar office where Doctor Dick sat in an old-fashioned swivel chair before a rolltop desk, both of which had belonged to his father.

He came to meet her, hand outstretched. "Elinor, I heard you were back. Sit down, my dear."

Dr. Richard Mallison (Doctor Dick to the people of Hastings) was a big vital-looking man of forty, with a fine forehead deeply grooved by worry, and the tired eyes of a man who never gets enough sleep. He was, Elinor thought, the kindest human being she had ever known.

"What's bothering you?" he asked quietly. "I can see it isn't yourself. Clay? Ginny?"

"Mrs. Martin."

"Mrs.—Oh, the mother of our skating champion. What's wrong with her?"

"I don't know, Doctor Dick, but she's been bedridden for four years and Betty's carried the whole load for the family. Mrs. Martin wants terribly to be able to work again, but—"

"What does her doctor say?"

"She doesn't have one. Betty says they can't afford it."

"Can't afford—Jupiter and all the gods! That's ridiculous!"

Elinor grinned. "Let me tell you a story. Most doctors make their patients pay for their services, and pay plenty. Haven't you heard? Anyhow, I wondered—do you think—I'm ashamed to ask when I know how busy you are—"

"That's what I'm here for. Ask your silly friend if she'd like to have me call on her mother."

"Oh, thank you," Elinor exclaimed, her face glowing. She made the call and turned to the doctor. "She—she was crying."

"I'll look in on her mother today. Fortunately, she's an adult. There's not another inch of space in the children's wing. People have money for everything, it seems to me, but the important things."

"Doctor Dick!" Elinor exclaimed. "Look, why can't we have a fair, an old-fashioned country fair, all the money to go for an extension to the children's wing at the hospital. Why can't we?"

"My God, that would be—" Doctor Dick shook his head speechlessly. He laid his hand gently over hers. "You're—quite a girl, Elinor. We need you here in Hastings. Don't you go away again."

"Not if I can help it," she said. She jumped to her feet. "I'm going to get to work on the fair right away. Hastings is going to make history," she boasted. "I can't wait to get started."

Clay was late that night, his face drawn with fatigue when he came in and dropped a heavy briefcase on the hall chair.

"Oh, Clay, you aren't going to work tonight, are you?" Ginny wailed. "There's a wonderful television program."

"Sorry, darling, I've got to go over some papers. You and Elinor can watch the program."

Ginny leaned against him, rubbing her bright head on his shoulder as though she were a kitten. "But it's no fun without you."

He smiled down at her tenderly and Elinor thought: I ought to forgive her for a lot. Clay loves her so much.

That night Mrs. Groom served a homemade vegetable soup, fried chicken that was so tender it fell off the fork, mashed potatoes like a fluffy cloud and fresh green peas she had put up in the deep-freeze the summer before. She came in with a plate of popovers.

"My favorite meal," Clay told her with a smile.

Mrs. Groom shot a quick look at Ginny. "I guess I ought to know what you like," she told him gruffly. "And that soup has a good nourishing stock. Ought to put some stamina into you."

Ginny eyed her plate with distaste. "Wasn't that Cornish game hen wonderful last night? Or perhaps it was just the change. Mrs. Groom tries so hard, but she has no imagination. Sometimes her meals just take away my appetite."

Clay, eating hungrily, made no comment.

"There are some new restaurants in New York that sound marvelous," Ginny went on. "A place where they make the most exotic curries right in front of you and you sit on cushions on the floor."

Clay looked up to grin at her. "I'm too old for gymnastics when I eat. I'll take a chair, if it's all the same to you."

"But it would be fun to try something different for once, Clay," Ginny said pleadingly, putting down her fork and leaning toward him. "Can't we go to the city just for two or three weeks? See some plays and eat decent food and do some shopping? It will be Easter before you know it and I haven't anything fit to wear for spring. Please, Clay. Please."

His face grew paler, more tired. "I wish I could say yes, darling, because I know your heart is set on it. But I can't."

"Why?" Ginny had leaned back in her chair, face set.

"In the first place, I can't get away right now. I'm swamped with work. In the second place, I can't afford it. The kind of outing you plan would cost a couple of thousand dollars. The thing is, we can't spend more now, Ginny, we have to spend less."

"I see," she said sullenly.

Clay's appetite was gone. He made a pretense of eating but he merely pushed the food around on his plate, watching his wife's disappointment and anger with pleading eyes.

Mrs. Groom gathered up the plates with an anxious glance at Clay's and came back with hot apple pie.

"Clay," Ginny said abruptly, "How much did that New York law firm offer you?"

"Twenty-five thousand."

"But there was more to it, wasn't there? Opportunity, expense account, a partnership in a year or two, and—"

"Yes, there was more to it," he said dully.

"So we just sit here and retrench when a job like that goes begging."

"Speaking of jobs," Elinor broke in, "I haven't had a chance yet to tell you my great news. I have a job!"

Clay was bewildered and angry. "But you don't need a job. This is your house and, heaven knows, so far as the money is concerned you—"

"But I must do something," Elinor interrupted. "I couldn't be happy if I were idle. And it's going to be fun."

Her earnestness convinced him as she had known it must if he were to accept the fact of her working.

"What is it?" Ginny asked.

When Elinor had finished her story Clay said, "Well, it sounds all right. If you're sure that's what you want to do—"

"I'll love it," Elinor assured him.

"But what about your painting?"

"I can be a week-end painter. What's good enough for Sir Winston Churchill is good enough for me."

"So that's what you and Mr. Sewell were discussing," Ginny said. "I wondered. You seem to have fascinated the whole family. I heard Mrs. Campbell ask you to lunch tomorrow—alone." She could not conceal her jealousy.

"Oh, that's another thing! She wants me to do a portrait of her little girl. It isn't a social lunch, Ginny, it's business."

Ginny brightened. "Oh, good. They've got an awful

lot of money. She'll probably pay well. Did you discuss price?"

Elinor shook her head.

"You and Clay! Anyone would know you were brother and sister. No money sense at all."

Elinor met Ginny's eyes in a long look and it was her sister-in-law who turned away first.

"I was certainly surprised," Ginny said, eager to change the subject, "to see how Jed had wormed his way into that house."

"Jed," Clay said, with his first touch of temper, "doesn't worm his way. He has talent and he's doing a fine job for Sewell. They like him for himself—as Elinor and I do."

"Mrs. Campbell certainly does. I saw her whispering to him all through dinner. And, Elinor, I think you ought to tell Jed that you're not children any more. The way he hugs you and all that, people will get the wrong ideas."

"Not about Elinor," Clay said levelly. "And not about Jed."

Ginny gave him a startled look. He had never spoken to her like that before. She glanced around to see whether they had finished and then got up from the table.

"Coffee in the living room," she ordered Mrs. Groom.

"Sorry," Clay said. "I'll have mine in the study. I've got to get to work."

"None for me tonight," Elinor decided. "I'm going up to go over my clothes and write some letters. I left New York in such a hurry—"

Clay put his arm around her and kissed her cheek. "Good luck on the job. Good night, Elinor, and sleep well."

Sleep well, she repeated to herself hours later, as she turned restlessly from side to side, more awake every minute. Because she was healthy and happy and fearless, she had rarely known what it was to be sleepless. But tonight her mind was a jumble of disturbing thoughts.

It had begun just after she turned out her light and got into bed. For a moment she had lain quietly, planning the day ahead, the highlight of which was to be her luncheon with Mrs. Campbell and an opportunity to do a portrait. How oddly different and yet how much alike that brother and sister were. They had the same narrow faces and deep-set eyes, but Julie Campbell was gay and Stephen Sewell was somber; she was warm and he was cold.

Julie Campbell, who gambled, who set such high stakes at bridge that Ginny had had to tamper with Elinor's check in order to pay her debt. "No one knows where the money comes from"—That had been Harold Brown's comment. Was Steve, like his sister, a gambler? "A perfect place for us to start over," Julie had said. To start over. Where had they come from, what had they done that they must start over, that they could start by buying the Rivers estate, which, house and land, had been priced at well over a million dollars?

Elinor turned over her pillow, shifted her position, eyes wide open in the darkness. What had Steve said about his houses? He was paying a debt. She turned from side to side. She wouldn't think of Steve or his sister any more. She—of course, she knew now why he had known so surely he could find her again. He had recognized her sketch of Jed standing beside the cannon on the Green. No one could mistake that battered cannon. The man and the place. No wonder he had been sure.

But why had he wanted to find her again? *A girl named Mary Todd. A little boy.* The sister, she remembered, was a widow—but where were Steve's wife and child? What was wrong? Was Steve divorced? Elinor hated divorce. Marriage was for keeps. Not just a business of trial and error and try again.

She turned her pillow again. Downstairs the grandfather clock bonged twice. She squeezed her eyelids shut and remembered the trouble between Clay and Ginny at dinner. He had been so tired, so worried, so over-worked, and Ginny had been blind to everything but her own discontent. Sick at heart, Elinor saw clearly that, unless a miracle happened, Ginny would win her objective, force Clay to move to the city.

If only Ginny could be like Betty Martin, who was nourished by crumbs from life's feast so long as the man she loved followed his own bent. It was a pity they should have to wait indefinitely to marry. How could the state trooper hope to capture the bank robbers at this late date? But the rest of the problems—Mrs. Martin's illness, Sue's selfish refusal to carry any share of the burden—there might be ways to solve them.

Slowly the tension left Elinor's face and her body relaxed. She was on the verge of sleep when she remembered Jed's blonde storming into Betty's shop, demanding to have her hair touched up. She might as well have come the afternoon before. Her friend hadn't kept the appointment.

Elinor was wide awake again. *Four o'clock. Usual place.* Had it been Mrs. Grant who had dropped that message? Or—she remembered Steve Sewell hunting through his pockets, a worried frown between his brows, looking for something he had lost.

She turned to bury her face in the pillow. "No, no!" she whispered. She knew then that she loved him.

Luncheon had been set at a small round table in the bay window.

"The dining table is so huge we'd have to use walky-talkies," Julie Campbell said, "and it's much nicer using the small table when there are only two of us. Just a light lunch, mushroom bisque and a crabmeat salad with little hot rolls. I hope you're not used to a heavy meal in the middle of the day."

"It sounds perfect," Elinor declared. "Where is your little girl? I'm so eager to see her."

"She has her lunch early and she is lying down. As soon as she has had her nap you'll see her. She's not at her best right now, of course. She picked up a throat infection in the fall and couldn't seem to throw it off. We've tried everything. Then we brought her here and, of course, after Arizona, the winter is so bitter she hasn't wanted to go out at all. I can't get her to take any exercise. She's just apathetic, not interested. When I do drag her out she droops around so it doesn't do her any good. I thought I'd keep her out of school for another month and try to build her up." Julie blinked back tears. "She's all I have left. Perhaps I make too much fuss and sometimes that's worse than none. Do you like children?"

Elinor nodded, smiling. "Of course."

"There's no 'of course' about it," her hostess retorted. "Some of the mothers I've seen—" she shook her head. "Steve adores Merry. I have to keep at him all the time to prevent him from spoiling her to death."

She smiled. "That red wool suit is madly becoming to you. It lights up the room."

"That's why I wore it." Elinor laughed. "I like red on a dark and gloomy day. In fact, I like color. I'm planning to splash color all over Mr. Sewell's houses."

Mrs. Campbell raised her brows. "Finished? Then let's move upstairs to my little sitting room. Merry should be awake now." In a hallway behind the circular entrance lobby she pressed a button and a tiny elevator, with a pearl-gray carpet and mirrored walls, took them up to the third floor.

Mrs. Campbell's sitting room, at the back of the house, looked down on what, in summer, would be a formal garden and, beyond, into woods and then, in the distance, rolling hills.

"I'm so glad you are going to work with Steve," she said suddenly. "You're going to be good for him. I can see that already. The other evening when he laughed I could have hugged you, I was so grateful. I haven't heard him laugh like that in three years."

She pressed a button and when a trim maid came to the door said, "Would you ask the nurse whether Miss Meredith is awake yet? I'd like to see her here as soon as she has finished her nap."

When the maid had gone she said, "I keep wondering how Merry will turn out. All the Sewell's divide into two classes: the reckless ones and the ultra-conservative ones. I'm the reckless kind myself. I'm a gambler at heart; that is, I love taking wild chances. Rod—my younger brother—was just the opposite. Rod was an architect, or rather he studied at the Beaux Arts in Paris. Then he—died. Be careful not to mention him to Steve, won't you. Poor Steve. He feels so tragically guilty. All those deaths."

Elinor's hands clenched and she hid them behind her. *So tragically guilty. All those deaths.* What had Steve Sewell done? Chills chased each other up her spine. Her throat tightened until she felt she would be unable to speak.

The door opened and a little girl came in quietly: a seven-year-old with the narrow Sewell face and deep-set eyes, with bony little legs and a small pale face. She walked listlessly, her head drooping.

"Hello, dear," her mother called cheerfully. She drew her into her arms and kissed her cheek. "Have a nice nap?"

"I guess so."

"This is Miss Parks, who is going to be our neighbor and our friend and help Uncle Steve."

The little girl turned politely to Elinor. "How do you do?" Then, unexpectedly, a three-cornered smile gave her face an unexpected pixy charm. "Oh, you're pretty!" She came closer and stood at Elinor's knee, looking into her face. "Tell me a story."

"Merry!" her mother protested.

"I'll tell you about Ho and Hum, two boxers who used to live down the road. Do you know what a boxer is?"

Merry nodded. "A big dog."

"They look like this." Elinor drew out her sketching pad and in a few vivid strokes had caught Ho. Then she added a girl sprawled on the snow with Ho nuzzling her face. While Merry stared, fascinated, she told her how Ho had tried to help her up and then had shaken hands with her. And while Elinor talked the pencil flew, illustrating the story.

"How did he get there? And where was Hum?" Merry said eagerly.

Julie Campbell watched her small daughter and her guest, a smile in her eyes. Unobtrusively she moved to a more distant chair, leaving them to become friends in their own way. In Elinor Parks's way. The girl was really irresistible, she thought.

Because Elinor had no intention of telling this fragile child of Hum's death she invented a story. Hum, she said, got bored with staying in the house. He was young and he liked to get out in the fresh air and play.

Mrs. Campbell looked up quickly and her smile deepened.

One day he packed his belongings in an old bandana handkerchief, which he tied on a stick. He hoisted the bundle over his shoulder and set out in search of adventure.

Merry looked at the picture of Hum marching off with his knapsack and let out a squeal of delight. She hopped up and down on one foot.

"And what then?"

Elinor went on with the story until she had brought Hum triumphantly home again.

"Where is Hum now?"

"Off on another adventure, I suppose. Life is so exciting and there's so much to see and do he can't bear to stay home. So poor Ho is all alone." Elinor told the little girl about the carpenter who had to go off and leave him. "He needs a home, poor fellow."

Merry scampered across the room to her mother. There was no listlessness about her now.

"Can I have him, Mummie? Can I?"

"You'll have to ask your uncle."

"Uncle Steve will say yes. I know he will. When can I have him?"

"But, Merry," Elinor said, "a dog isn't like a doll or a plaything, you know."

Merry came back and pressed against her knee, eyes anxious. "Why not?"

"You can put down a doll when you're tired of it, but a dog is real, he's alive. He has to be fed regularly and if someone else feeds him he's not truly yours. At least, he doesn't think so."

"I'd feed him."

"Every single day? You wouldn't forget? Imagine how hungry you would be if your nurse forgot your meals. Even one meal."

"I'd remember."

"And a dog likes lots of exercise. That's what keeps him healthy and happy. He likes fresh air and the warm sun on his head and the lovely cool soft feeling of rain and cold crisp snowflakes. He's curious and he likes to explore everything he sees and get acquainted with flowers and bushes and animals. He'd have to be taken for a walk every single day."

"Oh," Merry said flatly. "I don't go out much because it's so cold."

"What a shame! Because only when it's really cold can you build a snowman."

"What's a snowman?"

"Bless the child!" Mrs. Campbell exclaimed with a laugh. "It never occurred to me that, brought up in Arizona, she never saw a snowman."

Merry's eyes seemed very big. A thin hand plucked at Elinor's sleeve. "Can't I have Ho if I don't go out?"

"I suppose you could, but do you think it would be fair to him? Of course," Elinor said casually, "if you had a nice warm snowsuit, leggings and boots, we might see what we could do about building a snowman. And if we can do that, it might be possible to take Ho for a walk."

She turned around her sketching pad and Merry saw the snowman with a silk hat and a pipe in its mouth.

"Mummie!" She crossed the room like quicksilver. "May I go out? May I?"

While her nurse was bundling the eager child into

warm leggings and sweater, Julie caught Elinor's hand.

"How do I say thank you?"

Elinor showed her the sketches she had made of Merry. "She's a lovely elfin child. That's the way I'd like to paint her, half dreamer, half imp."

"You're not just good for Steve. You're good for all of us. I've got to call you Elinor. Miss Parks is too formal. And I'm Julie."

The next couple of hours were strenuous. Elinor and Merry rolled huge snowballs and pressed them together until they had an impressive snowman. Merry raced in and out of the house, tracking snow, screaming in her shrill little voice, wild with excitement. She found big buttons for the snowman's coat and small ones for his eyes. Elinor modeled his nose.

Merry, coming out of the house, brought a tall silk hat. "Uncle Steve's," she explained, "but he won't mind." She raced back and returned with a pipe, which they wedged into the mouth.

"He's beautiful!" Merry cried. Her cheeks were red with cold and exercise, and her eyes were sparkling. "What's his name? Elinor, what's his name?"

"There once was a man made of snow," Elinor declaimed . . .

> Who said, "I have no place to go,"
> So he took up his stand
> On Uncle Steve's land . . .

Behind her Steve Sewell completed the limerick:

> When the weather was sixteen below.

Merry ran to him and he swung her up in his arms. "Uncle Steve, look what we did. Elinor and me. A snowman! And he's wearing—"

"My silk hat," Steve told her. "And my extra-special favorite meerschaum pipe. Where did you get those red cheeks, youngster?"

"The wind did it. We had fun, Uncle Steve. And I'm going to have a dog, if you say I can. He's a boxer and his name is Ho. And he has a brother named Hum, only Hum's very adventurous."

Steve set the chattering child on his shoulder. "In you go for a nice hot bath and supper. Come have some tea and warm up, Miss Parks."

"Come in, Elinor, come in," Merry said.

"Come in, Elinor," Julie chimed from the doorway.

Laughing, Elinor refused. She had to go home. There were a thousand things to do.

"At least, let me drive you home," Steve said. "That's a long walk, and you've had your exercise for today."

Julie ran down the steps and kissed her warmly. "Thank you, Elinor. More than I can ever say. I'm so glad we've found you."

"So am I," Steve said quietly. "Very glad."

Elinor got out of his car at the Parks house. "Don't forget your hat and your pipe," she called gaily. "I hope we haven't ruined your lovely house, tracking snow all over."

"But that's the way a home should be, remember? So a child can run around without spoiling things. What you've done for Merry today—" He broke off and then added gruffly, "Neither my sister nor I are apt to forget it."

"I hope you won't mind being saddled with Ho."

"Oh, that reminds me." There was a glint of laughter in his eyes. "You'll have to go along with me when I get him. I'm not sure the carpenter would let me have him without your approval. And Ho has already pledged his allegiance to you." He looked at her steadily. "Both Ho and I."

He released the brake and the car rolled away from the house.

VII

"There's a good movie tonight," Jed said over the telephone. "How about a riotous evening? Popcorn and everything. We'll show New York it hasn't cornered the market on feverish excitement."

"Fabulous," Elinor declared.

"Who was that?" Ginny asked, as Elinor turned away from the telephone.

"Jed. We're going to the movies tonight."

Ginny shrugged. "Night life in the gay city of Hastings."

"Why do you mind it so much, Ginny? It's a nice village, a beautiful village. The people are kind and friendly. Both the people and the village have history and tradition behind them. Three hundred years. What is there about night clubs and mink coats and all those things that makes them so important to you?"

Ginny looked at her in surprise. "How silly can you be?"

"I'm serious, Ginny. What do they have that is more important that Clay's happiness and his peace of mind and his—" Elinor broke off.

"His what?" Ginny said in a challenging tone.

"His faith in you," Elinor said steadily. "He adores you. But every day you do little things that hurt, that sap his confidence in himself, destroy his peace of mind. And all for shallow values. Suppose someday he sees that? What then, Ginny?"

"I suppose you think it's right, wanting to give up a big career and stay in this poky village cutting down, when we could have all we wanted." Ginny's voice was shrill.

"It isn't a question of what is right. It's a question of what is right for *him*. Something deep-rooted in Clay would shrivel up and die if he had a city job. And so far as money is concerned, do you think you could ever have all you wanted?"

"Quite a preacher you turned out to be," Ginny said sullenly.

"I want Clay to be happy."

"So do I."

"Do you, Ginny?"

Elinor went upstairs to turn on the hot bath and change her clothes, wet and half-frozen from her romp in the snow. What a fool she had been! The one unforgivable thing was to interfere between man and wife. No wonder Ginny didn't want her in the house. She had only antagonized her sister-in-law and done more harm than good.

"I'm just a troublemaker," Elinor reproached herself. "Never, never again will I interfere."

Dinner was silent that night. Clay sat watching Ginny, who was sulking and did not talk. It was a relief when the doorbell rang.

Jed helped Elinor into the jeep and wrapped a rug around her in spite of her protests.

"How did the job work out?" he asked as they started into the village.

Elinor told him what had been decided.

"I knew it would work out all right. As soon as Sewell met you he'd be eating out of your hand."

"You and your Blarney Stone."

"By the way, at dinner Mrs. Campbell was explaining to me about this setup. There was a younger brother, Rodney, who studied architecture at the Beaux Arts in Paris. He was the one who was crazy about old-style houses and wanted to build them. Something happened to him—I don't know what—but he was killed. Sewell, for some reason, feels responsible for it. That's why he's doing this. For his dead brother. Mrs. Campbell wanted me to understand, but warned me never to mention it to Sewell."

Elinor's heart was cold. It felt like a stone. *All those deaths . . .* What had happned? If she only knew!

"She didn't tell you how the brother—died?"

"No, that's all I know."

The movie was gay and Elinor and Jed found themselves laughing wildly before it was over. As Jed had promised, they shared a bag of popcorn, with Jed solemnly checking to make sure she ate no more than her share.

They came out on the cold street and shivered in the icy air.

"Hot chocolate at the drugstore?" Jed suggested.

"Just what I want."

"And that's as well," Jed said laughing, but with a tinge of bitterness in his voice she had never heard there before. "It's all I can afford."

"But it's all I want, really it is," Elinor protested.

"I know." He grinned at her affectionately. "I never knew you to ask for anything for yourself. But sometimes I get fed up with having no money."

"I thought you were doing well on this job."

"I am. But I have all those school loans to pay back before I'll be free and clear and can afford to take a girl out in a nice way."

"That depends on the girl."

"Most of them expect more than hot chocolate in the drugstore."

"I saw you lunching with Mrs. Grant at the inn yesterday. That must have cut into the exchequer."

"It did," Jed confessed wryly. "But she's so lovely, Elinor, so darned attractive. I never met anyone like her before. And she—I think she likes me, too."

"Is this serious?"

Jed flushed. "As serious as it can be, so far as I am concerned. But it's no use, of course. She's too rich for me. Have you seen that mink coat? I can't afford to take her out properly, the way she'd expect." He added

defensively, though Elinor had made no comment, "The
way she deserves. She rates the best."

He paid the twenty-cent check and they went back
to the jeep. "Money is the devil, isn't it?" he groaned.
"When I think it will be years before I'll be free and
clear and making enough money to marry . . . ! And
by that time someone else will have seen Alice and
snapped her up. Sometimes I can understand why people do—desperate things to get money."

They drove back in silence. Jed was brooding over
his own problems, over the unattainability of a blond
woman with a dulcet voice and beguiling ways; Elinor
over the havoc that money caused with Jed and Ginny.

Money, or the lack of it, wasn't to blame, she
thought as she pulled an eiderdown over her shoulders
an hour later. What was at fault was the inability of people to find happiness where it existed, the idea that it
could be bought and paid for in coin. Poor Ginny. Poor
Jed. Poor Doctor Dick, who wanted nothing for himself
but desperately needed money to provide hospital beds
for sick children. She looked into the dark and began to
lay plans for the fair. She began to smile, turned on her
side, and slept.

Next morning she answered the telephone and
heard a deep, quiet voice say, "Good morning. This is
Steve. Do you feel up to collecting Ho today? Merry's
giving us no peace. Her mother has already driven to
New Haven to buy a proper kennel for him. And a supply of dog food."

Elinor laughed. "I seem to have started something."

"Julie is delighted. It's the first time Merry has
been eager—clamoring to go out of doors. She's like a
new child. The only hitch is that for some reason she's
not so well today and Julie has decided to keep her in
bed."

Elinor ran upstairs and dressed in the coral skirt and
matching sweaters. They were growing shabby. After
all, she had worn them for two seasons.

"Where are you going?" Ginny called from the living room as Elinor came downstairs.

"With Mr. Sewell."

"Back for lunch?"

"I don't know. Don't wait for me. Mrs. Groom can fix me a sandwich if I'm too late."

Ginny came to the door way, saw the glow in Elinor's face, the brilliancy in the larkspur eyes.

"Don't forget," she said sweetly, "Mr. Sewell is married." Seeing Elinor's suddenly blank expression she smiled and went back into the living room.

Elinor was very quiet on the ride to the Cape Cod cottage. She must wear love like a bright banner. She had betrayed herself to Ginny, who was not observant about anyone but herself. Perhaps she had been equally obvious to Steve. What had happened to him? In spite of everything—the warnings from Harold, the frightening hints his sister had let fall, the girl named Mary Todd—she loved him. She had never before been so conscious of anyone's nearness. She discovered that she wanted him to take her hand, to touch her.

She caught her lower lip between her teeth. You've got to get over it, she told herself grimly. You must not think of him, ever again, except as your employer. Never again.

Now and then, Steve stole a look at her but he made no attempt to break her silence. It was Elinor who forced herself to talk. She groped for something impersonal and then remembered the Martins. She told him about Mrs. Martin's illness and how, if Doctor Dick could cure her, she would set up a shop and make slipcovers and curtains for Steve's houses as well as for other people in the vicinity.

She told him about Sue, whose selfish unwillingness to take a job threw such a burden on her sister. Then, talking more and more rapidly to prevent any more disturbing silence between them, she told him about her idea for a fair to raise money for a children's wing for the Hastings hospital.

"That's a fine idea," Steve said. "I hope you'll let Julie and me have a part in it."

"Oh, would you?"

"Wouldn't we! And that gives me a brilliant thought. Why don't we get this Sue Martin to act as a kind of secretary for the enterprise? She'd find it fun and she would be useful for once."

"Steve! That's wonderful. Oh," she broke off in confusion, "I didn't mean—"

"I hoped you would call me Steve. And shall it be Elinor from now on? As long as Julie and Merry have adopted you, I hate to be left out in the cold. All right, Elinor?"

"All right, Steve."

As they reached the cottage, Ho growled a warning and again became ecstatic when he recognized Elinor. Gravely they shook hands.

The carpenter came around the house. "Ho! Down, Ho! Oh, it's you. I'm afraid always that there will be someone who acts ugly with him."

"But he wouldn't hurt anyone, would he?" Elinor asked.

"He never has, but there are people who don't like dogs and a dog can always tell."

"This is your show," Steve reminded the girl beside him in a low tone.

Elinor got out of the car. "Did you mean it when you said Ho needed a home?"

The carpenter nodded his head regretfully. "I hate to let him go, but what can I do?" He brightened. "For yourself, ma'am?"

"For a little girl who would love him and take good care of him."

He hesitated. "Well, I don't know—"

"A sick little girl," Elinor went on. "She hasn't been outdoors all winter because of the cold, but when she learned about Ho, and that he would have to have a walk every day, rain or shine, she spent two hours out in the snow to prove she could take care of him."

Elinor added earnestly, "I wish you could have

seen how happy she was about it. This morning her mother has driven to New Haven to buy a kennel and get the right kind of food for him."

"I guess you win," the carpenter said. "Only—could you wait until tomorrow? I'll be leaving then for my new job in Massachusetts and I'd like to keep him as long as I'm here. We're—kinda used to each other."

Elinor looked a question at Steve.

"Of course," he said promptly, "we don't want to take him away while you are here. We'll pick him up tomorrow morning. He moved off to discuss the price, and Ho tried to convince Elinor that she needed a walk.

"That's mighty nice, mighty generous," the carpenter said. "I didn't figure on anywhere near that much. In fact, I'd have let him go for nothing if I was sure he'd have a good home."

"He will have," Steve assured him and the two men shook hands.

"Now," Steve said as they got back in the car, "as long as we don't have to deliver Ho, suppose we go to the bank and arrange about a drawing account for you so you can get started on your buying."

As they turned onto the Green he said, "It's a lovely little village. A friendly little village. I hope Julie will make a place for herself here."

"How could she fail? She's so friendly herself."

"She has had an unhappy time of it," Steve told her. "She was very happily married. Then last year her husband had a minor accident, cut his heel, and within a few days he was dead of blood poisoning."

Elinor gave an exclamation of pity.

"Such a little thing. But it ended a good marriage. They were living in Arizona at the time. Do you know Arizona?"

Elinor shook her head.

"It's bright, arid, improbable country. Julie loved it while her husband was alive but after he died she couldn't stay there. She said it was too big and dry and empty. She longed for the smallness and the greenness of

New England. So I bought the Rivers place and now she is trying to build a new life."

"I do hope she will be happy here."

"So do I. Very much. The only trouble—" He hesitated. "Julie is—reckless. Sometimes, without meaning it, she does harm. I don't want anyone—hurt. It's just that, especially since John died, she has seemed to need more and more excitement."

"You mean playing cards for high stakes?"

"How did you know?" he asked quickly.

"Ginny told me."

"Ginny—oh, Mrs. Parks. I see. Yes, it's partly that. That's one form her craving for excitement takes. Well, perhaps Hastings will provide the miracle. Bring contentment too deep to need excitement."

He parked on the Green and they walked a short block to the bank, stopping continually while Elinor exchanged greetings with old friends who ranged from a stiff-necked dowager being helped into her car by an obsequious chauffeur to a mailman unlocking a box on the sidewalk. Her manner was the same with all of them, gay and unself-conscious and genuine in its simplicity.

The first person Elinor saw in the bank was Ginny, looking very smart in her sable coat and small sable hat. She was sitting at one of the desks behind the railing. Harold Brown's desk. They were deep in conversation.

Harold saw Elinor first and his eyes lighted up. They traveled on to the tall man behind her. He spoke and Ginny turned around. There was a trapped look on her face, instantly altered by a bright smile of welcome. Harold looked as though he was considerably amused.

"Nell! I thought you—oh, Mr. Sewell! How nice. Such a lovely evening we spent with you and your charming sister. Do let me present Mr. Brown, Mr. Sewell."

The two men shook hands and Steve explained that he had come to arrange a drawing account for Miss Parks, who had consented to be his partner in an enterprise of his.

"Glad to arrange it for you, Mr. Sewell," Harold said eagerly. He went to get another chair.

"Don't bother," Ginny said. "I'm going. Nell can have mine. Then we'll expect you for dinner tonight at seven, Harold."

He looked surprised and then pleased. "I'll be delighted."

Ginny gave Steve a glowing smile and went out of the bank.

While Steve and Harold discussed the drawing account, Elinor's attention wandered. Ginny hadn't come to the bank to ask Harold to dinner. That had been an afterthought to cover the real purpose of her visit. Had she overdrawn her own account as she had her sister-in-law's? Clay would be angry if he knew.

When the banking arrangements had been completed, Steve drove Elinor home.

"In the morning we'll pick up Ho," he said. "Perhaps you'll be able to start Merry's portrait. Then, the following day, if that's covenient, you can begin your shopping expedition."

"That will be fine."

"Oh, another thing. You'll need a car of your own if you're going to explore the countryside for old pieces of furniture. We have a Chevrolet convertible that we don't use. Just eating its head off without serving any purpose. I'll have it delivered to the house for you tomorrow."

He took her hand in his, his fingers tightening on hers. She saw the expression in his eyes and her heart soared with a joy she had never guessed could exist. For a breathless moment they looked at each other.

A girl named Mary Todd.

"Tomorrow, then," she said, and went quickly into the house.

Ginny, Mrs. Groom told her, had a lunch date and wouldn't be back before half-past three or four. Elinor longed to go to Green Pond to skate, to blow the wild thoughts from her mind, but it was too far to walk. She wished now that she had not sold her little Dauphine when she went to New York, but she had needed the extra money for a wardrobe and she didn't want a car in the city. Tomorrow she would have Steve's convertible.

She curled up in a deep chair near the fire in the living room, sketching pad in her hand, staring into the flames. The pencil began to move and Steve's face took shape under her fingers, a smiling Steve. She looked up to see Mrs. Groom standing in the doorway, and instinctively closed the sketching pad.

"What is it?"

"I'd like to talk to you for a minute, if I can."

"Of course. Come in by the fire."

Mrs. Groom sat down stiffly. "This morning I was offered a job. Housekeeper at the Hastings Inn. The job pays about fifteen dollars a week more than I'm getting, with room and board free just the same as here. The question is: Shall I take it or not?"

Elinor was troubled. "How can I urge you to stay if you'll get better terms somewhere else? But how can I bear to have you go? And Clay will be sick about it, too. I don't know what to advise you. Have you been looking for a job long?"

Mrs. Groom shook her head. "Never looked for one. Only way they'd think of making the offer is that they were put up to it."

"You mean Ginny?"

The housekeeper nodded. "She and a couple of young matrons lunch there once a week and drive over to New Haven to a show or a movie." She pressed her hands close together. "Well, what shall I do?"

"Would you be happier there?" Elinor asked, and saw the answer in the older woman's bleak face. "Wait a little longer. Be patient. Maybe things will iron themselves out."

"Maybe. All right, then, I'll stall them off for a while. They don't need me right away. This time of year there are only a handful of guests at the inn. But they are looking for someone for sure by April first."

She got up and rested her hand on Elinor's shoulder. "Like your mother you are," she said. "Well, I've got to see about dinner. Young Mrs. Parks just telephoned. That Brown boy's coming to dinner."

Rising young banker or not, he remained "that Brown boy" to Mrs. Groom, the little boy who ate all the cupcakes that had been baked for tea and let Clay take the punishment.

"Guess we'll have ham with pineapple and sweet potatoes and glacéed apples," she said. "And last night's pie. Not one of you even tasted your dessert last night."

She plodded out of the room and the swinging door to the kitchen closed behind her with a soft whoosh.

VIII

"It's always this way," Ginny said furiously. "Sometimes I don't see how I can bear it one more day. It's getting so I can't plan anything. Clay just comes home when he feels like it. He has no consideration."

"Probably he got stuck with a late client," Harold Brown said, trying to soothe his ruffled hostess. "These things happen." He turned to Elinor. "Your new boss Sewell seems to be quite an impressive guy. I never met him before. Looks to me as though you are in on a good thing there."

"Elinor is like Clay," Ginny said in exasperation. "She won't know how to make the best use of it. Oh, there's Clay now!" She ran to the door of the living room to greet her husband.

He kissed her gently. "You look lovely tonight, darling," he said. "Hello, Elinor. How's the working girl? Oh, how are you, Harold?" The warmth died out of his voice but his manner retained its invariable courtesy.

"It's nearly seven," Ginny said. "What in the world happened to you?"

"A beautiful woman," Clay teased her. "I simply couldn't tear myself away."

At dinner, Ginny went back to Clay's lateness in getting home.

"Actually," he told her, "I really was delayed by a woman. I suppose she was beautiful—if you like that type. I thought I'd never get rid of her."

"A client?" Ginny asked.

"A would-be client. She's a Mrs. Grant, who is staying at the Hastings Inn. In her own words, she was attacked by a ferocious beast and was in danger of her life. A valuable mink coat was ripped. She suffered from shock and nerve strain. She wants the poor devil who owns the ferocious beast to pay for the coat and the ferocious beast must be shot."

"If I had a valuable mink coat—which isn't likely—I'd want damages, too, if anyone ripped it," Ginny said. "What kind of ferocious beast would there be around here?"

"A boxer. It belongs to a carpenter who had been working for Sewell. The poor guy couldn't possibly pay for a mink coat. Anyhow, I'd hate to see him dragged into court, losing days of work as well as having to pay damages he couldn't raise without mortgaging his future, all for a rich woman who doesn't need the money. I got so annoyed by this Mrs. Grant that I felt like offering to take the carpenter's case for nothing."

"Clay," Ginny wailed, "you can't do that. Here you've got a rich client for once and you want to turn down her case. After all, whether the man is poor or rich, he is responsible for the way his dog acts, for the damage he causes. That's the real point, isn't it? There's justice on her side."

"I suppose so," Clay said reluctantly, "but I didn't like the woman. Under a soft beguiling manner she is hard as nails."

"But the law isn't just for people you like. It's for

everyone. Don't be childish about this, Clay. Please don't."

"I agree with Clay," Harold said unexpectedly. "Why don't you tell the woman she has no case? Anyhow, her coat is probably insured."

"This doesn't concern you, Harold," Ginny snapped. "Clay, will you at least look at the evidence before turning down the case?"

"All right. I'll go see the carpenter in a couple of days and find out about the dog."

"You'll have to see him tomorrow," Elinor said.

"How do you know?" Clay asked in surprise.

"Because he is an itinerant worker. He's leaving for Massachusetts tomorrow to take a new job. If you like, you could go with Steve and me when we pick up Ho in the morning."

"Steve?" Ginny raised her eyebrows.

"Ho?" Clay asked, puzzled.

"That's the boxer. Mrs. Grant's ferocious beast," Elinor said tartly. "Ferocious! He's a darling, the friendliest dog. He'd never attack anyone without a good reason. In fact, Steve bought him today for his little niece."

"So, actually, the dog belongs to Mr. Sewell. And heaven knows he could pay damages. Clay, you've got to take that case," Ginny said.

Harold grinned maliciously at Elinor. "This is going to be embarrassing for you, isn't it? Having your brother and your brand-new boss on opposite sides in a law case."

"They can both be trusted to deal with it on its merits," Elinor said coolly. "I'm not worried."

But while the others watched a television program she thought about Mrs. Alice Grant and the lawsuit. Why had the boxer attacked her? And why had she returned alone to the Cape Cod cottage? Jed would have been delighted to take her. Was she trying to decide about buying Steve's house?

Elinor's heart sank. Alice Grant, with the sweet voice that became so strident when she was angry, did

not belong in the Cape Cod cottage. If she settled in the
village Jed would continue to be unhappy about her,
dissatisfied with his burden of debts for his education,
wanting more money to spend on her.

But why did the woman want to stay in Hastings?
She didn't really like small towns. She had made that
clear enough.

The program ended and Clay turned off the television set without Elinor's being aware of the fact. She
came out of her absorption with a start when Harold
spoke to her and she realized that he had been watching
her for a long time.

"You seemed to be far away. Thinking about your
—job?"

"Making plans for an old-fashioned fair," Elinor
said, and told them about her idea for raising money to
add to the children's wing at the hospital.

"That's a good idea," Clay said. "You can count
on me."

"And me," Harold said.

"At least," Ginny said, "it's something different to
do. You can count on me."

When Harold had gone Clay said, "Tell me what
you know about this boxer, Elinor."

"He's friendly and harmless. He would never attack anyone unless there was a good reason. Come with
us in the morning and see for yourself."

"Don't be a fool, Clay," Ginny said. "As long as
Steve Sewell owns the dog there could be plenty of damages. Plenty."

"We'll see," he said lightly, "in the morning."

When Steve drew up before the house next morning he was surprised to see Clay Parks follow his sister
out to the car. Clay explained the situation as they drove
along.

"That's queer," Steve said, frowning. "I can't understand it. But if Ho is as dangerous as that I certainly
don't want Merry to have him."

When they reached the cottage, the carpenter, unrecognizable at first in a neat dark suit and white shirt, was waiting in a battered old Plymouth, his hand on the boxer's head. He got out of the car and came over to Steve.

"We've been having some trouble out here, sir. A woman came along yesterday and started to go through the house. Ho growled at her—after all, he's here as a watchdog—and she kicked him, hard, in the side. He jumped her and tore her coat. Mink, too. She acted like a wild woman. She said she would have Ho shot and I'd have to pay for the coat."

He swallowed hard. "So I guess the deal is off." He fumbled in his pockets and pulled out a billfold, searching it for the money Steve Sewell had given him the day before.

Ho had wriggled out of the front seat. He came up to the car. Elinor opened her window and held out her hand. Ho put his paw in it.

"Is this," Clay asked, "the ferocious beast?"

"That is the one," Elinor said.

"And the woman kicked him?"

The carpenter ran his hand over Ho's side. "There's a lump here." His fist clenched. "She can't have him shot, can she?"

Clay smiled grimly. "She was on property belonging to someone else. The dog warned her. Ho won't be shot."

The carpenter expelled a long breath. "Thanks for telling me. I was kinda scared about it."

A jeep rattled up and Jed got out. "So you're the guy who owns that man-killer," he said, striding toward the carpenter. "I suppose you know he nearly killed a woman yesterday."

"Oh, be your age, Jed," Clay protested. "I saw Mrs. Grant in my office late yesterday afternoon and she was nowhere near dead then. She was just plain mad."

"You don't understand her." Jed's face flushed. "She wasn't mad, she was almost hysterical from shock. I saw her myself last evening. Something has to be done to prevent dogs like this from running free, attacking women."

"Jed, you're talking like a fool," Elinor told him.

"You mean to tell me that Clay isn't going to handle this case for Alice—for Mrs. Grant?"

"I wouldn't touch it with a ten-foot pole," Clay answered. "Mrs. Grant was on property where she did not belong. The dog warned her off. She kicked him in the side and he jumped on her and tore her coat."

"She kicked—Clay, that's impossible! She's the gentlest, the sweetest woman in the world. Who told you that?" Jed glared at the carpenter. "The dog's owner, I suppose, trying to get out of it."

"I am the dog's owner," Steve said quietly. "I bought him yesterday for my little niece."

"Do you intend to have him shot or don't you?"

"I do not." Steve spoke each word distinctly.

"What kind of people are you?" Jed raged. "A woman is attacked, sent into hysterics, a valuable coat destroyed, a life endangered, and you don't do anything about it. Clay, I should think that as a matter of simple, common justice you wouldn't behave this way, unless you don't want to risk losing a rich client like Sewell."

"Jed!" Clay said explosively.

"And Mr. Sewell—just because you're so rich, you think you're above the law. You think you can get by with anything. Well, you can't. I intend to see that Alice is given a fair deal."

Jed plunged toward his jeep. Elinor tumbled out of the car in her haste and ran after him, clutched his arm.

"Jed! Wait, Jed."

The anger in his face faded when he looked at her.

"Jed, for the first time in my life I'm ashamed of you. You are behaving like a badly brought up small boy. You've been grossly rude to Clay. You haven't even been honest," she added stormily. "No one knows better than you that Clay is incapable of acting the way you accuse him of doing. You knew when you spoke to him there was no truth in that ugly accusation. And you were insulting to Steve Sewell, who was the only person to give you a break, to trust in your abilities more than you trusted in them yourself. And such a marvelous break . . .

"It's one thing to be head over heels in love, it's another to lose your judgment and your integrity and your sense of fair play. A love that makes you do wrong things is the wrong kind of love."

"Elinor!" Jed seemed very young and confused and ashamed. "I saw Alice last night, crying and hysterical, and then when I came here and no one seemed to care what happened to her . . ."

Jed's flood of justification stopped under the accusation in her eyes. "What do you want me to do?" he asked sulkily.

"You know as well as I do."

"Oh, all right," he said sullenly. He went back to where the three men were waiting. "I was way out of line. I was sore and I went too far—I guess. I apologize to all of you." He sketched a little salute and returned to the jeep. A moment later it jolted off over the frozen ruts in the road.

"He's sure sweet on that lady with the mink coat," the carpenter remarked. "But I'll take my oath any time that she wasn't hurt. She wasn't in hysterics when she left here. She was just plain mad, and using language that—Well, anyhow, there wasn't a mark on her. Nothing to worry about."

After a parting between the carpenter and the boxer that had brought a lump to Elinor's throat, she and Steve Sewell were taking Ho to Merry.

"I don't care about Mrs. Grant," Elinor said to Steve as they drove. "I do care about seeing Jed act that way. I told him I was ashamed of him. Thoroughly ashamed."

Steve gave her a quick look. "Jed Gordon is all right. He just lost his head for a moment. It happens to everyone."

"Just the same—"

"Let's forget about it, shall we?" he suggested gently. "He's sound all the way through. When he has time to cool down and think about it—"

"Do you suppose that woman really kicked Ho?" Elinor's fingers moved over the dog's side as he sat on the seat between them. "Oh, Steve, there *is* a lump here!"

"If it doesn't clear up in a day or so I'll take him to a vet. But we'd better get him home to Merry as soon as we can. That's why I had the carpenter take your brother back to Hastings. I'm worried about Merry."

"What's wrong? Did all that strenuous play in the snow upset her?"

"I don't think so. She loved every minute of it. She has been ailing all winter. I suppose we'd better find a good man in New York and put her in his hands."

"There's a good man right here in Hastings. Dr. Richard Mallison. Not just a small-town general practitioner. He's had dazzling offers from some of the big-city clinics."

The snowman, denuded of hat and pipe, still stood on the lawn as Steve turned into the driveway before the long fieldstone house. Elinor fastened Ho's leash to his collar and held it firmly as they got out.

Julie flung the door open. "I've been watching for you. Merry is all keyed up. Did you bring—Oh, what a beauty!" She stood quietly, hand at her side, while Ho investigated it.

"Will you take him up?" she asked Elinor. "Steve will show you the way."

They went up the stairs to the third floor. Merry's bedroom was next to her mother's, a big sunny room with fairy-tale characters on the wallpaper and open shelves stacked with toys.

Merry looked smaller than ever as she lay under the covers, her face flushed with fever, eyes too bright.

"Elinor," she cried, "did you get him?"

"Of course, we got him." Elinor led Ho to the bed. For a moment the child and the boxer regarded each other solemnly. A small hand reached out tentatively. Ho sniffed it.

Elinor held her breath. Ho raised his head and Merry patted it timidly.

"Ho!" she whispered. "Ho!"

He settled down beside the bed, on guard beside his mistress. Merry, an ecstatic smile on her lips, turned on her side and went to sleep.

Elinor and Steve tiptoed out of the room and went downstairs. Julie was waiting for them.

"All right?"

"Perfect," Elinor assured her.

"Is it all right to leave the boxer with her?"

Steve grinned. "He's going to look after her."

Tears spilled down Julie's cheeks. She brushed them away. "Sorry. I'm just tired. I didn't sleep much. We'll have to take her to New York—"

"Elinor says there's a good man here in town," Steve said.

At Julie's eager request Elinor called Doctor Dick. When she had put up the telephone she told Julie about him.

"But I must warn you," she said, laughing, "to look out for him. First thing you know he'll have you on the hospital committee. That hospital is his joy and his despair. His joy, because he was responsible for its being built. His despair, because he never has enough money for it."

To distract Julie's attention from her sick child, she described her plans for a fair to raise money for an addition to the children's wing at the hospital.

"I thought we'd have a booth to sell cakes and jellies, and one for handcrafts, and a fortuneteller, and—"

"The Ciano Puppeteers are in Boston," Julie said eagerly. "Why couldn't I hire them to come down? And they could put on a show for the children."

"Julie, that's an inspiration."

"I'll supply the ice cream and soft drinks and popcorn," Steve offered. He grinned. "How about getting hold of your friend Sue Martin? She can start writing the letters for us. And we'll want some big display cards made to put in store windows."

"But where can we hold the fair?" Julie asked.

"There's that deserted factory building near the river," Steve said thoughtfully. "I'll look it over. As a matter of fact, I was playing with the idea of starting a small industry here and the building seems to be in good shape."

The butler came into the big drawing room. "Dr. Mallison," he said.

Elinor went to greet him. "Mrs. Campbell, this is Dr. Mallison. And Mr. Stephen Sewell."

Doctor Dick smiled at them both. "Which one is my patient?"

While Julie took him upstairs, Elinor called Sue Martin and told her about the job.

"Working for a fair!" Sue exclaimed. "Oh, cool! That will really be super. When do you want me to start?"

"Tomorrow, if you can. There's a lot to do and a lot of people to see. Mr. Sewell will talk to you about it in the morning and make the arrangements."

"Gee, thanks, that ought to be fun."

Elinor hung up. "She thinks it will be fun."

"That young lady is going to learn to work," Steve told her. "She has a surprise coming to her."

When Doctor Dick and Julie came downstairs, Julie was radiant.

"Not too much exercise at first, but some every day," Doctor Dick was saying. "Get her outdoors with her dog. See that she eats properly. I'll leave a prescription with you. Three times a day after meals. I'll give her a few more shots. Bring her to the office if you can. There's never enough time for all the house calls I have to make. She ought to shake off that infection in a few days. And get her around other children if possible. She needs them."

Julie was glowing. "Oh, thank you, Dr. Mallison."

She made him sit down and ordered coffee. He leaned back wearily in his chair.

"I've been hoping that life in a quiet village would be good for Merry; it's so peaceful and uneventful."

"Uneventful!" Doctor Dick snorted. "A birth last night, a death this morning, influenza and whooping cough and arthritis and a broken hip and—"

"How is Mrs. Martin?" Elinor asked him.

"That's another thing," Doctor Dick said gruffly. "All that poor woman needs is the proper medication. And they wait for years because they can't afford a doctor. She'll be up and out of bed in a couple of weeks, if she responds to treatment as I think she will. And she'll regain her strength in a couple of months if she has decent care and some sort of incentive for living."

He smiled at Elinor. "And I gather you've given her that. She was talking about some work you have in mind for her and about making a shop of the lower part of the house and painting it a barn red. You're just the way you were as a kid. Full of ideas for helping people."

"Oh, I nearly forgot, Doctor Dick, I'm really going ahead with the plans for the fair. And Mrs. Campbell and Mr. Sewell are going to help."

"That's—wonderful. You don't know what it will mean. Right now there isn't a single free bed for a sick child."

He finished his coffee and got up. "Time for my office hours."

When he had driven off in his shabby car, Julie put her hand on Elinor's.

"Thank you again. I like him so much and he was wonderful with Merry."

"I'm so glad you like him. Sometimes his gruff manner puts people off."

"Gruff?" Julie protested. "He's not gruff. He's just bone-weary and overworked. He neglects himself. He needs someone to take care of him."

Steve looked at his sister in astonishment. Then he did a double take, a delighted expression on his face. He caught Elinor's eye and winked solemnly at her.

IX

Elinor checked her shoulder bag: sketching pad, pencils, lists, color chart, folding ruler, magnifying glass for examining old furniture, checkbook, driving license. All complete.

The green wool dress was brightened by the yellow scarf tied under her chin. She pulled the hood of the car coat over her dark hair and started down the stairs. Her first working day was ahead of her, a country tour in search of antiques.

The afternoon before, Steve had delivered the convertible to her and turned over the keys ceremoniously.

"Checked, greased, the tank filled and tires inspected all round. Snow treads on the back. You shouldn't have any trouble."

No, she couldn't possibly have any trouble. She could hardly wait to get started.

The doorbell rang and Mrs. Groom plodded heavily through the house from the kitchen to answer it.

A dulcet cooing voice asked for Mr. Clay Parks. Elinor stopped short. She had heard those ultra-sweet tones before. What was Mrs. Alice Grant doing here?

Mr. Parks was at his office, Mrs. Groom replied.

"No, he isn't." The voice lost its sweetness, became strident. "Or if he is, he wouldn't see me. I insist—"

Ginny came out of the little morning room.

"I am Mrs. Parks," she said. "My husband isn't here."

"I am Mrs. Grant."

"Oh, come in, Mrs. Grant," Ginny said cordially.

"My husband was speaking of you last night. You are a client of his, I believe."

Elinor came slowly down the stairs. Mrs. Grant was wearing a silver-fox cape over a smart black suit. There were pearls in her ears and around her throat. But what caught Elinor's attention was the dark bruise under one cheekbone. Neither Clay or Jed had said anything about a bruise. "Not a mark on her," the carpenter had sworn, and she believed him.

Ginny looked up. "Mrs. Grant, my sister-in-law, Elinor Parks."

Mrs. Grant nodded. "We've met," she said coolly. "Mrs. Parks, I would like to talk to you. Everyone says your husband is the best lawyer in town. I've got a damage suit. I've been frightened out of my life, my nerves have been put in a dangerous condition. I've been injured, my mink coat has been ruined. Someone is going to pay for this, and I insist that Mr. Parks take my case. I've just discovered the dog's owner is simply rolling in money."

Ginny hesitated, looking uneasily at Elinor. Then her lips compressed and she turned with deliberation toward the living room.

"Do come in and we'll talk it over, Mrs. Grant." She looked at Mrs. Groom, watching in disapproval from the dining room door. "Bring some coffee, will you?"

Elinor went out to the convertible and started the motor. For a moment she sat at the wheel. Where had Mrs. Grant got that bruise? Who had told her that Steve Sewell owned the dog? It must have been Jed. What did she hope to gain by coming to see Ginny?

The girl's heart felt pinched with cold. Mrs. Grant seemed to be sure that Ginny would back her claim. But what would Clay feel when he knew about it? What would he do? Indulgent as he always was to Ginny he would not permit her to influence him when he believed that he was right. Ginny was going too far.

There was only one bright element in the whole situation. Elinor knew, without knowing how she knew, that Steve Sewell had never made a furtive appointment with this vulgar woman. He couldn't have done it, unless she was entirely mistaken about the kind of person he was. Someone else had been intended to keep that mysterious four-o'clock appointment.

Elinor released the emergency brake and the car rolled down the driveway and out onto the road. Resolutely she pushed the dark thoughts out of her mind. There was nothing she could do about them. Better give all her attention to her plans for the day ahead.

And what a day! It sparkled. One of those February days when the sky is a deep blue and a sudden rise in the temperature melts the snow, clears the rivers of ice and foreshadows the coming of spring. Even when one knows that winter will settle down again in a few days, the promise remains.

In the distance the hills were a misty blue. Close at hand there were large patches of ground free of snow, revealing massed autumn leaves from the fall before. High on a hillside, standing in deep snow, etched against the sky, a deer poised motionless and Elinor caught her breath at that moment of frozen beauty. Then, without effort, it soared over the stone fence and was gone.

Hemlocks, whose great dark branches had been bowed under their weight of snow, stood like proud sentinels. A grove of white birch made slender silhouettes against the darker hillside. The ladies of the forest, Elinor remembered that they had been called.

I'm happy, she thought. I'm happy. I'm happy. Oh, it's good to be alive and healthy and have a worthwhile job to accomplish!

She pressed her foot harder on the accelerator and the little car leaped forward as though it, too, shared her joy in the day.

She stopped at the side of the road to consult a map and turned down a narrow dirt road to look for the first place she had marked as having possibilities.

By noon, she had visited a dozen side roads and negotiated, with her heart in her mouth, uncleared driveways that were still snow-and-ice bound. She had gone through over-crowded "parlors" and dim cluttered attics, and cold dusty barns stacked with the discards of generations. She had measured and examined and priced and bargained. She had made countless notes.

When she stopped at a back-roads farm, the owner opened the door for her.

"Miss Parks! You're a sight for sore eyes. Mother, it's Miss Parks, come back from the big city."

The farmer's wife drew her in and in a few minutes had forced Elinor to join them for a boiled New England dinner at the kitchen table. When she had finally refused a third helping she sighed with repletion.

"Heavens! I don't know when I've eaten so much. It was wonderful. I thought I was tired, but I was just hungry."

She told her kindly hosts about her work for Steve Sewell and they took her on a tour of the house, glad to be obliging, but finding it hard to believe that they had anything that would interest her.

"We haven't a thing to suit you, but you're more than welcome to look around."

At the end of an exciting tour Elinor sat in the parlor, whose shades were drawn to keep the carpet from fading.

"Well," she began, "first of all there are those patchwork quilts."

"But what good are they? My grandmother made them. Old-fashioned as they can be."

"But people love old-fashioned things. Would you be willing to sell them?"

"Beats me what people want. But if they'll pay decently we could get some of those new matching blankets. I've had my heart set on them."

"Then there are those pewter plates you've got on the wall in the kitchen."

"Pewter! Those were used by my husband's family more than a hundred years ago. I just keep them because they're kinda odd. And they look real nice when they are all polished up. What would people do with *them?*"

Elinor told them about the fair. "A booth with things like that in it would be able to raise a lot of money for the children's wing."

The farmer and his wife exchanged amazed glances.

"And that old organ. Someone would love having that just for fun, because it is so quaint."

"I'll be doggoned," the farmer ejaculated.

"Do you think," his wife asked shyly, "we could get enough out of these things to buy us a television set?"

Elinor smiled. "I'm sure you could." She got to her feet. "Thanks for everything, particularly that wonderful meal. I'll talk to Mr. Sewell and arrange about a check and send for the things some day next week."

"Thank *you*," the farmer replied. "My wife's thrilled pink. All I'm worrying about is we might be cheating you."

Elinor laughed. "Not a chance. But I do think you'll be pleasantly surprised when you get your check."

For a few breathtaking minutes the sun sinking in the west made the sky a kaleidoscope of orange and rose and gold. Then, almost at once, there was a gray twilight and Elinor switched on the headlights. Darn, she was going to get home after dark, after all. The afternoon had slipped by without her being aware of the swift passage of time.

She pulled her mind away from the engrossing and satisfying thought of the treasure she had uncovered during the day, not only possible additions to Steve's houses but some items that would be tremendously effective for the fair and that should attract people from far beyond Hastings.

A number of women had promised to bake pies and cakes and cookies, to supply homemade jellies and preserves and pickles, crocheted and knitted goods and hooked rugs. All in all, it had been a good day.

Just the same, she had better concentrate on getting home as soon as possible. The quickest way was by the use of back roads, which would take her past Steve's new houses. She turned onto a dirt road, reducing her speed. How unexpectedly darkness had fallen, and how different the country seemed at night!

The air became colder and she discovered that she was shivering. She rolled up the windows, switched on the heater and the blower. Something moved on the road in front of her and she eased on the brake. A raccoon stood pinned by the lights, its dark-circled eyes staring blindly, and then moved off awkwardly, like a small bear, its beautifully striped tail vivid in the high beams.

Curious how during the daytime she forgot the invisible life that moved through the hills and the underbrush at night, as at home in the darkness as human beings were in the light. Raccoons and flying squirrels and other small animals were around her, unseen. Queer how the thought of these harmless creatures gave her a sense of discomfort now.

There were few houses on the road, most of them unoccupied summer cottages. How still the country was. How empty. Elinor turned onto another back road. It ought to cut off five miles. There wasn't a house or a light. That, she remembered, had been Jed's worry about Steve's houses. They were so isolated. She had laughed at the time. She did not feel like laughing now. She had never felt so alone in her life.

Her headlights picked out a car drawn up at the side of the road. Lights out. Unoccupied. That probably meant a hunter, prowling somewhere through the woods. Darn him, anyhow! Illegally jacking helpless deer.

There was a report and the car swerved to the side. A shot! The hunter must be firing in her direction. The fool! The careless fool!

Then the car bumped along the road, the wheel pulling her arms as she tried to hold the road. It wasn't a shot. It was a blowout.

No use expecting any help on this deserted road. Elinor groaned to herself and got out. The air was icy cold outside the heated car. She had started around to the back of the car when a flicker of movement caught her attention. A man stood just at the edge of the light.

She ran forward. "Hi!" she called.

He turned then and, unbelievably, ducked out of the light and disappeared in the darkness. A man with thick shoulders, who moved clumsily. Something about him stirred a chord of memory but she could not place him.

"Hi!" she called again. "Will you help me, please? I have a flat tire."

There was a sound of breaking twigs and then nothing.

"Hi!" she called a third time.

He wasn't coming back. He wasn't going to help her. How very odd, she thought. In all her years in the country she had never known anyone who refused to help a person in trouble, particularly a woman in trouble.

She lifted the top of the luggage compartment and took out the jack. She worked fast because, she told herself, she was cold. But she was also frightened. She assembled the jack, raised the car, and, using a flashlight, got the tire off. She rolled it to the back of the car. Queer how exposed she felt, as though she were clearly visible to someone unseen, someone who was watching her. It was a horrible feeling.

Then lights illuminated the open trunk of the car, brakes squealed, and a car pulled up behind her.

She whirled around, her heart thudding.

"Elinor!"

"Steve!" She found herself running toward him, running straight into his arms. It seemed to be the most natural thing in the world.

The arms closed around her, held her warmly, securely. His head was on her hair from which the hood had fallen back, then his cheek against hers, hard and warm, and then his lips.

"You're trembling," he said. "What's wrong? What happened to you?"

Elinor could feel the hard hammer beat of his heart. She stepped back from his arms.

"I'm sorry," she said huskily. "I don't know what got into me. I guess I was scared."

"Get into the car where you will be warm. I'll finish changing the tire for you. What a lousy job of inspection! You might have been hurt!"

She sat huddled in her coat while he worked. What had made her run to him like that? As though he were her natural refuge? What would he think of her? Practically throwing herself at him . . . Her cheeks burned with humiliation, but, in spite of herself, she still remembered the hard warmth of his cheek against hers, the faint brush of his lips.

At last she heard the top of the luggage compartment slam down. Steve came around and she opened the window.

"What frightened you?" he asked quietly.

"Just my own stupidity, I guess. There was a man—"

"He bothered you?"

"No, no," she answered quickly, startled by the swift anger in his voice. "He just," she tried to laugh, "ignored me. When the tire blew out I called to him and he—"

"He what?"

"He ducked out of sight into the darkness." She was shaking again. "But all the time I was getting the tire off I felt he was there, close by, watching me, waiting for something."

"I'll look around," Steve said. "Wait for me."

He went back to his car for a heavy flashlight and walked away from the road. She could see the light moving in wide arcs from side to side. She watched breathlessly, her heart pounding, her blood like ice in her veins. Something about that silent stalking terrified her. As though something dangerous, something evil, lurked in the dark.

Then the light was still, pinning against the night a man's thick figure. There was an exclamation and then the man was running, plunging away into the woods, down the slope. His footsteps died away. The flashlight searched among the trees in vain. The quarry had vanished.

In the distance a car started up, a motor raced, the sound died away.

Then nothing. No light. No movement. No voices. It seemed to Elinor that she had been sitting alone in the dark forever, alone in the night, alone in the world.

Steve returned so silently that she had no inkling of his approach until he spoke beside her.

"He got away," he said briefly. "I'll follow you back to Hastings and then call the State Police. That guy's up to no good. I can't imagine what he would be after on a deserted road like this, but they had better look into it."

"I thought—at first I thought he might be a hunter, but—"

"But?"

"The way he came up to the light and then ducked back when he saw who I was—I think he was expecting to meet someone else."

"Don't sound so little and frightened," Steve said unexpectedly. He leaned in at the open window. "This," he told her, "is a calculated risk." His mouth covered hers in a long kiss. Then he drew back, his eyes searching her face.

"Keep straight ahead until you reach the fork. Then turn left."

In a moment she heard him start his car. She turned the key in the switch, her fingers shaking, released the brake, drove slowly back to Hastings. She could see Steve's lights in her rearview mirror. They were close behind until she reached a lighted street in Hastings. Then he sounded his horn in farewell and turned off on another road.

X

Earlier that day, Steve had taken Ho for a walk. Merry was sitting up in bed and was to be allowed to walk around her room the next day. If she ate her meals properly, so that she could grow strong and well, Doctor Dick promised that the following day she could supervise Ho's meals and after that she could exercise him every day.

Steve had walked around his property, planning gardens and tennis court and a swimming pool as spring projects. A pity that this beautiful place had been neglected and untended for so many years. The house had now been restored but there was still much to be done on the grounds.

In a way, he ruminated, it was fortunate that there had been so much to do with the house. Julie had found her time so occupied with redecorating and furnishing the many rooms that there had not been much leisure for mischief.

He stopped to light his pipe, shielding the flame of the match from the wind. Not that Julie ever intended mischief. But since John's death she had not known what to do with herself. She seemed to need feverish excitement. That was why she had started bridge games, playing for preposterously high stakes. Well, he had stopped that, at least, though for a time Julie had been out of temper with him. But she hadn't realized how awkward it might be for some of her new acquaintances to meet heavy losses at cards.

Thinking deeply, he stood still, looking into the

woods without seeing them. Ho, who had been in charge
of the expedition, as was only proper, turned, came
back, tried to make him move.

Steve looked down at the boxer and laughed. "All
right, Ho. Good for you. Keeping me up to the mark."

He walked on. Poor Julie! She had been heartbro-
ken when her husband died so unexpectedly, so quickly.
And Merry had been ailing all fall and winter. Things
hadn't been easy. He should not be so critical. After all,
Julie was one of the reckless Sewells. And so, he admitted, was he. Only Rod, in their generation, had been a
conservative in his thinking and his living.

Steve bit hard on his pipe. Rod! His younger
brother. Brilliant, gay, full of ambitious dreams of creat-
ing a new demand for the graceful old houses which he
loved. And all his dreams had perished in a sheet of
flame. All his promise had died before he had been giv-
en an opportunity to reveal what he could do.

"Rod!" Steve groaned.

How long would this pain be with him? This sense
of poignant loss? This terrible, devastating sense of
guilt?

"I killed them all," he said aloud. "Mary and Jimmy and Rod."

As clear as the hemlocks on the lawn, as the ma-
ples in the woods, he saw the plane at the Texas airport.
How hot it had been that day! Over a hundred in the
shade and heaven knew how high in the sun. The
ground wavering in heat waves. His wife Mary was taking their eight-year-old son Jimmy to visit her mother in
Oregon. Rodney had just completed his studies at the
Beaux Arts and had gone from Paris to Texas to visit
his older brother before taking a job. He was under-
weight and run down from working too hard. Rod always went at everything he undertook with all his
strength and all his heart.

It was Mary who had urged him to go with her to
Oregon where he could escape the heat and be able to
build himself up. Rod had balked. Not because he did
not like Mary. Because he hated flying.

And I was the one who overruled his objections, Steve thought, as he had thought over and over for three terrible years. I persuaded him to go. I laughed at his prejudices.

Mary, small, fair-haired, devoted, had kissed him warmly and cried—it wrenched his heart to think of it —"Take care of yourself, dear!"

Jimmy, excited over his first plane ride, had shaken hands with his father, suddenly self-conscious, suddenly grown-up, and gone up the ramp without a word.

Rod, looking like a younger Steve, a lighthearted Steve, had called gaily, "Well, if the plane smashes, I'll call a taxi."

"You'd take a covered wagon if you could," Steve had laughed back.

The plane had taxied up the runway, started to take off, turned over and burst into flames.

That had been three years ago. There had followed a month in which Steve had been benumbed by shock. A frozen, white-faced man who withdrew from his friends and plunged frantically into work. Sewell the Madman, his business associates had called him, watching with alarm while he took crazy chances, risked his entire fortune over and over in gambles that paid off. It seemed as though now, when he no longer cared, he could not lose.

After that, he regained his balance. During the daytime even his close friends were unaware of the change in him. But his nights were horrible. As soon as he dropped to sleep, the plane turned over and the dark was lit by the flames, seared by their heat. The screams of the dying rang in his ears.

Was that Mary's voice seeking her son in the horror? Was it Jimmy yelling in agony, "Dad! Come help me! Dad!" Was that Rod, laughing through his pain, shouting, "I'll call a taxi."

There had been more than a year of that suffering. At length, Steve was able to sleep again without nightmares, but by that time a feeling of guilt, that he was responsible for the deaths of the three people he loved most in the world, had become deep-rooted. Only when his sister's husband died did he rouse himself from his absorption in his own grief and learn to think of the unhappiness and the emotional needs of someone else, which, if he had known it, was the beginning of his cure. He had bought the Rivers estate and brought Julie and her small daughter to Connecticut to build a new life.

While he had been brooding about these unhappy, far-off things, Steve had turned back toward the house. As he passed the snowman on the lawn he found himself smiling. Then Ho bristled and growled—a low, menacing sound.

"Ho! Quiet!" Steve looked up and saw the woman standing on the lower step that led to the front door. Brassy blond hair under an extreme hat tilted on one side, silver fox dripping from her shoulders. He bent over and snapped Ho's leash to his collar, holding it firmly in his hand.

Ho growled again, and the woman whirled around.

"That dog! That horrible dog! Don't dare let him come near me!"

"He won't hurt you."

"That's what *you* think," the woman said shrilly. "I tell you he's dangerous."

Steve had reached her side now. A quick searching glance showed him the artificial lashes, the heavily made-up mouth, the bruise below her cheekbone. His eyes rested thoughtfully on the bruise. "Not a mark on her," the carpenter had sworn. Even Jed had made no reference to a bruise.

"I think," he said slowly, "you must be Mrs. Grant. I am Stephen Sewell."

The china-blue eyes surveyed him in turn, weighing him shrewdly, his cultivated speech, his poise, his air of unstressed command, his unusual good looks. They went back for another look at the imposing façade of long fieldstone house. Her manner changed. The challenging tone died out of her voice.

"Mr. Sewell!" she exclaimed, fluttering the long lashes, her voice like honey. "How nice! I didn't dream that the Stephen Sewell I've been hearing so much about was so young and charming. Somehow I had the impression that you were old and unattractive." Her laughter rippled.

"You wanted to see me?" Steve's deep voice was gravely polite.

"Yes, I did. About that bad dog of yours. He's really very naughty."

As the door opened, Steve motioned for her to precede him and turned the boxer over to the butler. In the great drawing room Mrs. Grant stood looking around her. Watching in amusement, Steve felt that she was busy affixing a mental price tag to everything in the room.

"Won't you sit down?"

"Oh, thank you. Such a lovely house you have here." Again a ripple of girlish laughter. "But it must be sad for you. Rattling around in this great big house—all alone." The preposterous lashes fluttered.

Steve restrained a grin. "I don't suppose you came here to discuss my solitary state."

"Well—no; actually, I—you see, it's like this, Mr. Sewell. The day before yesterday, that boxer of yours—"

"Oh, you mean poor Ho? Did you see what happened, Mrs. Grant? I'm looking for a witness, so you'll be providential. Someone kicked him, raised a big lump in his side. May have cracked some ribs. I don't know yet how serious it is. The vet will be able to tell me. But as Ho never went off the property—I do have witnesses for that—we can only imagine that someone tried to break into my house."

The woman looked at his blandly smiling face. The wind had been taken out of her sails. She was not sure how to proceed, busy rearranging her story.

She held a handkerchief daintily and wiped dry eyes. "It wasn't really the boxer's fault," she said. "I'm sure he's a gentle creature."

Steve put up a hand to conceal a broad grin.

"But that beastly carpenter—I was just walking by the house, admiring it, you know—such a darling little place—a real dream house. And the carpenter made the dog jump on me. He simply ruined my mink. And knocked me down, and I got this bruise. I may be disfigured for life. I think—just possibly—when I fell, my heels might have touched his side, only grazed him. I was so shocked, of course, I didn't know what I was doing, I thought I was going to be torn to pieces. Simply petrified with fear. My nerves are in a highly dangerous state as a result of the experience."

"What does your physician say?"

"My—oh, I wouldn't trust a hick doctor!"

"Then you've consulted nobody about your state of shock—and your nerves?"

"Well," she hesitated, "not yet. I didn't feel up to driving to New York in my condition."

"But you were well enough to consult a lawyer, and, when he wouldn't take your case, to drive out here to collect damages."

"I don't see what business that is of yours!" Her voice was shrill again.

"And that bruise—you didn't have that right after you encountered the dog."

"What do you mean by that?"

"Jed Gordon came raging around in your defense. If you had had a bruise when he saw you, he'd have told us about it."

She sprang up from her chair. "You think you're being pretty smart about this, Mr. Sewell. I was hoping we could be friends, but if you want trouble you can have it. I mean to collect damages. Plenty."

Steve grinned. "Then you have come to the wrong person," he told her calmly. "I'm not to be bluffed or blackmailed. I'll shoulder my responsibilities any time, but I'm not an easy mark. If you want damages I suggest you appeal to the person who gave you that bruise."

"You—you—" she sputtered.

He escorted her to the door. "And a word of warning," he added. "Unless you are looking for trouble, don't try to enter strange houses unless you have someone with you who is authorized to visit them."

For a moment she stared at him, the china-blue eyes blank, the bruise standing out darkly on a chalk-white face. Then she went outside and ran down the steps.

Steve Sewell looked thoughtfully after the running figure of Mrs. Alice Grant. Well, well, that had all been very odd. She had come to bluff him into paying damages. Then she had decided to try blandishments, with the idea of acquiring a wealthy husband. Then she had revealed her true nature. What on earth had he said that had startled her so much at the end, that had driven her into headlong flight from the house? Was it his comment about the person who had given her that bruise?

He shrugged his shoulders and went back in the house, closing the door. So that was the woman over whom Jed Gordon had lost his head! Jed, who had talked to him about Elinor Parks, admitting he had loved her all his life. Jed, whom Elinor loved. How could he look from this cold, calculating, artificial woman to the loveliness and gaiety and warmth of Elinor and choose the one who was obviously untrustworthy?

Jed was headed for trouble. He had turned on his life-long friend, Clay Parks. He had made stupid and ugly remarks to the man who was not only his employer but his friend.

How badly Elinor had felt about it! Elinor, who did not attempt to deceive herself, who saw honestly. He did not want her to be unhappy, but he could not escape a feeling of elation that this infatuation of Jed's must alter her attitude toward him.

He remembered his first meeing with her. He was watching the little boys skating, thinking that Jimmy could have been with them if he had not taken that plane. The sketchbook was knocked at his feet and he had bent to return it to the girl. Stopped. A glowing face with skin like cream and flushed by the wind. Larkspur eyes. The beautiful mouth curved in an amused smile. It was not merely her beauty that stunned him, it was some quality—some . . .

And then he had looked at the sketches, seen his own face. Stern, withdrawn, brooding. That was what those honest eyes had seen. In a flash he had realized what he had done to himself. How he had permitted his grief and his senseless feeling of guilt to withdraw him from the main current of life and hope.

When she had left him he could not have let her go if he had not recognized the sketch of Jed on the Hastings Green. He had known then that there was a way to find her again.

He lived over again the moment when she had nearly slipped under the truck and his heart tightened. To have found her and then to lose her!

He laughed jeeringly at himself. To lose her! What did he mean by that? What was he allowing himself to hope? She loved Jed, didn't she? And he—how could he ever dare to marry again, knowing how responsible he had been for Mary's death? For all the deaths.

This was morbid and cowardly. He had to stop thinking in circles like this. He must learn to think straight and honestly once more. And instead of indulging in all this self-pity it was time he remembered to live in the present and build for the future, to pay attention to all the needs around him. If Hastings was to be his home, then he must learn to be a responsible part of Hastings.

The immediate job was to look over the empty factory building and see whether it would serve for the fair. When he had inspected it, he went on impulse to the small professional building beside the bank where Clay Parks had his offices.

Clay came out to meet him and took him into his private office.

"Mrs. Grant put in another appearance," he said with an amused smile, "and I sent her packing."

Steve laughed. "So did I." He described her visit to his house. "One thing I'm sure of, Parks, she didn't have that bruise when Jed was with her, or in his desire to protect her interests he'd have told us she was disfigured for life—which she suggested herself."

Clay shook his head. "I've known Jed all his life. I'd never have thought he would fall for an obvious phony like that. Wonder she doesn't trip herself up on those eyelashes. She can use them next summer in place of a palmleaf fan."

He grinned in amusement and then sat back with a questioning look.

"The reason I came in here," Steve said, "is that I'd like to have you take over my affairs for me here in Hastings. First, I want.to rent that empty factory building down by the river to hold the fair in. We can't have it out of doors in this weather."

Clay grinned. "I see Elinor has dragged you into this project she has for a fair."

"She didn't have to drag me. I was eager." Steve stopped short. He didn't want Clay to feel that he was turning business over to him as a way of winning his support with Elinor.

Clay shot him a quick look from eyes that were disconcertingly like his sister's.

"Then," Steve went on in a more businesslike tone, "if there's a clear title and the price is reasonable, I'd like to buy the building. Hastings needs a small industry of some sort to help employment and I'd like to provide it."

"This is going to be good news for the entire village," Clay declared, while he made some rapid notes. "What do you have in mind?"

"Several ideas. Nothing definite. If possible, some product that won't be affected by hard times, that will provide steady employment. We'll have to so some research on it."

The two men talked for half an hour, exchanging ideas, and so became acquainted with each other's minds, liking what they discovered.

"Today, with industries pulling out of New England and heading South, isn't it risky to bring one in?" Clay asked.

"I've always been a gambler in a way," Steve confessed. "But somehow or other, it seems to pay off."

Clay doodled on the pad in front of him. He didn't particularly care for that comment. Someone else had referred to Sewell as a big gambler. Oh, yes, it had been Harold Brown. Clay didn't like Harold, never had, but there was no getting away from the fact that he was in a position to know about the financial standing of the people of Hastings. Nobody, he had said, knew where Sewell's money came from. The man had appeared out of nowhere.

Later in the afternoon, Steve drove to the shabby Martin house. Sue came to the door.

"Are you Susan Martin?"

"Yes, Mr. Sewell. Please come in."

For an hour Steve talked briskly.

"Goodness," Susan exclaimed at last, flexing her fingers with which she had been making shorthand notes, "that's going to be a lot of work, isn't it?"

Steve nodded. "A great deal of work. First, we'll get the announcements to all the papers in the nearby towns. Then we want to get off the letters to people who can contribute things for the fair. Then we want to find people to take charge of the booths. And we'll have to arrange for someone from the local paper to interview Dr. Mallison and get the story of the great need for more beds for the children's wing."

"It will be sorta exciting, won't it!" Sue exclaimed.

Steve smiled. "There's no excitement like the feeling of accomplishing something worthwhile."

"Yeah," Sue said thoughtfully. "You know I never believed that before, though Bert Jackson, who is going to marry my sister, says it all the time. Well, I'll get to work right away."

When he had left her opening her typewriter, Steve got into his car. It was growing late but he felt restless. He would drive for a while before he went home. Outside the hospital he parked for a few minutes, looking at the building. Actually, what was needed was not just an additional wing with a few more beds, it was a hospital devoted entirely to children, one that could handle more than local cases; one, perhaps, with a laboratory for research in children's diseases.

Suppose, Steve thought, I should endow such a building. Pay some of my debt to little Jimmy. Help other children. Perhaps have Jed as the architect. He did well with the houses.

On impulse, he took the side road that led to his three new houses. Twilight fell swiftly. This was foolish. He wouldn't be able to see anything. Would people be willing to buy houses on this deserted road? No one seemed to come this way. . . . Yes, there was a deserted car, pulled off the road.

In the distance he heard a report. A shot? He slowed up, trying to see into the darkness at the sides of the road. A hunter? Then his headlights picked out a car, an open trunk, someone trying to lift a tire. A girl. Elinor!

How immense her eyes looked as she whirled to look at him. How white her face. Then she was running headlong, straight into his arms, clinging to him, shaking. Something had terrified her.

When he had put on her spare tire and tossed the other into the luggage compartment, he went around to the side window where Elinor told him about the lurking man who had scared her.

Steve went through the woods searching. His flashlight picked up a man trying to hide behind a tree trunk. A big fellow with heavy shoulders. The man lunged down the hillside and vanished among bushes at the bottom of the gully. Steve was torn between the desire to track him down and the fear of leaving Elinor alone any longer.

He went back to the car, saw her huddled on the seat, fighting her fear which he could not understand.

"This is a calculated risk," he had said unsteadily. He had gathered her into his arms and kissed her soft mouth. His heart leaped up. Surely the warm lips had moved, had returned his kiss!

He released her abruptly and went back to his own car, followed her into Hastings, cursing himself for an impulsive fool. He had risked everything! Why had he gambled his future, his hope of happiness for a moment's delight?

When she reached a lighted street and he knew she was safe, he turned his big car, heading for the substation of the State Police.

A tall good-looking young man in a trim uniform introduced himself as Trooper Jackson.

Steve explained the reason for his visit.

"Of course, the man may have been perfectly harmless. At worst he might have been breaking the hunting laws. But Miss Parks felt sure he had been spying on her, though he refused to help her. She had an impression that he only showed himself in the first place because he had been expecting someone else. And by the way he ducked and ran when I showed up, he certainly didn't want to be recognized."

"Word will go out to the prowl cars," Trooper Jackson assured him.

"I hope I haven't taken up your time for nothing."

"That's what we're here for. Anyhow, I have a bee in my bonnet, I guess. It's just about time for another big bank robbery and I have my own theories about it. All these jobs are the same: three people involved. They always get away. So does the money. The descriptions are never satisfactory and they differ so much that my own hunch is that the third person varies, is local. A different one every time."

"How do you think they work it?"

The trooper looked at him intently for a moment. Then the friendliness died out of his face. He was official.

"Sorry, sir, but I can't go into that."

"Of course not," Steve said lightly. He went out to his car and drove off, while the trooper looked after him thoughtfully and then made a note of his license number.

"You never can tell," Trooper Jackson said to himself.

XI

Elinor drove home, her thoughts in a turmoil. "This is a calculated risk," Steve had said. Then he had kissed her. The feeling of his lips on hers still remained. Her mouth trembled with the memory of that warm pressure, which had been so sweet. Had she returned his kiss? Had she? Her face burned at the thought.

A girl named Mary Todd. How could Steve have done this to her, roused this emotion in her, when he had a wife? But where was she? Had there been a divorce? "All those deaths," Julie Campbell had said. Was she dead, then? Was Steve guilty of her death? But how could he be? Steve with his fineness, his generosity, his tenderness with Merry, his wise understanding of his sister, his tolerance with Jed's ingratitude. No, her heart could not be so wrong about him.

"A calculated risk." What an odd expression. A gambler's expression. Was Steve a gambler? What was the mystery about the man? If she only knew!

Except for the day when he had spoken of Julie's tragedy—and Julie's weakness—he had never discussed his past. He had stepped out of the shadows into Hastings. And yet somewhere he had made—or inherited —a great deal of money. He lived like a man accustomed to money. There was none of the ostentation that appeared with sudden wealth.

As she stopped the convertible in front of the house and pulled on the emergency brake, the outside lights flashed on and Clay ran down the steps.

"Thank heavens, you are all right! I was beginning to worry. Do you know what time it is?"

Elinor shook her head and slid out from under the wheel.

"Nearly seven. And with you out after dark in a strange car on bad roads I've been having a fit. If something had happened to you, on top of everything else—"

"Everything else," Elinor repeated. "What's wrong, Clay?"

He summoned up a wry smile. "Ginny planned a dinner party and things went wrong. She asked Mrs. Grant to dine here tonight."

Elinor looked up quickly and saw his grim expression. Then he was on guard again.

"She asked Harold Brown and Jed—a bad combination at any time. Then, at the last minute, the guest of honor telephoned to cancel, and you didn't show up. Harold and Jed have been glowering at each other. Ginny's party is spoiled, and—"

Elinor laughed and tucked her hand under his arm. "Poor Clay! We'll have to do something to salvage the evening."

Ginny came to the door. "Well, at last! Clay was ready to call the State Police. Don't change for dinner. Everything is probably spoiled, anyhow."

When Elinor had hastily washed, brushed her hair and powdered her nose, she ran down to join them at the table. Clay was courteous but withdrawn. Ginny was almost silent. For the first time, she was aware that she had gone too far in interfering with Clay's professional life and, in the face of his controlled anger, she was a little frightened. Harold and Jed seemed unable to speak to each other without exchanging jibes. It was a horrible dinner.

Elinor did her best to break down the atmosphere of hostility. Gaily she told them about her experiences in hunting antiques. She concluded with an account of her adventure on the road, when she had the blowout; about the strange man who had escaped in the dark, and Steve's opportune arrival.

Opportune. The moment she used the word her heart did a flip-flop. *Opportune.* What had Steve been doing on that dark, deserted road at that time? Could he, by any possible chance, have planned to meet the other man? Had his plans been changed by her unexpected presence there?

No, she told herself fiercely, it isn't true. I don't believe it. I won't believe it.

"That's darned queer," Jed said, perplexed, when she had finished her story. "I never heard of a man refusing to help a woman change a tire."

"Did you see him clearly?" Harold asked.

"No, he was a little more than a shadow."

"Sure he *wasn't* a shadow?" Harold grinned at her. "In the dark, you know, especially if you were nervous, you might have imagined him. What's that line of Shakespeare, something like, 'And in the dark how easily each bush becomes a bear'?"

"He was real," Elinor said firmly. She shivered. "He frightened me."

"I am sure he did." Jed laughed. "Your eyes are as big as these dinner plates."

"But why did he frighten you?" Clay asked. "What did he do? That's what I can't understand."

"N-nothing."

The three men laughed and, for the first time since dinner began, Ginny joined in. That moment of shared laughter broke the tension.

Clay sobered first. "I know you too well, Elinor. You don't scare easily. What was wrong?"

"I don't know. At first I thought he was a hunter. Then—I can't explain—the way he edged into the light when my car stopped. The way he ducked out of sight when I called to him. I had a feeling he expected to meet someone else. There was something furtive about the way he vanished in the dark. And yet—" She was shivering again.

Jed put his hand over hers and Harold scowled at the gesture.

"Pull yourself together, gal," Jed said cheerfully. "You're getting the heebie-jeebies."

"Laugh if you want to. I don't blame you. But I was scared silly. All the time I was getting that d-darned tire off, I felt his eyes—he was lurking there in the d-dark, w-watching me. I hated it." She blinked back tears.

"I'm going to call the State Police," Clay declared, pushing back his chair. "It sounds darned queer."

"But what, after all, could the guy be up to?" Harold asked in perplexity. "There's nothing—nobody—on that road."

"You needn't bother about the State Police," Elinor said. "Steve was going to call them himself."

"It seems like a lot of fuss about nothing, to me," Jed said.

"It isn't nothing if Elinor was frightened," Harold retorted.

"At least," Jed sneered, "Sewell doesn't waste any time looking after Elinor's interests. After the way he acted about Alice Grant, giving her the brush-off when she could have been torn to pieces by that boxer—"

"Steve knew it really happened. He saw the man," Elinor said quickly, noticing Clay's expression. "He knew he was there. He followed him into the woods. Turned his flashlight on him, when he was trying to hide. The man got away."

Jed laughed. "Apparently Sewell preferred to let him get away. He doesn't seem to have done much chasing after him in the woods."

"What's wrong with you, Jed?" Elinor exclaimed, exasperated. "I've never known you to be so unjust before."

"What did you mean by that crack—*Steve knew it really happened?* And why didn't he believe Mrs. Grant about the dog?"

"Who is this Mrs. Grant?" Harold asked.

"She's our missing dinner guest," Ginny explained, with a side glance at Clay's set face.

"I didn't know you had met her," Jed said in surprise.

"She called on me this morning. Actually, she was looking for Clay. Thought she'd catch him at home. We talked. I—liked her so much. Thought she was a client of Clay's and that it would be nice to have her to dinner. Then, late this afternoon, she telephoned. She had a terrible headache. I imagine she'd been in some sort of accident. She had a bad bruise on her cheek when she was here. May have hurt her head. The poor woman looked as though she had really been through something." Ginny stole a look at Clay.

"Badly hurt! A bruise!" Jed pushed back his chair. "Forgive me, Ginny, will you? I'm really worried about Alice. Something else must have happened. She didn't have any bruise on her face when I saw her."

He broke off, apologized awkwardly for breaking up the dinner party and almost ran out of the room. A minute later the jeep's lights went on and it roared down the driveway.

"Well," Harold exclaimed, "he seems to have it bad. Who is this fatal charmer?"

"More fatal than charming, if you ask me," Clay said. "She's as synthetic as though she came out of a bottle. Not my type. I like women who are real and—and—dependable."

"Oh, Clay, sometimes I—I hate you!" Ginny exclaimed and she burst into tears. She ran blindly out of the room and stumbled up the stairs. The door of her room banged shut behind her.

"I'm sorry," Clay said stiffly. "Ginny has had a difficult day. Her nerves are all shot."

"Of course," Harold said amiably. "It was a grand dinner. I'll be getting along. Ginny will want peace and quiet so she can get some rest. How about going to the movies with me, Elinor? There's a good picture in Newcomb."

"Thanks a lot, Harold. Not tonight. I've had a tiring day."

She sighed with relief when the door closed behind

him and turned to Clay. The look of sick misery in his face pinched her heart. She wanted to put her arms around him, to comfort him—and knew it would be a fatal mistake. The problem could only be handled between Clay and Ginny. Even a devoted sister would be an intruder. Her pity would be an insult, her sympathy could only hurt.

She could not stay in the living room looking at his unhappiness. Yet if she, too, went to her room it would seem like an escape from an intolerable situation.

"I'm going to call on Mrs. Martin for a little while," she said. "I won't be late."

She slipped into her car coat, pulled on driving gloves and went out to the Chevrolet. It had been a relief to get home this evening. Now it was an even greater relief to be leaving the house, putting behind her the rift between Clay and his wife that, so rapidly, was widening into a gulf.

Elinor parked outside the Martin house and rang the bell. Sue opened the door.

"Hi, there," she said. "Come in."

"Elinor!" Betty came out of the little living room to meet her. "How wonderful! I meant to call you and thank you for Doctor Dick. Mother feels better already. We're both so grateful. And Sue's job—"

Elinor smiled at the big plain girl, whose face was radiant with happiness.

"And this," Betty said proudly, "is Bert."

Trooper Jackson was tall and well built, with an open, attractive face and a firm jaw.

"I think," Elinor told him, holding out her hand, "that you're a very lucky man. I congratulate you with all my heart. People like Betty are pretty special."

He shook hands warmly. "You're telling me!" He slid his arm around Betty's shoulders. "I still can't believe my luck."

"Is that Miss Parks?" Mrs. Martin called from upstairs.

"Will you go up to see her?" Betty asked.

Elinor ran up the stairs. Mrs. Martin raised herself on her pillows and held out both hands.

"My dear, I'm so grateful! Doctor Dick says he'll have me out of bed before long, and that I'm going to get well, be able to work again and support myself."

Elinor brushed a hand across her eyes. "Of course, you will," she said gaily. "Doctor Dick is wonderful!"

"And so are you. Sue is so excited about her job that for once there's no holding her back. She even has ideas of extra things she can do to help."

Elinor giggled. "Don't discourage her."

Mrs. Martin gave her a conspiratorial grin. Was this the wan discouraged woman of so short a time ago?

"I'll keep my fingers crossed," she whispered. "Maybe Sue will learn that work can be fun if you put your heart into it."

She closed her eyes as Elinor lowered her head gently, took out one of the pillows and switched off the light.

"Don't try to do too much at once, Mrs. Martin. You'll have lots of time ahead," she said, and went softly out of the room.

Betty was waiting for her at the foot of the stairs. Elinor squeezed her arm. "I think your Bert is marvelous," she declared enthusiastically.

Betty glowed. "He's grand. And so kind and thoughtful. And reliable as the mountains. Stay a while. I want you to know him."

"I want to know her, too," the trooper laughed. "And, especially, I want to know what happened to you this evening, Miss Parks."

"Happened to Elinor!" Betty exclaimed.

"A Mr. Stephen Sewell came to the barracks with an odd story. I'd like to hear your side of it."

Your side of it. What did he mean? That her story would not match Steve's?

She told him about it from the moment when she had seen the empty car on the road to the moment when the strange man had run away from Steve.

Trooper Jackson—he wasn't Betty's fiancé Bert

now, he was all official—listened as though he were mentally checking off points. Then he nodded.

"It's the same story."

"Of course, it's the same story," Elinor said indignantly. "Why on earth shouldn't it be?"

"Well, it's odd, you know. The man's actions were certainly queer."

"Very queer," she agreed.

"Did you notice his license number?"

Elinor shut her eyes, trying to see the license plate in her mind. She shook her head regretfully. It had been an out-of-state license. That was all she noticed.

"And the car? Make? Color? Approximate year?"

"Dark. A sedan. Not new. That's all."

"What's so exciting about an old car parked on the road and a man who didn't do anything but run away?" Sue demanded. "I can't see anything in that to get so hot and bothered about."

"He frightened Miss Parks," the trooper said quietly, "and I don't get the impression, somehow, that she is easily frightened. Exactly what did frighten you?"

"I don't know," Elinor admitted. "That's the silly part of it. I felt he had expected someone else and didn't want me to see him. But I felt—he was watching me. He was—evil." She added, with an embarrassed smile, "Don't laugh at me, if you can help it."

"I'm not laughing," he assured her.

"Do you think you'll find him?" Betty asked.

"A man no one recognized in a car no one can identify? Afraid not. The prowl cars have been looking for him. The car was gone, of course. Not a trace of the man. Anyhow, there is no conceivable charge against him. You can't arrest a man because he runs away from a woman who asks for help."

"But you are really interested, aren't you, darling?" Betty said. "Do you think he could be part of—" She broke off. "Oh, sorry, I didn't mean to bring that up."

Bert Jackson had an engaging grin. "Okay, my pet. No harm done." He explained to Elinor, "Betty thinks I am hipped on the subject of bank robberies and try to tie everything that happens in with them."

"She told me you were investigating them as a sort of special assignment."

He nodded. "Now and then, I get cold chills for fear I am on the wrong track. But ever since that big bank robbery in Newcomb last year I've been studying the way it was done. First thing I realized was that it was just like the one the year before in Caldwell and the one the year before that in Asbury."

"Tell me," Elinor said. "This is thrilling."

Bert Jackson leaned back on the couch and reached for Betty's hand. "In case I get scared," he explained, "while I tell this gory tale.

"Well, I went to Caldwell and Asbury and got all the first-hand information I could, after I had studied all the reports. Everything checked with the Newcomb robbery. The pattern was exactly the same. Each crime was committed in the middle of April. Each time, the robbery coincided with the time when the most currency was in the bank vaults. Each time, two men and a woman entered the bank at about ten o'clock at night."

Elinor laughed. "Entered! It sounds as though they had just walked in."

"That's about the way it was. No breaking in."

"But that seems incredible!"

Bert nodded. "The burglar alarm had been disconnected. The safes were emptied of currency and negotiable bonds. Roadblocks were set up but the robbers were never caught. The money was never recovered.

"The theory I've been working on is that there is a reason for this particular pattern. That three people are always involved. The trouble is," he ran a hand through his hair and it stood up boyishly, "that the descriptions of the three people just don't tally. They differ wildly every time. That's where I had my biggest argument with the brass. They wouldn't go along with it at first. They said I was wrong about the robberies being the work of the same gang."

He chuckled. "You should have heard the descriptions: the woman was fat, she was thin; she was dark, she was fair; she was young, she was old. Same for the men. Well, that's where my girl came in."

Betty giggled. "That was fun."

"What happened?" Elinor demanded. "I'm all a-tingle with suspense."

Bert laughed. "Well, Betty dressed up, different styles, different ways of doing her hair, a wig, I don't know what all. She made three appearances at the barracks in one day and the men thought they had seen three different women. So they got the idea. They've given me a lot of rope. Now it's up to me to make good."

"You think these people are always disguised, is that it?"

"I can't prove any of this, of course," Bert said. "Not yet. I think there are two people running this, and a third who varies each time. The third one is local. And I think the next robbery will take place next month. If I'm right about the pattern."

"But can't you alert all the banks?"

"We've done about everything we can. No telling where they will crop up next."

"But," Betty began, caught Bert's look, saw the slight shake of his head, and was silent.

"How do you think they get away with the money?" Elinor asked.

"My idea is that they don't get away with it. Not at the time of the robbery. I think they find a safe hiding place and one of them leaves it there. For weeks, if necessary. They drift out of town, one by one. Then another one retrieves the money when it is safe. They live high on the hog for a year while they prepare for a new *coup*."

"I don't," Sue admitted, "see how you can do anything about a setup like that. Seems air-tight to me."

"Bert will find a way," Betty said with quiet confidence.

"Bert's got to find a way," he said grimly. "It means promotion—and you."

"But this local person," Elinor said. "Can't you check up on all suspicious characters?"

He grinned. "We'll never find what we are looking for among suspicious characters. Remember, there is a lot of money involved. The person we're looking for won't arouse suspicion. He or she will be beyond suspicion, established in town, respected. Plenty of money to spend. That's the kind of person I'm looking for. Someone you'd be inclined to trust. But someone who gets his or her thrills by taking risks. Someone who gambles his freedom on the chance he'll get away with it."

"You're terribly white, Elinor!" Betty exclaimed. "Are you ill?"

"Just tired. It's been a rugged day. I must be getting home to bed."

"Thank you for coming and for all you've done for us," Betty said.

"Miss Parks—" Bert Jackson stopped her at the door—"I've been talking in confidence tonight. You must not repeat a word of this!"

"Of course not."

"To anyone." He held her eyes. "Anyone," he repeated slowly. "Promise?"

She held out her hand. "I promise."

She summoned up the courage to smile radiantly at them all. Then she went out to her car.

"How beautiful she is," Sue said enviously.

"How kind she is," Betty said warmly.

"How white she was," Bert said. "Her hand was like ice."

"I think that experience this evening must have been more of a shock than she admitted," Betty said.

"It's a cinch that something was," Trooper Jackson remarked.

XII

The next two weeks were a whirlwind of activity, the days devoted to scouring the countryside for local products and handcrafts for the fair—which Steve had decided was to have priority over the furnishing of the houses —and the evenings busy with dinner parties and dances.

Much as Elinor had always loved fun and parties, she found that she was going out, more often than not, to escape the tensions of the house: Ginny's sullen moods broken by feverish gaiety, and Clay's restrained quiet and brooding watchfulness over his wife.

Something, as Mrs. Groom confided to Elinor, was bound to happen before long.

"The fires are too banked down," Mrs. Groom put it. "One of these days there is going to be an explosion and what's blown up won't be put together again."

But that couldn't happen, Elinor told herself. It couldn't. Clay loved Ginny profoundly. For keeps. He would hate a divorce. And even if that was what Ginny wanted, there would be no other woman for him. Ever.

But was it what Ginny wanted? Sometimes Elinor thought it was. Sometimes, seeing Ginny watch Clay, with tears sparkling on her lashes, she thought it wasn't. Ginny loved Clay. Really loved him. The trouble was that she loved herself more. As an only child, she had never learned the basic principle of sharing. She assumed that she had a right to the first consideration.

Strangest of all the unexpected features of those two weeks was that Jed had apparently dropped out of the social activities of the younger set in Hastings. Elinor rarely met him at all, and never at the parties. Now and then, she saw him at the inn, lunching with Alice Grant. Now and then, she saw them driving together. But not in the jeep. Jed had acquired a new car that was more worthy of the glamorous lady of his dreams.

"She's nothing but a gold digger," Elinor stormed to herself. "She's ruining Jed. He's not even spending much time at his office any more; he's neglecting his job, and he must be head over ears in debt. Why does she stay here? Is she really in love with Jed? But she must know he has no money. She doesn't like small towns. Oh, I wish she'd go away! Before it's too late. Before she spoils Jed's life."

For the first time she remembered the scrap of conversation she had overheard at the inn when she saw the glamorous blonde at the next table. Her companion had been pointing out various village people, among them Clay and Ginny. The man had mentioned Jed as a young architect with—how had he put it?—unlimited money behind him.

Was that the real secret of Jed's attraction for Mrs. Grant? Unlimited money. But the money was not Jed's, it was Stephen Sewell's. Surely she had discovered the mistake by now!

Or—Elinor's heart did a nose dive—had Jed deliberately allowed her to continue in her deception? Had he been afraid to have her learn that he was penniless?

The person who profited most by Jed's absorption in the blonde woman was Harold Brown. Night after night, he appeared as Elinor's escort. Or, if someone else took her dancing, he managed to cut in most of the time. Ginny, looking on, was pleased, but careful not to say so. Clay was less pleased, but he made no comment. Elinor had a right to make her own decisions.

Only now and then did Steve telephone with suggestions. During those two weeks Elinor did not see him at all. Since the night when he had said "This is a calculated risk" and kissed her, he had not come near her. His voice, during his infrequent telephone calls, was impersonal and businesslike. He was so much older than the group of young people with whom Elinor ran around that he was not included in their parties.

That's fine, Elinor told herself firmly. That's the way it should be. We'll maintain a purely businesslike relationship. That's what I wanted, isn't it?

It was only toward the end of the second week that she acknowledged to herself that her heart leaped every time the telephone rang, and sank when she heard another voice. That her eyes were engaged, whenever she was out of the house, in seeking for him on the sidewalks or in a passing car.

Pain, she learned in those long days, wasn't the worst thing that could happen. Emptiness was worse.

Then the intensifying crisis in the affairs of Clay and Ginny made her put aside her own unhappiness and uncertainty.

One morning at breakfast Ginny looked over her mail, one letter and a stack of bills, her face paling.

"I'm going to New York," she said. "I've simply got to go. I'm—stifled here. And you can't stop me!"

"I won't try to stop you, Ginny," Clay told her quietly. "Is this for keeps, or do you plan to come back?"

"I don't know," Ginny said steadily.

The telephone rang and Elinor hastened to answer it, to escape from those two stormy faces.

"This is Steve," said the deep, quiet voice she loved, and her heart turned over. "Will you lunch with me at the inn? . . . One o'clock? . . . Thank you."

The day, like the emotional atmosphere in the house, was stormy. Bare trees bowed under the rush of wind. A driving rain was mixed with sleet. Dressed in red in defiance of the gray weather, Elinor drove cautiously to the inn. In spite of the impending disruption of Clay's marriage, she could not prevent her heart from singing. She was going to see Steve!

He was waiting in the lobby; he checked her coat and took her into the dining room. They sat at a table by the window, hearing the gusts of wind roaring in the trees, the sleet clawing at the window with angry fingers.

Steve's manner was impersonal. That kiss might never have happened.

When he had ordered, he smiled at her. "Jed was right. You belong in a garden."

"Br-r-r, not today," she protested, laughing.

He squinted out of the blurred window. "Your time is coming. I can see spring on its way."

"What signs do you see today? The hills blotted out by rain . . . The wind like galloping horses."

"Remember the Millay poem—

> Spring rides no horses down the hill
> But comes on foot, a goose-girl still . . .

—a poem about the importance of simple things, honest things?"

"Millay knew a lot about spring, didn't she?" Elinor said. "And love mixed with laughter, and love mixed with tears." She raised a glass of water but could not swallow because of the lump in her throat.

"What's wrong, my—What's wrong, Elinor?" he asked. "Something is worrying you, driving all the brightness from your face."

"Clay and Ginny," she surprised herself by admitting.

He waited and she found herself pouring out her worries to this stranger. She described the growing tension between her brother and his wife. She told him about Ginny's sudden determination to go away, to live in New York, perhaps not to return.

"Eat your soup while it's hot," he said, when she had finished.

"Soup of the evening, beautiful soup," she laughed.

"So you read *Alice,* too. One of my bitterest disappointments as a child was failing to find any talking flowers in our garden." Without any transition he went on, "I think you are worrying too much. Let Ginny go to New York and have her fling. Work it out of her system."

"But suppose she doesn't come back?"

"We will see that she comes back."

"We will?"

Steve smiled and the stern face was suddenly boy-
ish and alight with mischief. "I'm full of plans. I've been
wanting to go to New York with you to visit some of the
Madison Avenue shops and complete the furnishing of
my houses. Get the show on the road before late spring.
The trouble is that Julie isn't willing to leave Merry until
she is stronger. But if Mrs. Parks is going, we can make
up a party, take in some theaters, go dancing—I've
waited a lifetime to dance with you—see the bright
lights."

"Oh, Steve, that would be wonderful."

He laughed. "Your eyes lit up like neon lights.
Fine. Now all we have to do is to sell your sister-in-law
on the idea."

"When do you plan to go?"

"The sooner the better. Tomorrow, if you can both
be ready by then."

"Tomorrow," Elinor said gaily. "It's a deal."

Twenty-four hours later, Ginny and Elinor were
unpacking their suitcases in the suite at the Waldorf that
Steve had taken for them. When Elinor had exclaimed
that they didn't need two bedrooms and a sitting room,
he had silenced her.

"You are here to help me with a job and you are
on an expense account. Mrs. Parks is included because
she has been kind enough to act as chaperon for you. I'll
be at the Plaza. I've kept a suite there for years so I'll
always have a place to stay in New York. You girls will
want to rest after that long ride. Suppose I pick you up
here at seven for an early dinner. I'll see what I can get
in the way of theater tickets."

"That sounds wonderful."

"Not for me, I'm afraid," Ginny said. "I have a
date for dinner." She avoided Elinor's eyes.

Elinor's lips parted. She closed them firmly. But
the unasked questions almost choked her. Who is he?
What did you make a dinner engagement for? When did

you make these plans? Do you care more for this man than for Clay?

"How about dancing later?" Steve suggested smoothly, appearing to be unaware of Ginny's embarrassment, of Elinor's shocked surprise. "Shall Elinor and I meet you and your escort at 11:30? There's a new night spot with good music—the Peppercorn Club, on Fifty-second Street."

Ginny hesitated, biting her lips. Then she agreed, a trifle reluctantly.

Now, a half hour later, she was shaking out a silver sheath evening gown and hanging it carefully.

"Ginny, how stunning! I've never seen that before."

"Bergdorf. I couldn't resist it but there's been no place to wear it in Hastings."

Elinor gave a gurgle of laughter. "I should think not! It must have cost hundreds."

"It did. Oh, Elinor, I do love beautiful clothes!"

"But, Ginny, Clay isn't a rich man and you'd never have any use for a dress like that," Elinor began helplessly.

"I have use for it tonight. I must say your boss is giving us the red-carpet treatment. Too bad he's married. What are you going to wear?"

"That yellow dress. It's all I have."

"But you can't afford to look shabby. Mr. Sewell wouldn't like it. Look, I have two other dresses I've never worn. Which one do you like best?"

Elinor looked from the black net to the pale green velvet and chose the latter. It revealed her creamy arms and shoulders and her beautiful back.

"You're breathtaking in it," Ginny admitted. "I'm glad we're not the same type. Too much competiton. Fortunately, gentlemen prefer blondes."

"Ginny, who is this mysterious escort of yours for tonight?"

"You'll meet him later at the Peppercorn Club."

"Ginny—"

"Look, Elinor," Ginny said impatiently. "Don't start preaching at me. I know what I am doing."

"But Clay—"

"I'm doing this for Clay's own good."

"He loves you, Ginny, but there are some things he won't permit anyone to do."

"I love him, too. Don't think I could ever stop loving Clay. But this is the only way I can think of—" Ginny's fingers caught at Elinor's arms, tightened on them.

Elinor looked into the desperate eyes. "What do you mean?" she asked gently, trying to conceal her growing alarm, to hold back the comments on the tip of her tongue.

"I'm trying to save our marriage," Ginny said. "This is the only way I can do it now." She relaxed the frenzied grip on Elinor's arms. "Only don't ask me any more questions now. Please. Please." She whirled around. "I'm going to take a nap. See you later."

Elinor looked after her sister-in-law in dismay. Who was this escort with whom she had made the secret appointment! What did she mean by the only way she could save her marriage?

The green velvet dress lay over a chair and Elinor took it into her own room to hang it up. She looked at the label. No wonder Clay had cut Ginny's allowance!

Fourteen stories below an endless stream of cars moved up and down Park Avenue. Lights blinked green and red. The muffled roar of the traffic from this height was like the sound of the wind in the trees at Hastings.

Elinor glanced at her watch. Only three o'clock. It was weeks since she had been in New York and it was a pity to stay cooped up in a hotel room, even one as luxurious and comfortable as this.

Down a long corridor and another. A crowded elevator. The lights of the huge lobby. People meeting for tea and cocktails. Bellboys rushing. The door at the foot of the broad flight of stairs constantly revolving. Wasn't that a famous politician whom she had seen on television? And that was the new sensational night club sing-er. Faces in the news. People making news. The world swirling around her. Furs and the scent of perfume.

The revolving door deposited her on Park Avenue. She waved away the doorman's offer of a taxi and walked swiftly. Everyone in New York walked swiftly. Trucks rumbled. Taxis stopped with a squeaking of brakes. Impatient motorists sounded their horns. Sirens of fire engines, ambulances, police cars. The unceasing sound of riveters, building a bigger, a higher city. Voices. Voices. Speaking French, Spanish, German, Russian, Japanese. All the languages of the world. All the races. And emerging out of it one nation, one people.

Elinor's heart lifted. No wonder Ginny longed for New York. Surely no place on earth was more exciting. On Madison Avenue she paused to look at a chest of drawers. An exquisite piece. But time enough for that tomorrow when she made her tour with Steve. And she should have at least half a day for study in the American Wing at the Metropolitan Museum.

New York, once a city of gleaming, towering steel, seemed rapidly to be turning into a city of glass. Great soaring buildings of glass. Unreal. Fragile yet indestructible. And the cascades and fountains outside so many of them gave a magic touch.

Elinor was conscious of an increasing number of lights in the buildings and saw that the sky was darkening. She went back to the Waldorf to prepare for her evening with Steve.

Why, she thought in surprise as she re-entered the lobby, that's all I've done for the past hours. Wait for the evening. Wait for Steve.

The suite was empty when she let herself in. On a table in the sitting room was a scrawled note from Ginny: *Having my hair done. We'll meet you at the Peppercorn Club at 11:30. Have fun. Ginny.*

Slowly Elinor tore the note and dropped it into the wastebasket. Ginny was determined to postpone explanations as long as possible so that Elinor could not interfere with her course of action. Whatever it was. There was nothing Elinor could do about it.

Elinor bathed in scented water, took her time dressing, studied her reflection in the long mirror. The pale green velvet was the loveliest dress she had ever worn, the most beautifully cut, the most becoming.

A tap at the door. The bellboy handed her a transparent box. Nesting inside were two gardenias. She looked at the card.

I hope you'll wear these tonight. Steve.

She pinned them on the dress and put on her fur coat and went out to the elevator to meet Steve. He glanced at the gardenias and smiled.

"Thank you for wearing my flowers."

"Thank you for sending them. They are perfect."

Even among the distinguished-looking men in the small, exclusive restaurant to which he took her, he stood out.

"You're very beautiful tonight," he said as he lifted the coat from her bare shoulders. "Every man in the place is envying me. If there's a riot, the fault is all yours. What would you like to eat?"

"Order for me. You'll know better than I what they do especially well."

"Oysters to start with," he suggested. "A clear soup. Roast lamb with mint sauce. All right, so far?"

"Perfect. I'm starving."

Steve laughed. "I like to see a woman eat as though she enjoyed it. It's an insult to good food to toy with it. By the way, I got tickets for the Mary Martin show. Will that suit you?"

They talked of plays and music and books, of pictures and sculpture and foreign travel. With the last sip of perfect coffee it seemed that the hour had flown.

Then a taxi, bumper to bumper traffic, and the flashing lights of Broadway. A crowded lobby, no time to look at the program, the dimming of lights, the strains of the orchestra, the swift rise of a curtain and all the magic of theater.

Beside her, Elinor was aware of Steve, dark sleeve against her bare arm, the gleam of his white shirt front. Once, for a breathless second, she met his eyes in the darkened theater. Met and held and turned away with an effort to the lighted stage and music.

Then the curtains closed, opened again while the cast bowed, and the lights went up in the theater. Steve lifted Elinor's coat and laid it over her bare shoulders. For a moment his arm held her lightly and then dropped away and he stood back to let her precede him out of the theater.

"Let's walk," she suggested. "It's not far and after the theater I'd like some fresh air."

"In those shoes?" he asked doubtfully, looking down at the fragile, high-heeled evening slippers.

At her nod he slipped his hand under her arm and guided her through the after-theater throngs.

"It's been a perfect evening," she said, taking a deep breath of the cold air. "Mmh! Fresh air."

"Mostly gasoline fumes," he laughed, "but at that it is better than a stuffy taxi."

They paused for a moment to look at the brilliant lights of Broadway and then walked across Fifty-second Street to the Peppercorn Club.

"It's listed among the quiet ones," Steve assured her, "and the music is out of this world. I wonder if your sister-in-law is here yet. I reserved a table."

The club was small and tastefully decorated, and the music, as Steve had promised, was out of this world. His table was on the edge of the dance floor at a distance from the orchestra. Ginny was already there, exquisite in the silver dress, seated beside a distinguished-looking man in his middle fifties, with silver hair and a beautifully tailored dinner jacket.

"Elinor," Ginny said, her expression half-defiant, half-triumphant, "let me introduce Mr. Lightwood. My sister-in-law, Miss Parks. Mr. Sewell."

The two men shook hands and Elinor gave Ginny a bewildered look. Lightwood? Who was he? The man was old enough to be her father.

"Lightwood, Mueller and Grantlin?" Steve asked, and the pieces of the puzzle fell together.

Mr. Lightwood was the senior partner of the law firm that had offered Clay a position. This time Ginny had really overstepped the bounds. Clay would not forgive her for this. What on earth was she trying to do? Force Clay's hand? Make him accept the New York position?

Whatever plans Ginny might have discussed with the famous lawyer, she put them aside for the balance of the evening.

Lightwood looked from the fair girl in silver to the dark girl in green velvet. He lifted his glass in a toast.

"To two beautiful women," he said, smiling.

The music throbbed. "Dance?" Steve asked, and they moved smoothly away from the table, stepping, gliding, turning.

"Made to dance together, weren't we?" he said.

Elinor smiled. "You're right. The music is wonderful."

"Is that what makes you breathless?"

She swayed in his arms to the pulsing rhythm of the dance and in a dark mirror saw the tall man with the narrow face and the dark-haired girl in green velvet as they swirled past. Stopped at their table with the last note of the music.

Ginny, who had been leaning forward, talking earnestly to her partner, sat back as Steve drew out Elinor's chair. The lawyer, Elinor thought uneasily, was studying Ginny's face with a cryptic expression.

As the orchestra began again, Steve said, "Will you dance, Mrs. Parks?"

"Thanks," Ginny said, then realized she would have to leave Elinor alone with Lightwood. "Sorry, but we must be getting back to the hotel. It's late."

Elinor saw the lawyer's lips lengthen in a grin of amusement.

After three days of shopping with Steve, three evenings of dining, dancing and theater with Steve and Ginny, Elinor was surprised to hear Steve say, as he left them in the lobby late one night, "I've got to get back to Hastings in the morning. Business. I know you can finish here by yourself, Elinor. Mrs. Parks, would you care to drive back with me?"

Ginny's hesitation was only for a moment. "I'd love to," she agreed.

"Shall I pick you up here at eight?" Steve was gone before Elinor could say anything.

Ginny was silent while the elevator carried them up. Before going to her own room she said abruptly, "I can't wait to get back. Clay hasn't called once since we came. Not once. I'm scared, Nell."

"If you've been up to what I think you have," Elinor told her frankly, "you have every reason to be scared."

"You don't understand. I did it to save my marriage."

"I suppose," Elinor said bitterly, "that means your marriage isn't worthwhile unless Clay has lots of money."

"I guess I deserve that. But it's not what I meant. I've been a fool, Nell. An awful fool. And I've got myself in such a—an awful mess I didn't know what to do."

Ginny straightened her slim shoulders. "Well," she said, trying to steady her voice, "here I go to face the firing squad. Don't get up when I leave in the morning. You'd better catch up on sleep after the hours we've been keeping. See you in Hastings."

She was gone when Elinor awakened late the next morning. So, Elinor remembered with a pang, was Steve. She set briskly to work, planning the purchases she still had to make, listing the most likely dealers, and trying to arrange her time so as to be able to see some of the current art shows.

For the next five days she filled the hours so full, and walked so much, that she was glad to tumble into bed at night, too tired to worry about what might be happening in Hastings, about what Clay would think and do when he learned that his wife had got in touch with Lightwood.

The fifth day brought her four brief notes from Hastings. One was from Clay, saying that he had already thanked Sewell for being so perfect a host to Ginny on her New York trip—and for bringing her home again. He added that the change seemed to have tired her. She didn't look well. He didn't think she was sleeping. She barely ate anything.

There was no word from Ginny herself.

Betty Martin wrote to say her mother was sitting up and was doing hand-sewing for two hours a day. Sue was working like mad on the fair and loving it. Bert was working even harder on his special assignment, but he looked haggard.

There was a queer-sounding note from Jed, saying he missed her, that Hastings wasn't the same place without her. In fact, Hastings wasn't the same place. Maybe he should go north, young man, go north, and grow up with the new State of Alaska. Though they had panned out all the gold a long time ago . . . An oddly disturbing note.

And there was a short note saying that, if she was ready, Elinor might come back to concentrate on the fair. There was a lot to do. Ho was pining away without her and so was Merry and so was Julie. It was signed "Your Steve."

She peered at the signature again. He must have meant to write "Yours."

She had stretched out her hand to wire Steve that she would be back on the 4:10 when the telephone startled her by ringing. Harold Brown greeted her exuberantly. He was down in New York for a day and driving back in the morning. Would she have dinner with him and let him take her back? That is, if she was ready to go back.

Elinor inspected the green velvet dress and decided that the old yellow one would do for Harold. When she went down to the lobby she did not see him on the Park Avenue side, and she walked through toward the Lexington Avenue side. He was not looking for her. He was standing, talking to a man who sat on a couch with his back to her. Elinor saw only his shoulder. Then Harold looked, recognized her, said good-by hastily, and came to meet her.

"Elinor!" he said huskily. "I always forget in between times how darned beautiful you are!"

"What brings you to New York?"

"Business for the bank. They sent me down yesterday and kept me so busy I didn't have a chance to call you until now. How about Twenty-One? Okay?"

"Fabulous. But expensive, isn't it?"

The beaming smile faded. "What good are all my savings if I can't share them with you? That's all I ever saved and invested for."

"Oh, Harold!"

"Sorry. I'll be good."

All during dinner he told her the small gossip of Hastings. A friend had been married since she went to New York. Another had been in an automobile accident. The fair was getting to be big news. The factory was being fixed up, booths arranged, everyone in the village seemed to be contributing.

Over a flaming dessert he said casually, "I ran into Ginny yesterday. She seems to have enjoyed her New York jaunt. So far as I could make out, Sewell took you girls stepping. Fine restaurants, famous night spots, theaters. You'll find Hastings pretty stodgy when you get back."

"How's Clay?"

"I see him going in and out of his office quite often. He looks tired. Working too hard, or something on his mind."

"And Jed's great love?"

Harold shrugged. "I never see Jed if I can help it. We never did hit it off. Even as kids. But he must be doing all right professionally. He's throwing money around like a drunken sailor. And speaking of money—"

He leaned forward, his round face sober. "Look here, Elinor, I know a banker—like a lawyer or a doctor—is supposed to observe professional secrecy and all that. But this thing is too much for me and I think you ought to know what is going on."

"Ginny?"

"Ginny," he said grimly. "I don't know how much she has told you, or whether you've guessed about the mess she is in."

"Only hints. But I guessed it was pretty bad. Has she—has she overdrawn her account, Harold?"

She sat, her cheeks whitening, while Harold told her just how bad it was. Ginny had not only overdrawn her account. She had borrowed money repeatedly from Harold. Over four thousand dollars—and that wasn't the worst of it. She had run up big accounts at half a dozen New York stores.

"God knows how much the total is," Harold groaned. "The silly kid must have lost her head and gone on a buying spree. And, besides that, she has been playing cards for terrific stakes. Gambling. She is probably in the hole for somewhere around fifteen thousand dollars."

"Oh, no!" Elinor pushed away her plate with shaking hands. "Oh, you must be wrong! That's impossible, Harold. Clay can never cover anything like that unless —unless he sells the house. Our family has lived there for over a hundred and fifty years, and it would break his heart to part with it. There must be some mistake."

"Some weeks ago," Harold told her, "just before you came back to Hastings, in fact, Ginny asked me to make her a new loan for fifteen thousand. To cover everything, so she could get clear."

"But how on earth did she expect to pay it back?"

"Well," Harold said slowly—"well." He fumbled for a cigarette and lighted it. His eyes were on the match he dropped into the ash tray. "Ginny has always hoped —that is, she thought someday I might be the luckiest guy in the world. That you'd marry me. And she knew, in that case, I'd never press her for the money."

XIII

Elinor spent a sleepless night. Harold's bombshell had left her stunned. Ginny had run up fifteen thousand dollars worth of debts. Fifteen thousand dollars! No wonder she had been desperate, ready to do anything to prevent Clay from knowing about it.

Now it was easy to understand her frantic moods. But nothing—nothing in the world—excused the fact that, in order to save herself, she had deliberately tried to force Elinor into marriage with Harold Brown. Sold for fifteen thousand dollars. The shame of it was unbearable.

The sleepless girl got up and slipped a black velvet robe over white silk pajamas, thrust her feet into velvet mules and pulled a chair close to the window. A spring rain was falling and the streets were wet. Tops of cabs and private cars gleamed. Red and green traffic lights threw colored shadows on the pavement.

No wonder Ginny had come to New York to see Mr. Lightwood, to persuade him to re-open negotiations with Clay for a job in his law firm. Lightwood was no fool. He probably understood a great deal more than Ginny had intended to reveal.

Elinor's heart felt as though it had been squeezed by a giant hand when she thought about her brother. His integrity. His pride. When he learned, as he eventually must, about Ginny's debts, he would strip himself of everything he owned in order to pay them. But, in doing so, he would lose more than the family home he loved, in which he had his roots. He would lose forever his profound trust in Ginny. Whatever they might make of their lives in the future, that would be gone. Always there would be lurking doubts about her.

Elinor got up to pace the floor. She did not need to switch on the lights. The shapes of the furniture were revealed in the glow cast by New York, the city that is never completely dark.

Up and down. From wall to window. How could it have happened? Was it just mad extravagance on Ginny's part? Had she spent money as a kind of defiance of Clay's determination to remain in Hastings? Had she, like Julie Campbell, a reckless streak?

From window to wall, her velvet slippers noiseless on the thick carpet. After all, the thing had happened. The reason for it was not important now. The essential thing was to know what could be done. There were only two possibilities that Elinor could see. The first was the one Ginny had ultimately hit on herself: Clay would sacrifice all that he loved and move to New York to become a part of the rat race he hated.

Elinor's imagination pictured swiftly what would happen. The gaiety and boyishness would die in her beloved brother. He would grow disillusioned, bitter, hard. . . . She could not bear it.

The second possibility was the one that had been Ginny's first choice. Elinor would marry Harold. Ginny's debts would be canceled. Clay would be free. Harold would be "the luckiest guy in the world," he had said. And Elinor . . .

From window to wall. She felt as though she were on a treadmill, that she could never get off. Am I being utterly selfish, she wondered. Can't I do this for Clay, and do it gladly? Harold loves me. He'll be happy. It will solve everything. When we drive back in the morning . . .

From wall to window. Morning had already come. The street lights had been switched off. Across from her a window caught fire. The reflection of the sun. And with the morning light came sanity and clear thinking.

I can't marry Harold, Elinor told herself. I cannot

make a mockery of my marriage, even to save Clay's. Sacrifice is a fine-sounding word. The thing itself is uglier. A sordid bargain: myself in exchange for fifteen thousand dollars. No. A thousand times no.

Her heart flooded with relief at her decision and she packed briskly, showered, dressed and looked around for the small things she was always apt to leave behind her.

Harold was waiting in the lobby. "Have you had breakfast?" he asked. At her nod, he had her suitcases taken to a taxi.

"I left my car in a garage," he explained. "We'll pick it up there."

They spoke very little until they were driving along the Henry Hudson Parkway. The sun had come out and the early April day was behaving with typical capriciousness. The Hudson sparkled and the great steel span of the George Washington Bridge reflected back the morning sun.

"What a wonderful day!" Elinor exclaimed. "Did you see that forsythia? And we'll be hearing the peepers in Hastings. Before long there will be crocuses and daffodils; the robins will be strutting across the lawns. There's something about beginning things that always excites me!"

Harold's sober face lighted with a smile. "You carry your own built-in sunshine. That's one of the things —one of the many things—that I love you for."

"Please don't, Harold!"

"Why not, dear?" he asked quietly. "I've always loved you. Why won't you let me tell you so?"

"Because I can't marry you, Harold," she said steadily. "I can't marry anyone without love and I don't love you. There's nothing I can do about it."

They drove past the Cloisters in silence, went through the toll stations, turned east and finally headed north on the Merritt Parkway.

"I'm sorry," Elinor said miserably. "Terribly sorry. The last thing I'd want to do is to make anyone unhappy."

"I suppose you know," Harold told her simply, "I'd settle for affection, if that's the most you can give me. Perhaps someday I could teach you to love me."

She shook her head, realized that, with his eyes on the road, he could not see the gesture.

"I couldn't settle for affection. Not for second best."

"I see." Harold's hands tightened on the wheel. "Well, that seems to be that."

Elinor looked at his white, unhappy face. There was nothing, after all, that she could say. After a while he switched on the radio and let the noisy gossip of the world fill the strained silence.

A long time later, Elinor ventured to say, "Harold, how do you suppose Ginny ever got herself in that kind of mess?"

"You can't blame Ginny altogether," Harold said thoughtfully. "She got mixed up with some gamblers. She just didn't know the score."

"You mean Mrs. Campbell," Elinor said, keeping her voice steady with an effort.

"Mrs. Campbell and her brother. The mystery man —Stephen Sewell."

"What makes you think . . . ?"

"This is confidential," Harold warned her. "Don't breathe a word. Sewell bought the old factory building down on the river last week. Do you know how he paid for it? Never heard of such a thing in my life. Bearer bonds!"

"Well?"

"Well, it's the first time in the years I've been in banking that I have known of such a situation."

"But bearer bonds are perfectly legitimate, aren't they? I don't understand what is wrong."

"Not wrong," Harold explained patiently. "Not illegal. But when a man is attempting to establish himself in a community and buy property, it is customary for him to indicate, one way or another, his sources of income, to show some evidence of his financial background. For a man to have the greater part of his available resources in bearer bonds—as though he were ready to pick up and run at any time—"

Elinor was silent, hands clenched, face set.

Harold stole a look at her. "Well, at any rate," he concluded, "I can tell you this: people just don't do business that way. You can figure out for yourself what it means."

Mrs. Groom opened the door. "You can just leave the suitcases there," she said to Harold. "We'll get 'em upstairs later. Young Mrs. Parks is resting and I don't want her disturbed."

Harold nodded, said good-by to Elinor and went back to his car.

"I'll make you some tea and sandwiches," Mrs. Groom said. "You look tired. As you're going out to-night you'll be eating dinner late, so you'd better have something now. I'll take it into the living room."

"I'll come out in the kitchen with you," Elinor suggested after a glance at the housekeeper's set face.

Mrs. Groom gruffly refused her offer to help and Elinor pulled out a chair at the kitchen table.

"All right," she said at length, "you might as well tell me. What's wrong with Ginny and what is all this about tonight?"

"The inn is starting its Saturday night dine-and-dance parties. You are all invited. Clay and young Mrs. Parks and you, to go with Mr. Sewell and his sister."

Mrs. Groom set a pot of tea and a plate of sand-wiches in front of Elinor.

"Well?" Elinor prodded her anxiously.

"It's a celebration," Mrs. Groom said so lugub-riously that Elinor laughed in spite of herself.

"It might be a funeral, the way you say it!"

"Might as well be a funeral, the way I see it."

"Tell me," Elinor said, exasperated. "You've got me on tenterhooks. What's wrong with Ginny?"

"She cried all night. There was an awful scene. Clay was madder than I ever knew him to be. You know how controlled he generally is. Lets her get away with anything. Thinks she's such a cute litte trick. I guess he found out—"

"Mrs. Groom!"

"Well, you wanted to know. He got a letter from that New York firm, a bigger offer than the last time. He said no. Then young Mrs. Parks—I heard her talking and carrying on—and he shouted, 'Good God! How could you, Ginny?' and they had an awful argument. Went on all evening. Then he calmed down, sounded tired, and said. 'All right. There's no choice. I'll take the New York offer. Let's not discuss it any more.' And she said, 'Don't look like that, dearest—as though you didn't care for me any more,' and he sort of laughed, not as though anything was funny, and said, 'Do you remember those lines—

> "No love," quoth he, "but vanity, sets
> love a task like that . . ."'

"And he got his topcoat and went out for a walk. Didn't come back until all hours, and then he slept in the guest room.

"Well, she went up and cried. Something awful. Got right hysterical. Finally I got her some hot milk and a sleeping tablet, though I don't usually hold with them. This morning she looked awful. Then Mr. Sewell called about the dance at the inn and Clay accepted for all of you. 'A celebration,' that's what he said it would be.

"You finish those sandwiches, Elinor, and I'll make some more for young Mrs. Parks. I made her rest but she didn't touch her lunch. You know, I'm kinda sorry for her. Whatever she's done, she is being punished."

"She ran up fifteen thousand dollars' worth of debts by buying clothes and gambling at cards," Elinor said briefly. "Clay has to take the New York job in order to pay them. And he'll probably have to sell this house as well."

"So that's it," Mrs. Groom said thoughtfully. "Well, it's spilt milk now. Nothing left to do but mop up as well as can be done. You get out the dress you're going to wear tonight so's I can press it for you."

When Elinor went downstairs later in the evening, Ginny was in the living room standing in front of the fireplace. She wore the new black net dress, which dramatized the gold of her hair. Careful make-up helped to cover the reddened and swollen eyelids but could not conceal the dark shadows under her eyes. She held her small head proudly but she shivered and huddled closer to the fire as though she were chilled to the bone.

There was no brittle assurance about Ginny tonight. She had been frightened by her husband's anger; but, worse, she had been stunned by the loss of his faith in her. Elinor understood at first glance why Mrs. Groom, who had so disliked Clay's wife, was sorry for her now.

"Hello, Nell," she said listlessly. "I see Mrs. Groom told you we're going to dine and dance at the inn."

"Yes. She said it was a celebration."

Ginny's lips quivered. "I didn't think Clay would mind so much. I thought if he'd just be sensible and take the New York job everything would be fine. But now he *is* going to take it, and everything is—awful."

"Does he know you saw Mr. Lightwood in New York?"

"No, I didn't dare tell him that. But I had to tell him—"

"About the money you owe?"

"How did you know?" Ginny asked sharply.

"Harold."

"He had no right to tell you."

"He was just protecting his investment," Elinor said. "He hoped I would marry him and cancel your debt."

Ginny looked as though she had been slapped. Color drained out of her face leaving her ghastly. "Oh," she whispered, "I never saw it clearly before. You make me feel so ashamed."

The doorbell rang and Mrs. Groom clumped down

the hall to answer it. Then they heard Clay's quick steps on the stairs. He had remained in the guest room until Sewell arrived.

Steve exchanged friendly greetings with Ginny and Clay and welcomed Elinor home. As she got in the back seat of the long sleek car beside Julie Campbell she thought: "Harold is crazy. There is some mistake. Steve can't have an ugly or dishonorable past. I don't believe it. I refuse to believe it."

Julie greeted her with her usual warmth. Merry had sent a dozen messages.

"And," Julie admitted, "I took a chance and promised her you'd come to lunch tomorrow and start work on her portrait. She can't wait to see you and to show off the tricks she has been teaching Ho. Do say you'll come."

"Of course I will. How is Ho?"

"Dennis the Menace," Julie laughed. "The bull in the china shop. I had to lay down the law. If Merry is to give him the run of the house she must teach him manners. Right now he seems to think he's a lap dog."

"Whose lap was he on yesterday?" Steve jeered from the driver's seat, and Julie joined in the laugh against her.

She turned to the silent Ginny. "Mrs. Parks, I can't begin to tell you how grateful we all are to your sister-in-law. Why, if it were only for giving us Doctor Dick, our debt would be more than we could ever repay."

Elinor laughed. "I warned you about him. Has he put you to work yet?"

"There's so much to do about the fair I haven't had a minute for any of his other projects."

"I wish you'd give me something to do to help," Ginny said unexpectedly.

"You angel! Come with Elinor tomorrow to lunch and we'll talk it over. We need people to handle the food booths, and to put the proper price tags on the hooked rugs and the patchwork quilts, and someone to—"

"Hey!" Steve called. "This is an evening of fun.

Remember? You are as bad as Doctor Dick. You're supposed to take time off for f-u-n."

"I'm going to," Julie declared. "And so is Doctor Dick. I told him if he didn't stop work for one evening he would turn into such a grim forbidding man that he would scare his patients to death."

Steve turned his car over to a parking attendant and Clay helped the three women out. Elinor noticed that he did not look at Ginny.

When they reached the table Steve had reserved, Julie, radiant in orange satin that looked like a flame, looked around in disappointment. Then Doctor Dick, seeming years younger in a dinner jacket, stood smiling down at her.

Julie welcomed him with a smile so warm, so tender, that Elinor recognized the unmistakable signs of a woman in love.

"Doctor Dick," Julie said eagerly, "I've found you a new recruit. Mrs. Clay Parks."

"Julie," her brother said firmly, "one word more about the fair and you get no dinner. That's a warning."

"Well, since you've practically stopped helping—" she began.

Elinor looked at Steve in surprise. "Have you lost interest in the fair?"

"Not at all. But I'm delegating most of the work I undertook to do. There's something rather important coming up, and I have to give my time to that."

"You're taking on a new job?"

"Well, you might put it that way." Steve looked up, saw Clay's eyes watching him, and changed the subject. "There's Jed Gordon! I called him several times today to suggest that he join us tonight, but I couldn't reach him."

Elinor followed his eyes and saw Jed sitting at a table for two with Mrs. Alice Grant. She wore a strapless gown of black velvet, deeply cut. Long diamond pendants dangled from her ears, diamonds sparkled at her throat. She was smiling at Jed, who looked at her with hopeless adoration.

"He's gone down for the third time," Clay commented in a disgusted tone.

When the members of the small dance band had taken their place, there was a moment's confusion, the sound of tuning, and then they broke into the lilting strains of "I'll see you again."

"Shall we dance?" Steve asked and drew Elinor away from the table.

They made the circuit of the room in silence, swirling to the lovely music of the waltz. Ginny and Clay had joined the couples on the dance floor but still without speaking. So, to Elinor's surprise, had Julie and Doctor Dick. They were laughing uproariously.

"He really is having fun," Elinor said, smiling.

Steve chuckled. "The poor man hasn't a chance."

"What do you mean?"

"Julie has fallen in love again. I'm so glad for her. The one right thing. And I think she'll sweep the poor man off his feet before he can put up any defenses."

"I shouldn't think he would want to. Against Julie."

A scent of cloying perfume made her turn her head. Jed danced by with Alice Grant.

"The music isn't bad for a hick village, is it?" Alice was saying. "Did anyone ever tell you that you dance divinely, my sweet?"

Jed looked through the artificial lashes into the hard china-blue eyes and gulped.

Steve's arm swept Elinor past the bemused young architect. He looked down at her troubled face.

"He's a young fool, of course," he said gently, "but that sort of thing is like an illness. He'll get over it."

"I hope so," she replied. Heard the fervency in her voice. "For his own sake," she added hastily.

"You're not engaged to him, then?"

"Heavens, no. Just old friends."

"Then there's no reason, is there," Steve said, "why I shouldn't tell you that I love you."

Elinor stumbled, his arm steadied her, guided her through the dancing couples. Her heart pounded. He couldn't have said that. Looked up. Saw the deep-set eyes intent on her face.

"There's one reason," she said, trying to speak quietly, to control the trembling of her lips, the shaking of the knees that would barely hold her up. "Your wife. Have you forgotten your wife, Steve?"

He saw her face. Still and white and cold. His own was as white.

"No," he said, "I haven't forgotten Mary. I intended—sometime I meant to tell you about her. I didn't realize that you already knew."

"It was almost the first thing that I heard about you," she said stiffly. "Will you take me back to the table, please?"

XIV

Have you forgotten your wife? The words followed Steve Sewell like a drumbeat. Have you forgotten your wife? Forgotten Mary? Gentle, devoted, sweet. The childhood sweetheart for whom he had had so warm an affection, for whose deep love he had been so grateful.

He had married her because they were old friends, their familes and acquaintances took for granted their mutual devotion, and Mary loved him. He had made her happy. That he knew. If something had been lacking in his marriage it had been, he always assumed, because he was unreasonable. He expected too much. Dreamed too much. That kind of love, the transcendent kind he wanted, probably did not exist except in the imagination of poets.

After Mary's tragic death he had punished himself like a guilty thing. He realized now, belatedly, that he had felt guilty not because of the unavoidable death but because he had never been able to love her as he had wished to do.

Then, when he had regained his balance, he had looked across a field of snow in a park one morning and seen Elinor Parks. Love at first sight! How childish could a man be? But it was true, no escaping it. Her beauty had been the first thing he saw. Then the other discoveries had come: her honesty, her sweetness, her radiance, her capacity for bringing happiness to everyone about her, her exceptional talent as an artist, her steadfast loyalty. There seemed no end to the discoveries he made. And with each one his love had deepened.

At first, his pointless sense of guilt about Mary's death had held him back. If he was responsible for that, he had no right to marry again, to risk another woman's happiness. Then he had believed Jed to be his rival. What a fool he had been, when he learned Elinor's heart was free, to tell her, without warning, without preparation, that he loved her!

And yet there had been moments—surely she had returned that impulsive kiss! He had seen her color come and go when he looked at her, she had grown oddly breathless when he held her in his arms the first time they danced together.

Fool! Fool! Imagining that she could return his love. And she had drawn away from him, her face white, and said, "Have you forgotten your wife?"

She knew, then, how Mary had died. Blamed him as he had blamed himself. She had been cold—cold.

Well, he was not a schoolboy to whine because life had withdrawn from him its loveliest gift. He had spent too much time living in the past. He would put aside his dream—forever—and get on with the thing he had planned, in a mad moment, to do. And if he lost—what difference did it make now? At least, there ought to be some moments of excitement ahead.

Trooper Jackson looked up as Steve came into the

barracks the next morning. Looked again. Brought a cup of hot coffee and set it before the white-faced man.

"You seem to need that."

Steve forced a grin. "Thanks. I gather from your hospitality that you've been checking up on me."

Bert Jackson flushed under the ironic eyes of the older man. "We have to do that, sir."

"Of course you do. Be very careless if you didn't."

"It was routine," the trooper explained, "but there were a lot of rumors about you. No one knew your background. You came out of nowhere and you were loaded. Money somewhere and plenty of it. And there was talk—you know how villages are—about your being a big gambler."

"So I am, in a way," Steve admitted.

"I suppose so," Jackson agreed, "but not in the way people took it here. You come from a very wealthy Massachusetts family. Old stock. Started with millions. Then you plunged in Texas oil and really cleaned up."

"Where did you learn all this?" Steve asked curiously.

Jackson started to speak, checked himself. "Sorry, sir, I can't tell you my source of information."

Steve was amused. "Are you sure it is reliable?" he joked.

"Yes, sir. My—my source of information is completely trustworthy."

"And just how did your source happen to find out so much about me? What was the reason for this private investigation?"

"He had a reason, all right, Mr. Sewell. He didn't tell me what it was."

"At any rate, you are satisfied?"

"Yes, sir." Unexpectedly, Bert Jackson grinned broadly. "One thing sure. You're a gambler, all right, in your own way. What you are doing is taking an awful chance. It makes my blood run cold just to think of it."

"I'm aware of the chance. But if it pays off, it will be worth it."

"And if it doesn't?" the trooper asked curiously.

"Then," Steve said calmly, "we'll try something else. We'll keep on trying something else."

"Yes, sir!" the trooper agreed enthusiastically. "That's the spirit."

"How long do you think it will take the story to trickle out?"

"My guess is that half the people in Hastings have heard it already. Now, shall we just go over the plans and see that we haven't overlooked anything? This means a lot to me, too. I want to get married without waiting any longer." His face set. "I'm gambling a lot, too."

Clay was at breakfast when Elinor came down. How pale she looked!

"Hello, early bird!" she said gaily.

"Early bird yourself." He gave her back smile for smile. "What are you up to, today?"

"This morning I'm going out to start getting the garden cleaned up after the winter and check on the seeds and bulbs we'll have to order."

Clay's smile faded. "What's the use?" His voice was flat. "We probably won't be here this summer. Ah, thanks, Mrs. Groom. Waffles and sausage! How did you guess what I wanted?"

"I ought to," she said gruffly. "Seeing that I've been watching your tastes all your life."

Clay made a gallant pretense of eating and enjoying his breakfast and then pushed back his chair.

"Back to the salt mines. Tell Ginny I won't be here for lunch. A lot to do."

When he had gone, Elinor went to the small room beside the kitchen where she kept her gardening gloves and tools, and pots and vases for arranging flowers. In a moment Ginny came into the room in a trailing robe of red chiffon.

"Has Clay gone?" she asked almost timidly.

Elinor nodded. "He asked me to tell you that he won't be home for lunch."

Ginny swallowed. "He's going to arrange to put the

house on the market," she said. "I didn't even know before that it was part yours, Nell. That you'd given him your share. I didn't know."

She dropped into a chair, her face in her hands, rocking herself back and forth.

"I didn't understand anything!" she wailed. "I knew I wasn't clever like you and Clay. I wanted to be something he could love. Something special. That's one reason why I wanted pretty clothes. And I changed the house so it would seem mine and not just yours. I was jealous. I didn't realize you could love anyone and be unselfish.

"Then things began to go wrong and I spent too much money. And I thought I could get it back by playing cards and I lost more—I lost—"

Sobs stifled the words.

"I lost Clay. I lost everything."

"Here," Mrs. Groom said sharply. "Stop crying this minute, Ginny, or I'm going to slap you hard. Drink this coffee while it's hot."

"I—d-don't—want—"

"Drink it. You're acting like a silly child, but at least you're not as bad as I thought. Silly, all right. But we can fix that. I've fixed enough things for the other young ones. But you didn't seem to need me. Guess I should have taken you in hand a long time ago."

Her work-worn hand went into the deep pocket of her apron and came out with two small passbooks.

"This family has kept me for nearly thirty years, good times and bad. Paid me well and all my living besides. I've had no call to spend a cent. I've got about eight thousand dollars in savings in a New York bank and five thousand in the Hastings bank. That ought to see you and Clay through well enough and save this house."

As Ginny started to speak, the housekeeper added hastily, trying to sound severe—failing—"I'm not doing it for you. But this is my home, too, and it's only common sense to try to keep a roof over my head."

Ginny jumped up, spilling the coffee, threw her arms around Mrs. Groom, sobbing.

Two tender arms held her close. "There, now," Mrs. Groom said. "Now, now. No more tears. You get dressed and go down and see Clay. Tell him he doesn't need that New York job nor to sell the house, either."

"You're so good," Ginny wailed.

"Well, I guess you're part of my family, too," Mrs. Groom said sternly, and tears rolled down her cheeks. "And mind you get back in time to go to Mrs. Campbell's for lunch. Clay says you both got an invitation." She patted Ginny's shoulder. "Silly puss," she said gently.

Ginny sniffed and blew her nose. "You're just about tops in this world, and I'll make it up to you some way. Maybe I can get a job. I know I can be useful."

"Make it up to Clay, that's all you need to do. And don't you go upstairs, Virginia Parks, until you've eaten some breakfast."

A smile quivered on Ginny's lips. "I won't," she said obediently. She added in surprise, "Why, I'm hungry!"

Mrs. Groom beamed. "I'll have a waffle and some sausage ready for you in two shakes of a lamb's tail." She clumped out of the kitchen.

When Ginny returned from Clay's office her manner was very subdued.

"All right?" Elinor asked her.

"He—" Ginny kept her voice steady with an effort. "Clay nearly broke down when I told him about Mrs. Groom's offer. He's going to accept it, because he said we couldn't refuse an offer of love. He won't sell the house. But he plans to take the New York job so he can pay her back a little at a time. He said, if we were careful, we could do it in three or four years."

Elinor made no comment. There was nothing she could say.

"But I won't let him go to New York," Ginny said fiercely. "I won't. I've been figuring things out. Just driving around and thinking things out. You remember that job I had before Clay and I were married? Planning wardrobes for girls getting married and people going abroad. Well, I was thinking—I could do it by mail, from here. Or, better, I could do the shopping myself in New York, on commission. There's a need for that sort of thing and never enough people to fill it. On a commission basis I could easily clear five thousand a year until we've paid back Mrs. Groom. Nell, help me persuade Clay! I could do it well. I want to do it."

"Good for you, Ginny! It sounds super to me."

Ginny brightened. "Then you'll back me?"

"To the hilt."

"Swell! Heavens, we've got to run. We'll be late for lunch."

As Ginny parked in front of the great stone house, she heard a low threatening growl.

"Good heavens," she exclaimed. "That dog sounds dangerous to me. I hope they've got him chained up."

The door burst open as though flung off the hinges and Ho tore out with Merry hanging on to the end of his leash and shrieking with excitement.

"Elinor!" she cried. "Look at Ho! Look at me, Elinor! Ho's taking me for a ride."

Ginny cowered behind Elinor, who laughed.

"There's nothing to be afraid of!"

Ho recognized her and leaped around with mad excitement.

"Down, Ho!" Merry said firmly. "Now shake hands."

He held out his paw and Elinor took it with grave politeness.

Julie, laughing from the doorway, instructed the butler to remove the boxer and then sent Merry upstairs for her nap.

"Oh, Mummie! I want to see Elinor."

"You'll see her after your nap," her mother assured her, and Merry went off reluctantly, her feet dragging on the stairs.

Julie drew the two girls in with a warm welcome.

"The difference in that child!" Elinor exclaimed. "I can't get over it."

"She's so full of vim and vigor I can hardly get her to take her nap," Julie said happily.

Through the delicious lunch Elinor sat quietly, hardly aware of the delectable food. After a searching look, Julie turned all her attention on Ginny and talked about the fair with enthusiasm.

Elinor withdrew into her thoughts. *There's no reason, is there, why I can't tell you I love you.* The words were like molten metal in her heart. She had not known she could suffer so. He had no right to speak, no right to tell her how he felt, even if he really loved her.

A girl named Mary Todd. Where was she? What had happened to Steve's wife? *Sometime I meant to tell you . . .* he had said. The pain seemed to be more than she could bear. He had had no right to speak. She had had no right to listen.

I love you, said the deep quiet voice in her ear. *I love you.*

"Steve was sorry he couldn't join us for lunch," Julie startled her by saying. "He seems to be working at fever pitch on something, but he's very mysterious about it."

Again Elinor felt her hostess's eyes on her face and she hastily lifted her napkin to her trembling lips, kept her revealing eyes on her plate.

When lunch was over, an endless meal during which Elinor was careful to maintain a smiling face and appear to listen to the eager chatter between Julie and Ginny, her hostess took them up to her sitting room.

"Have you everything you need?" she asked Elinor, seeing the easel and canvas and boxes of paints and brushes that the butler had brought up from the car. "Merry will be with you in a few minutes. Do you mind if I take Ginny down to Steve's study where all the lists are? You can be setting up your easel."

Elinor got to work. *Keep your hands busy and don't feel sorry for yourself. Remember the Dreadful Warning.* She walked restlessly to the window, looked out at the lawn where the snowman had stood. The grass was already green. In so short a time the sullen winter had slunk away and spring had come, bearing promise of the summer.

"What's the use?" Elinor thought, echoing Clay's disheartened words at breakfast.

She was aware that someone was watching her and she turned to see Julie standing in the doorway.

"Merry's having her dress changed and her hair brushed so she'll be pretty for her portrait." She sank into a chair. "I've been so glad, for Steve's sake, that Merry and I could be with him," she went on casually. "Steve adores her. I suppose you know he had a child of his own and lost him."

"Lost him?" Elinor said huskily. "No, I didn't know that."

Again Julie's eyes swept her face. Looked away again.

"Do you mind if I tell you about it?" she asked impulsively.

"Mind? Why, no, of course not."

"Because I'd like you to know. It helps to explain Steve. When he was just a boy he married Mary Todd, the girl next door. A sweet kid. They had played together as children, got invited together as they grew up. Everyone assumed they would marry. Especially Mary herself. She idolized him. Well, one day, Steve realized it after everyone else knew it, and asked her to marry him. He was awfully fond of her but—you know . . ." Julie's voice trailed off.

"They had a little boy. Jimmy. A darling. Well, Steve's kid brother Rodney came back from Paris to get a job as an architect. Steve was living in Texas at the time and Rodney went to visit him. He wasn't well. Mary was going to fly north to visit her family and urged him to go alone for the change. Rodney hated airplanes. He had an obsession about them. Steve used to joke and tell him he'd have been much happier in the days when men wore armor. Anyhow, he urged Rodney to fly with Mary and Jimmy. The plane never left the airport. It turned over and burned. They were all killed in the crackup before Steve's eyes. He just about cracked up himself. It took all the gaiety and lightheartedness out of him. The last three years have been simply horrible because he blamed himself. As if he could have helped anything that happened!" She clenched her hand and beat it angrily on the arm of her chair.

"It was all tragic enough—those three heartbreaking deaths. But for Steve to add to his own pain by feeling guilty! That's what changed him so, made him stern and withdrawn. He used to be the gayest—"

"I—see." The words were barely audible. The lump in Elinor's throat choked her. Her self-contempt made her ill with rage. How much harm she had done!

"Of course," Julie said after a long silence, "I hoped, in time, he'd marry again. This time marry some woman he deeply loved. Steve has so much love, so much tenderness to give. I don't think I could bear to see him hurt again."

She turned to the door with a smile. "Hello, there, darling! Let's see what Elinor can make of you." Her eyes flickered questioningly over Elinor's face. "Remember, this is to be our birthday present to Uncle Steve."

Color rose in a soft tide over Elinor's face. Her cheeks burned with it. And it seemed that with that blush a warm tide swept over her bruised heart, healing it.

She met Julie's eyes. Smiled. "We won't disappoint Uncle Steve, will we, Merry?"

Julie's eyes shone. She bent over and kissed Elinor's cheek. "Bless you," she said softly. "You're a darling. I knew the first time I met you that you were going to be good for all of us. But I couldn't guess how good."

She went downstairs to help Ginny work on the lists.

Elinor placed Merry in a natural pose, leaning against a chair, looking out into the garden. She wore a soft blue dress and stood beside a primrose curtain. What Elinor wanted to catch was a mingling of Merry's elfin charm with the quality of dreamer.

She worked rapidly at first and then with more difficulty. Merry had turned into a breathless chatterbox. Her expession changed constantly. In her exuberance she hopped up and down on one foot.

To keep her still Elinor began to talk quietly, to tell her of the lastest adventure of Ho's restless brother Hum. One day he wandered down to the river and there he saw a raft that had been pulled up on the bank. He climbed up on it to see how the river looked from there.

Just then a man came along. "Darn those boys. Building another raft instead of doing their chores! I'll show them!"

He gave the raft a shove and it floated out on the river carrying Hum along with it.

Merry stood stock-still while Elinor painted and the story went on and on. Hum had looked over the side and watched the fish in the river and they had flipped their fins at him in a friendly way as he floated past. He had drifted under shady trees on the shore and heard the birds talk to each other, while they fed their young and gossiped about their neighbors. Then they soared up into the deep blue vault of the sky, singing their hearts out for very joy in being alive.

All day Hum floated along the river on the raft and saw the world go past and thought, "This is the life! Adventuring forever. It's fine to be Hum and dull to be Humdrum."

Merry giggled appreciatively.

"And then," Elinor went on, while her brush snared the line of Merry's cheek, caught the half-dreaming rapture in her face as she lived in the enchanted world of make-believe, "the sun went down in splendor. And then it began to grow dark. Hum was all alone, and hungry and a little lonely, too. He thought of Ho, who had a home where he was loved. And suddenly he remembered the house he had left. Adventuring was fine for a while. But not for all the time.

"Then the raft was caught in an eddy and went round and round. Hum hung on the best he could. Adventuring was fine in its way but it wasn't good for a dog to be alone. He needed friends to help him when he was in trouble.

"Just then a boat came along. A man said, 'Why that's the raft the Marshall boys next door lost this morning! I'll just tie it on to the boat and take it back to them.'

"So the raft floated safely to the bank of the river. Hum could see the door of the house standing open, the light shining out. He could sniff the good smells of dinner. And he discovered that the best part of adventuring was coming home again.

"And that," Elinor concluded briskly, "is all for today. Get your coat, Merry. We'll take Ho for a walk."

XV

"Betty Martin telephoned," Mrs. Groom said when the two girls returned to the house. "She wanted to know if Elinor would come to dinner tonight."

"I'd love to," Elinor said. "I'll call her right away." She smiled at Ginny. "Tell Clay all about it," she advised her. "Don't hold back anything. And be sure to tell him about the work you have in mind. You won't need me here. This must be between the two of you."

"I don't deserve Clay," Ginny said somberly. "Or you. Or Mrs. Groom. But I hope some day I will."

"In that mood you can't fail."

Elinor found Mrs. Martin on the couch in the little living room.

"Bert carried me down," she explained, her face glowing. "I'm not strong enough to manage the stairs yet, but every day I feel my strength seeping back through my very pores. And I've been sewing. Wait until I show you. I've done most of the curtains, and as soon as I can sit up at the sewing machine I'll get at those draperies you had delivered here. What heavenly material!"

Sue called from the dining room where she was setting the table: "What you'd better concentrate on, Mother, is Betty's trousseau. All those napkins to embroider!"

Betty came out of the kitchen, flushed from heat. "It's just a pot roast," she said, "but I got started late."

"Mmh, it smells good."

"I have a new chef," Betty laughed, and Bert Jackson loomed up behind her, wearing a big apron, a high chef's cap perched rakishly on his head.

"Madame will be *servi* in *un peu* time," he said.

"If you cook as well as you speak French," Elinor assured him gravely, "the results should be—ah—"

"Alarming," he suggested. "Don't worry. Betty does all the work and I get in the way. Fair division of labor."

"That's what you think," Betty retorted. "Go back and finish peeling those potatoes."

"Slave driver!" he hugged her.

"Elinor—" Betty extended her left hand proudly —"see my ring."

"How beautiful!"

"Isn't it?"

Bert frowned. "I wish it could have been a bigger diamond. You should have seen the stones Jed Gordon was looking at when I got this. Regular headlights. We were in the same jewelry store in New Haven."

"Jed was buying diamonds?" Elinor asked slowly.

"Well, pricing them. If he hasn't the money now, it looks as though he expected to have some before long."

"I suppose it's that dizzy blonde," Betty commented. "She was in my shop half the afternoon. Eyebrows shaped. Two shades of lip rouge to blend. A facial. Jed's going to find the upkeep pretty high for that gal." She and Bert returned to the kitchen.

Sue went to answer the doorbell. "Doctor Dick! Come in. Mother is downstairs."

"She is, is she? Now who told her she could do that? Getting too smart, if you ask me."

He came in, smiling. "Hello, there, Elinor! Looks as though your fair is going to be a great success. Well, how's my patient tonight?"

"Fine," Mrs. Martin assured him.

"Not overdoing it?"

"No, I stop the minute I get tired."

Elinor joined Sue and Betty in the kitchen where the trooper was peeling potatoes and Betty was mixing a salad. "How's the special assignment?" she asked the trooper.

"Not long now until we know. If the pattern holds, a bank in this general vicinity should be robbed within a couple of weeks."

"Have you learned anything more?"

"Quite a bit more."

Doctor Dick called Sue and she went out reluctantly, eager to hear Bert's news.

"You can trust Elinor," Betty said.

The trooper nodded. "I know the identity of one of the robbers, the gang leader. I have a hunch that I could name the second one. I still haven't a clue as to the third."

"You know who the gang leader is?" Elinor exclaimed. "Tell me!"

"I can't tell you that. I won't tell even Betty. All I can say is that you'd never guess." He broke off as Sue came back to join them.

"How's your job coming?" Elinor asked.

"I love it. Mr. Sewell is swell to work for, though he certainly expects a lot. But what he is doing for the fair and for the hospital—he's really wonderful."

Doctor Dick had come to the kitchen door. "Your mother is progressing beautifully. Don't let her overdo, that's the one danger. She has to build her strength, not exhaust it." He turned away. Turned back. "Heard what you were saying about the fair. I don't deny Sewell is doing a lot. But I might point out that Ju-Mrs. Campbell is doing just as much. She has practically made it her full-time job. I wouldn't have expected a wealthy woman to do more than let her name be used on a committee. But she is working like a coolie."

"Julie Campbell isn't a typical wealthy woman," Elinor said quickly, struck by something in the doctor's voice. "Personally, I don't think that she cares about having a lot of money. She really wants to be useful. She doesn't want a society woman's life. She wants a—a woman's life. Someone to love and cherish and take care of. A job that has meaning."

"You think so?"

"I'm sure of it."

"I suppose, to a rich woman, this village life seems amusing for a change," he remarked.

"It's the kind of life she wants to put down roots in," Elinor retorted. "The way she wants her little girl to grow up. The simple things. The real things."

Doctor Dick eyed her in sudden suspicion. "Why are you telling me this, young lady?"

"I don't want you to—underestimate Julie, Doctor Dick."

"No danger of that," he said gruffly. Flushed. Then he flipped his fingers lightly against her cheek. "Hey," he said, "look who's being the doctor. I'm supposed to be the diagnostician around here."

"Oh," she answered with a twinkle, "I thought it might be a case of 'Physician, heal thyself.' "

Elinor was smiling as she drove back to the house. Perhaps she should not have spoken about Julie as she did to Doctor Dick but it had been obvious that he was deeply attached to her and afraid of the money barrier between them.

Somehow, with the coming of spring, the dark clouds of winter were being dispelled. The problems of the Martin family were on their way to being happily solved: Mrs. Martin getting well, Sue self-supporting, Betty with her glowing face and her engagement ring.

Elinor's smile faded as she thought of Bert's comment about the diamonds the size of headlights that Jed had been pricing. As though he expected to have money before long. She remembered the trooper saying that he knew the leader of the bank robbers, and that she would never guess who it was.

Her heart jumped. Stopped. Beat wildly. Not Jed! Surely not Jed! What had he said about people doing desperate things for money? Had his infatuation for Alice Grant driven him to crime?

Don't look for our man among suspicious characters, Bert had said. They would be more likely to find him among the established, the respected, those with plenty of money.

Bearer bonds! Was that what Harold had tried to tell her? Tried to warn her?

Steve. *There's no reason, is there, why I can't tell you I love you.* And she had hurt him. Hurt him profoundly. Hurt him about the one thing in which he was most vulnerable, most defenseless, most sensitive. How could she make it up to him? How could she undo the harm she had done? She wanted to tell him, "I didn't know. I misunderstood."

She locked the car and went into the house. There were voices in the living room, and she thought she would slip quietly upstairs, not disturb the talk between husband and wife.

"Elinor?" Clay called. "Come in."

She looked in the door. "I'm going to bed."

"Please come." His face was younger, alight. The ring was back in his voice. "You know about this crazy girl of mine, don't you?"

His arm was around Ginny, whose gold head rested against his shoulder. The sight of the quiet radiance in their faces reassured Elinor.

"Have you heard about the job she plans to do?" Clay asked proudly.

Elinor nodded, smiling.

Clay rubbed his cheek on Ginny's hair. "We're going to keep the house and I'm going to stay right here in Hastings and we're going to work out our debt to dear Mrs. Groom. At least, the financial part. There is no repaying her loyalty."

"But we have to see the fair through first," Ginny reminded him. "Only a few days more. Can you help set up the stuff in the booths tomorrow, Nell?"

"In the afternoon, yes. But I want to hang the curtains in the Cape Cod cottage in the morning. Mrs. Martin finished them and if I keep them in the boxes for days they'll have to be pressed again."

"All's well, Elinor!" Clay said.

"All's well. Good night, you two."

That night Elinor slept soundly.

She was the first one down to breakfast in the morning. Mrs. Groom was beaming.

"Our young people have got themselves straightened out, thanks to heaven!"

"Thanks to you," Elinor said softly. "You've been a mother to us all. Clay and me and now Ginny."

"Well, you've been like my own."

"And Jed, too. He told me not long ago he'd never be able to pay his debt to you."

"He's a good boy," Mrs. Groom said stoutly. "Only one of the young people around here I never could stand was that Brown boy."

"And yet," Elinor said soberly, "Harold is the one who has made good. And Jed—Oh, Mrs. Groom, he's making such a mess of things!" She blinked back tears.

"Don't try to shoulder the world's burdens," Mrs. Groom warned her. "People have to work out their problems by themselves. You can't do it for them."

Elinor grinned. "Listen to who is saying that."

"Run along now and get those curtains hung so you can help Ginny down at the fair. I'm going down myself as soon as I get my work done."

When Elinor reached the cottage she sat in the car for a few minutes, smiling with sheer pleasure. With the beneficent change of season the little house began to look as though it had been there for a long time. Taken root as a house should if it is to be transformed into a home.

She carried in the hardware, and the big box of curtains Mrs. Martin had made, and set to work. For some time the vigorous sound of hammering as she put up the curtain rods drowned out every other noise. Then, little by little, she became aware of a different kind of hammering. Someone knocking at the door. Knocking? He was banging.

She climbed down from the window seat and went to open the door. A big man in overalls stood on the front steps, a toolbox dangling from his right hand. A man with heavy features and massive shoulders and a cruel mouth. The expression in his eyes sent a chill coasting down her spine. A nerve twitched at the corner of his crooked, smiling mouth.

"Miss Parks?" he said in a hoarse voice.

"Yes," she said in surprise.

"Mr. Sewell sent me to check up on the oil furnace." He ducked his head toward the truck that stood behind the convertible as though to establish his credentials. PLUMBING & HEATING appeared in large letters on the side.

Elinor hesitated. Instinctively, she distrusted the man. She did not want to admit him to this charming house.

"I don't understand. Mr. Sewell didn't tell me that he expected you."

"He asked me to come. I helped put in the oil furnace. He wants a double check to make sure the connections on the tank are okay."

Her curious reluctance deepened. "I'm sorry. Perhaps you had better bring me a note from Mr. Sewell."

His mouth grew uglier. He stepped forward almost shoving her out of his path. Instinctively she backed away from him to avoid his touch.

"Sorry, miss," he said brusquely. "I've got my orders."

He was inside now. Helplessly she led the way to the kitchen.

"Which door to the cellar, miss?"

Her distrust sharpened. "Don't you know? You said you had worked here."

"Sure I worked here. But I always used the bulkhead."

The voice sent a shiver through Elinor. Foolish or not, she was scared. Only once before had she been as frightened as this. As pointlessly frightened . . .

Without waiting for her help, the man flung open the door that led to a closet. Slammed it shut. Opened a second. Went down the stairs.

It was then, as he turned away from her, that she knew without doubt that this was the man who had ducked out of the light the night the Chevrolet had had the flat tire. She couldn't prove it. Only an impression of a thick shoulder, of the carriage of a head. But there was no possibility of mistake in her mind.

She waited, heart racing, knees trembling, for him to come back. No sound. What could he be doing down there? Feeling half ashamed of herself, she tiptoed back to the window seat and picked up the hammer. She held it behind her, comforted by its solid weight in her hand. At least she had something with which to defend herself.

Defend herself from what, for heaven's sake? There was the truck. This must be an accredited workman. He had known her name. Steve had sent him.

Her heart missed a beat. Steve! But Steve had not dealt personally with the workman. That had been Jed's job.

She was completely bewildered now. Then she heard heavy steps as the man came up. He looked at her and her hand tightened on the hammer she held behind her.

"Okay," he said. "Knew it was all right, but we like to keep the customers satisfied." He looked around him, saw the curtains. "Someone moving into this place?" he asked sharply.

"No. Mr. Sewell wanted it furnished as a kind of *model* home."

"Oh, yeah." He paused, examining her in a leisurely fashion. She felt color burning her cheeks with embarrassment and anger at his insolent look.

"If you went with the house," he leered, "the prospective buyers would be lined up outside. Sewell sure knows how to pick 'em."

He went out to the truck. Elinor watched until it drove away. Before she went back to work she bolted the front door. Perhaps it was like locking the barn door, but at least it made her feel safer.

She was still upset by the oil furnace man's manner when she reached the fair building early that afternoon. She would ask Steve about him. Anyhow, an impersonal subject would help bridge over the awkwardness of their first meeting, since he had offered her his love and she had been so unspeakably cruel to him.

She walked into a deafening uproar and a beehive of activity. The noise was from the hammering of temporary partitions and the sawing of boards for counters. The activity, she discovered, was, for all its apparent confusion, beautifully organized. Everyone seemed to be going about his appointed task in an orderly fashion.

After wandering about, watching the installation of exhibits, she realized that Steve was not there. She realized, too, in profound surprise, that it was Ginny who was directing the work, assigning booths, keeping order with confident efficiency. Julie Campbell was standing on a ladder, tacking up a sign over a booth.

"Hi, there, lazybones!" she called. "Hand me another box of tacks, will you?"

"What can I do?"

"Help Mrs. Robinson in booth four. She's got about sixty different kinds of knitted goods and she wants to display as many of them as possible. We'll never be done in time to open in the morning. Never. Stuff is still pouring in. We'll have to get paper plates and cups somewhere to serve food. Darn Steve, I told him we needed him, but he's off in his own mysterious way."

"How about me, Mrs. Campbell?" Jed asked.

"Your brother suggested that you could use a pair of willing hands."

She promptly climbed down the ladder and presented him with a big hammer and a banner reading: CIANO PUPPETEERS.

"It's all yours," she said fervently. "The age of chivalry still lives. But when I get my hands on that elusive brother of mine—"

"I saw him a while ago. He was just hanging around the bank. Didn't seem to be busy."

"The wretch!" Julie directed the placing of the banner, handed Jed more signs—BAKED GOODS; HAND-CRAFTS; ANTIQUES; HOMEMADE PRESERVES AND PICKLES —and dashed to the booth where Elinor was arranging scarfs and mittens and babyshawls as light as gossamer.

"I haven't had a chance to tell you—I saw what you've done so far on Merry's portrait. Already you've captured that—special quality of hers. As though all life were a lovely dream and she was wandering through it like Alice in Wonderland. I nearly cried. And Steve said—"

"What did he say?" Elinor asked, trying to sound only casually interested.

"I'll let him tell you himself."

"Oh." Elinor worked in silence. She held up a knitted cap. "Pretty color, isn't it?"

Julie's eyes were on her face. "Very pretty," she agreed. She grinned.

Elinor felt her color deepen. Then she laughed. "By the way," she said with mischief in her voice, "I saw Doctor Dick last night."

"Oh?" It was Julie's turn for studied indifference.

"He's—rather cagey—about women with too much money. Afraid of them. He doesn't have a high income, himself, because he felt he was needed here."

"Oh," Julie said again. "How darned silly! That is, not silly to stay here, of course." She stopped abruptly.

"Very pretty color," Elinor said demurely, and they laughed together.

Late that night, or early next morning, when the lights in the fair building were finally turned off, Clay took Ginny and Elinor home.

"I'm so tired that it doesn't even hurt any more," Ginny said.

"I was numb for an hour or so," Elinor said sleepily, "but unfortunately it wore off and now every muscle aches."

"It will be worse in the morning," Ginny said cheerfully.

"I warn you right now," Elinor yawned, "that I intend to sleep for the next twenty-four hours."

"We have to be up in exactly five hours to get down to the fair." Ginny was merciless.

Clay smiled proudly at his wife's efficient, crisp tone.

"The farm people will be there by eight o'clock," Ginny explained. "I promised to help serve food."

"But, Ginny," Elinor protested, "that's one of the hardest jobs."

"Well, if I leave some other woman free, maybe she'll weaken and buy things. And you're to handle the decorating of the second floor for the country dance tomorrow night. Tonight! Wonderful of Mr. Sewell to provide a dance band."

"Dance!" Elinor groaned. "Any dancing I do will be from a wheelchair. Ouch! I feel like Jenny Wren in the Dickens novel: 'I can't walk because my back is bad and my legs are queer.' "

She yawned again and stumbled upstairs. She fell asleep the moment she got into bed.

XVI

The ladder looked as high as the kind firemen use, and Elinor eyed it warily before she started up, holding on with one hand, the other clutching yellow crepe-paper streamers. Thank heaven, she had decided to wear slacks. She'd never have been able to climb that monster in a skirt.

The fair seemed to have attracted everyone for miles around. If all five days were to draw as large crowds as the first one, plenty of money should be forthcoming for children's beds in the hospital. Around the factory building no parking space could be found for blocks. People had come in sports cars and sedans, in station wagons and in jeeps, in sleek streamlined cars with huge fins and in battered old-timers, in trucks and on bicycles.

Every inch of space on the first floor was thronged with viewers of the exhibits. Business in Hastings had come to a virtual stop for the day. Even on the second floor the sound of voices rose in a muffled roar, like the sea in a storm.

"Hey, need any help?"

The unexpected voice startled Elinor and she nearly lost her balance. Hanging on to the ladder with one hand, she looked down at Sue Martin.

"Hello there, Sue!"

"You certainly look on top of the world, Miss Parks," Sue laughed.

"From here I feel like a space man or as though I

had gone into orbit," Elinor said feelingly. "You startled me so I nearly pitched down on my head."

"I wouldn't. It's a long, long way to the floor."

"I'll say it is."

"My boss sent me over to help. Mrs. Parks says everything is under control downstairs but that you might be able to use me."

"Can I!" Elinor declared. "We're going to need at least fifty yards more of that crepe paper and the hardware store is holding a baby spotlight. Can you get them?"

"Sure. On my way. Be careful, Miss Parks. Look out for that ladder. It seems shaky to me."

"Famous last words," Elinor commented. "A cheerful comment, if I ever heard one."

Sue waved her hand and went out of the big loft room that had been transformed temporarily into a ballroom.

Elinor climbed cautiously to the very top rung of the ladder. She was afraid to look down, the floor seemed so far away. Carefully she reached out to tack a crepe-paper streamer in place, felt the ladder sway, dropped the streamer, clung to the ladder. Choked back a cry of terror.

"Careful, my dearest! Don't move. Don't shift your weight."

She held on to the swaying ladder, eyes tightly shut.

"All right. Come down slowly. Slowly. Hold on with both hands." In spite of Steve's calm voice there was a strained note in it.

She couldn't come down. She couldn't move. The ladder was—no, the ladder was steady now. It was she who was swaying. Dizzy.

"Hold on," Steve said sharply.

The ladder vibrated as he climbed up to her. The ladder was whirling now. The room growing dark. He'd never reach her in time. She was going to release her frenzied grip, pitch headlong down onto the floor. She was . . .

"Steve's hand was on her back, steadying her.

"All right," he said in an easy, conversational tone. "You are all right, Elinor. You understand? *All right.* Perfectly safe. Do you hear me? You can't fall."

She nodded her head. Her jaws were clamped tight together. She could not get out a word.

"Now, you are going to climb down the ladder."

"I—I can't." The words were wrested out of her by sheer terror.

"Oh, yes, you can. You can't possibly fall, you know. I'm right behind you. One step at a time—don't hang on so hard—loosen your grip."

"I—I can't."

"Oh, don't be so childish," he said sharply. "I thought you had more sense. Acting like a baby at your age!"

The words sent a flame of fury through Elinor. A baby, was she? Here she was on the verge of falling into space and he dared to laugh at her. She'd show him.

Step by careful step, she went down the ladder. Steve's arm supporting her, Steve's body like a wall between her and that awful drop, Steve's voice goading her on, mocking at her, talking her down the ladder so that she forgot her fears.

When both feet were on the floor she leaned weakly against the wall.

"That's the second time you've saved my life," she said at last.

His voice was still quiet and conversational, but there was something deadly in it that sent ice through her veins.

"I'd like to kill the man who left that kind of ladder here for women to climb. Sit down, dar—Elinor. I'll finish putting up the decorations for you."

He pushed her into a chair with gentle hands and quickly mounted the ladder. He seemed awfully far away. She couldn't shout what she wanted to say to him. It would have to wait until later, when there wasn't all this distance between them.

For a while he worked quietly, without speaking. It

occurred to Elinor that he was consumed with anger over the carelessness that had so nearly caused a fall that might have killed her; that, at least, would have caused serious injury and crippling.

An hour passed. Two. Except for brief directions from Elinor, brief questions from Steve, no words were exchanged between them. For a while she hoped that he would say something, anything, that would make it easier for her to tell him that she had made a mistake, that she was sorry. Then she realized that he was not going to reopen the subject. Ever.

Did that mean that he no longer loved her? That she had killed his feeling for her when she had hurt him so brutally about his wife? She couldn't bear it.

"Steve!" she called impulsively.

"Yes?"

There were footsteps mounting the stairs. Her opportunity was gone.

Sue came in with her arms filled with packages.

"Sorry to be so slow. There was only one clerk in the hardware store. Everyone else is at the fair. It looks as if the whole world is there. And Mrs. Parks says to ask you can you come down and help for a while. That bunch of early-rising farmers is all ready to eat. At eleven o'clock! She can't handle the mob by herself. You need anything else here? If not, I'll pour the coffee for her."

"No, that's all. Thanks."

"Don't you just love all this excitement?" Sue waved her hand and ran down the stairs, thrilled by the crowds and the noise. "What did you want to ask me, Elinor?" Steve said.

His back was turned to her while he screwed colored lights in place. She couldn't talk to the back of his head.

"I was just wondering about that man you sent out to the Cape Cod cottage this morning."

She had his attention now. He turned to face her, eyes alert. But the look he gave her was impersonal, as though he were hardly aware of her.

"What man?"

"The plumbing and heating man who came to check on the oil furnace."

"I sent no one out there," he said slowly.

"But he knew my name. He knew yours. He said you asked him to make the inspection, that he had been the one who installed the furnace in the first place."

"Tell me about it."

When she had finished, his eyes were shining. At last, she thought, he was aware of her.

He dashed her exultant mood by saying sharply, "Could you describe him?"

"I thought—maybe I'm crazy, Steve, but I thought it was the man who lurked in the woods that night and ran when you turned the light on him."

"Well," Steve said. "Well!"

"You act pleased."

"I couldn't be more pleased," Steve assured her. "Hadn't you better run down now and help your sister-in-law?" He turned back to the colored bulbs. "See you later," he added in a tone that was less a promise than a cool dismissal.

Oh, you will, will you? Elinor stormed to herself. Her heels clicked angrily on the stairs as she went down into the noise and the gaiety and the excitement of the fair.

At half-past nine that night, the rather bleak-looking loft had been transformed into a brightly lighted dance hall. Streamers fluttered. Lights sparkled. On an improvised platform the dance band had begun to play.

The room was thronged with couples dressed for an evening of country dances. Men in blue jeans and bright-colored shirts, girls in cotton dresses. A few of them wore sunbonnets.

"Swing your partners!"

Ginny, in a pink cotton dress, her gold curls shining like a soft mist, eyes sparkling, flashed across the room. Clay set down the rake he had balanced over his shoulders, wiped his hands awkwardly on his blue jeans, bowed like a yokel.

"Lady, kin I have this dance?"

Elinor, in soft blue voile with a dainty lace apron, her dark hair burnished from brushing, her fatigue forgotten, was dancing with Jed. Her eyes roamed over the dancing, laughing couples, seeking for Steve.

There was a stir at the doorway; heads turned; someone smothered a giggle. Mrs. Alice Grant had made her appearance wearing an exotic slack suit of black velvet trousers and a Chinese-red jacket. She looked like an orchid in a kitchen garden, Elinor thought, choking back a laugh.

Jed's step faltered, came to a halt.

"Excuse me, Elinor," he muttered and cut his way through the crowd, drawn, like a magnet to the north, toward the glamorous blonde.

"Well," Harold Brown laughed, "this I never expected to see. Elinor Parks left stranded on a ballroom floor! That guy needs his head examined."

Elinor made no reply. She was staring, dumfounded. Steve and Julie had appeared in the doorway behind Mrs. Grant. Before Jed could reach her, Steve had touched her arm, spoken softly, and she had glided away in his arms. Jed looked after them, mouth open, bewildered.

Harold chuckled as he saw Jed's expression. "That will teach him not to desert the prettiest girl in the room."

"What a crowd," Elinor said, making an effort to be gay, though her head felt like lead. "The whole thing is a tremendous success, isn't it? They cleared more today than they expected to get out of the whole five days. And this dance, at five dollars a person, is going to add hundreds. Doctor Dick will be a happy man."

"I must say, he certainly doesn't look like a happy man to me," Harold grunted.

Elinor saw the doctor dancing with Julie. As Harold had said, he didn't look happy. The deep furrows were back in his forehead. He danced as though he were tired, barely speaking to the vivid woman who moved like a feather in his arms, talking eagerly and vivacious-ly.

The next time they passed, Elinor saw that Doctor Dick's mood had dampened Julie's gaiety. The vivacity was gone from her face. She was as silent as her partner.

Sue Martin was dancing, but Betty was without a partner. Bert was working, of course.

When the dance ended, Elinor was claimed for the next one. She nodded and smiled.

"Harold," she said in a low tone, "ask Betty to dance, will you? I hate to have her miss things."

He smiled at her. "Sure," he said good-humoredly. "Glad to. Anything you say—always."

After the next dance, she found herself beside Clay and Julie.

"Having fun?" she asked.

Julie summoned up a tired smile. "It has been a strenuous week."

Elinor leaned forward, whispered against her cheek. "He's scared of your money. He'll never dare ask you."

Julie managed a gay smile. "If he wasn't like that, I probably wouldn't—like him so much."

"There's always Leap Year," Elinor suggested.

"It's a long time to wait," Julie admitted, "though it's a sound idea."

"What's the secret?" Clay demanded.

Elinor laughed without answering and danced off with her next partner. Harold was dancing with Betty, who revealed on the dance floor the same unexpected grace that distinguished her ice skating. Steve was danc-ing for the third time with Alice Grant. He had not once come near Elinor.

Then Jed, his face hard, touched Steve's shoulder, and moved away with Alice, talking fast. In a moment, Steve cut in on Elinor's partner.

She had looked forward eagerly to dancing with him again; but, though their steps matched as flawlessly as ever, there was no joy in this dance. Steve seemed to be remote, barely conscious that he held her in his arms. She might have been any woman. A total stranger. She sensed a kind of tension in him. His eyes constantly searched the room.

Clay had cut in on Betty now, and in a few moments they began to try out some fancy steps. Clay had always been a superb ballroom dancer but recently he had not been light-hearted enough to bother. Little by little, the dancers moved back, giving them more space, until they were dancing alone, swirling, dipping, swooping, while the room lights dimmed and the spotlight was trained on the two dancers.

In the darkness of the room, Elinor became aware that Julie was beside her.

"Dick had to leave," she whispered, disappointed. "He got an emergency call. I offered to drive him, but he wouldn't hear of it."

"That's the way it would always be," Elinor warned her. "Emergencies. Night calls. Overwork. You would never be able to plan things and be sure that they wouldn't be upset at the last minute."

"I wouldn't care," Julie said passionately. "As long as that was what he wanted. Oh, Elinor, he's so kind and good and—and—"

She looked around in surprise. "Where's Steve? I thought he was dancing with you."

"Why, I don't know. He just slipped away. He's probably looking for that siren again," Elinor said rather tartly.

"She doesn't seem to be here either," Julie said. "You can't miss that black and red velvet outfit. She must have thought this was a fancy dress ball."

There was no sound now but the throb of the music and the tap of the dancing feet. Yes, someone was running down the stairs, the sound clear in the room. Then a movement. The turning spotlight caught a white face. Jed. He turned, thrust his way to the door, ran down the stairs. What was wrong with him? Why had he gone like that? His face had been set and terrible.

The dance ended, the audience burst into applause, Clay and Betty bowed, laughed, bowed again; and the lights went up in the room.

"My dance, I think."

Elinor smiled at an old friend and moved out on the floor.

"That was quite an exhibition dance," he said. "They were both terrific. I've seen Clay dance before, when he was in the mood, but Betty Martin was a surprise to me. Sensational."

Betty was surrounded by would-be partners now, all clamoring for her to dance with them. Julie passed, so did Sue and Ginny and Clay. But the blond woman was gone. And so was Steve Sewell.

Someone cut in on Elinor's partner, who protested, "Hey, we've hardly started."

"Your hard luck, buster."

There was the thin, ominous sound of a siren.

Elinor shivered. "I hate those things. They always mean disaster: fire or ambulance or police. Or—air raids. Hate them!"

"Maybe there is a fire somewhere. Seems to be a lot of confusion." He nodded his head toward an open window. "I was leaning out a while ago, getting some fresh air. Something going on down there."

"I wonder—" Elinor broke off.

Doctor Dick had returned. He stood looking around, frowning.

"That was a short visit," Elinor called.

He shook his head. "I couldn't get through. The roads—all blocked."

As people heard him, they stopped, turned toward the doctor, listening.

"What!"

Doctor Dick nodded. "Hell to pay down there. The bank has been robbed."

The dance ended then and there. The Hastings bank was a part of the village. It was concerned in the lives of almost all the people. On its safety they rested. This was something that mattered to them all, as a public disaster cannot have an individual meaning or application in a large city.

The dancers crowded to retrieve their wraps and hurried down the stairs. Though what good could they possibly do? They would only complicate matters for the authorities.

The authorities! That meant Bert Jackson. Elinor looked around the nearly deserted room, which, only a few minutes before, had been filled with music and laughter. The musicians were packing away their instruments.

Betty, her face pale and controlled, was tugging at Sue's arm.

"We're going straight home," she said firmly.

"No! I don't want to miss the excitement."

"Home," Betty repeated. "I mean it. We'll only be in the way here. Anyhow, if there is any rough stuff I don't want you to get shot. Mother will be frantic as it is. The news is probably on the local radio by now. Come along. This is what Bert would want us to do."

"You and your old Bert. I'm not taking orders from him, even if you are."

"Come along," Betty said in exasperation.

Clay came to where Elinor and Ginny were standing with Julie. He held their coats for them.

"I'll get you girls home."

"Thanks," Julie said, "I'd better wait for Steve. He'll worry if he doesn't find me here."

It was the gravity in Clay's face that stopped Elinor's heart. Set it racing again.

"You'd better go along with us, Mrs. Campbell. I don't think Sewell is likely to come back."

"I'll take Mrs. Campbell home," Doctor Dick said abruptly. "Can't get out of town to see my patient. The roads are blocked off and the fools wouldn't let me through, though I've known them since they were young pups."

Julie nodded mutely and let the doctor lead her down the stairs. His old car was parked near the entrance where he had left it after his abortive attempt to reach his sick patient.

They drove slowly, the doctor's thumb on the horn, forcing the excited crowds to move aside and let them pass.

"Sheep!" he snorted. "Just a bunch of sheep."

He drew a breath of relief as he cleared the mob and moved more quickly toward the center of town. The bank was a blaze of light. Police cars at the curb. Men moving in and out of the building. As the doctor involuntarily slowed down for a view of what was happening, the town constable peremptorily waved him on.

"How on earth could it happen in a peaceful village like this?" Julie asked.

"Peaceful," Doctor Dick said thoughtfully. "There are no peaceful places, Julie. The places where men live are places of strife and violence and aggression and discontent and self-seeking. That's why we have law. To keep society on an even keel, to avoid chaos. Eternal vigilance. That's what it takes. No, my dear, a man or woman has to provide his own peace in his own spirit."

"But can it be done?" she asked, hesitantly.

"Oh, it can be done! If one works hard enough at it." He was silent for a moment. "If one learns not to— want too much."

"To much what, Dick?"

"Too much that is out of reach."

"In that case," Julie said, "perhaps he should learn to extend his reach."

The car slowed down, stopped. He turned to face her. Saw her shining eyes. Saw the message in them.

"Julie?" he said incredulously. His hands tightened on the wheel. "I'm a country practitioner. My annual income wouldn't support the place you live in for two months. I haven't anything to give you."

"Nothing at all?" she said in a small voice.

His hands reached for her. There was tentative hope in his shaken voice. "Julie?" He drew her gently into his arms. "Will you take me as I am?"

A long time later she drew away from him.

"It's late. I should be getting home. There is all the rest of our lives for us to talk in."

He started the car. "Wasn't there," she said vaguely, "some sort of trouble?"

He flung back his head and shouted with joyous laughter. "Nothing important," he said between broken gasps. "Just a bank robbery."

"I'd forgotten," she admitted. Then her voice rose in sharp alarm. "Dick, what happened to Steve? Where is he?"

XVII

Clay had scarcely started the car before he was stopped. He rolled down the window.

"What is it, Trooper?"

Bert Jackson looked at the two girls on the front seat. "When you've taken your wife and sister home, we could use you. There are more men being assigned to Hastings but, meanwhile, we need some one to help us search. They got away, as usual. Five people missing."

"Five!" Elinor exclaimed. "But I thought—that is, I understood—"

"Be with you in ten minutes," Clay promised.

"If you have a revolver, bring it with you."

Clay indicated the glove compartment. "I've been carrying it for a week," he said grimly. "Has there been any shooting?"

It occurred to Elinor that Clay and Bert were saying more than she understood, that there was a current of meaning between them they were not putting into words.

"Yeah. One of them was shot. Don't know how badly, of course. Be seeing you."

Clay nodded. The car shot down the road. They drove in silence to the house.

"Don't worry," he told Ginny as the two girls got out of the car. "You'll hear from me as soon as there is any news."

"You won't be in any danger?" Ginny's voice quavered.

"I won't be in any danger." He bent over to kiss her on the lips.

Ginny stared after him. "I guess I'll go up to bed. I'll connect the telephone in my room. If I hear from Clay I'll let you know. You probably won't be asleep either, until you know."

"No, I won't be asleep."

Elinor waited until Ginny had dragged herself wearily upstairs. Then moving, quietly, she let herself out of the house and the Chevrolet coasted down the driveway. On the road, she started the motor and switched on the lights.

There was no hesitation in her mind as she drove away from Hastings toward the deserted secondary road that led to Steve's three new houses. From the beginning, something had been wrong. In some way she failed to understand, the houses had some connection with the bank robbery. It all fell together, a jigsaw puzzle whose pieces fitted. And the picture they made was a portrait of Steve Sewell, bank robber.

Was it only yesterday that she had felt she had discovered the meaning of suffering because she had hurt Steve Sewell? Now she knew what real suffering was, raw, brutal, agonizing. She was heartsick. All that she had loved proved to be wrong. And the awful thing was that she still loved. She could not help it.

But there was no time for her own pain. Her love did not alter the fact that she was going in search of Steve Sewell. If she found him, she would do her best to persuade him to come back, to face the music, to take his punishment. She had no choice about that.

And if he had been hurt—*one of them was shot*—
she could, at least, see that he had the proper care.

The visibility was terrible. She discovered that she
was blinded by her own tears and brushed them away
angrily.

Something important coming up. (That was
Steve.) *Going his mysterious way.* (That was Julie.)
Hanging around the bank. (That was Jed.)

Those bearer bonds that Harold had mentioned . . . Were they the form in which he had
put away his share of the last robbery?

She turned onto the narrow road. How empty it
was! How still! Along here she had seen the abandoned
car. Along here the man with the heavy shoulders had
lurked. Along here Steve had come and the man had
gone away. Driven away by Elinor's presence.

In a way, she had known then. If she hadn't deliberately blinded herself because of her love for him, she
would have seen clearly that Steve's opportune arrival
could not have been a matter of sheer chance. But then
he had said, "This is a calculated risk," and kissed her,
and everything else had been crowded into the background.

This morning, when the man with the thick shoulders had come to the house, she had had that sense of
recognition, that stirring of memory, that same unrea-
soning fear. And Steve had been pleased, excited by his
visit. It was something he had half expected but had not
quite dared to hope.

What was wrong with the little Cape Cod cottage?
What attracted people to it? This was where Alice Grant
had been the morning Jed took her to see his houses.
This was where Alice Grant had tried to force herself in
a second time and kicked Ho when he attempted to
ward her off.

Alice Grant! In her surprise, Elinor's foot came
off the accelerator, the car slowed down. Alice Grant
and the man she had dined with at the Hastings
Inn . . . the man with the heavy features and the thick
shoulders. . . . *That* was why he had seemed familiar!

Her heart raced—thudded against her side. Her breath came short. The man with the thick shoulders must be the gang leader. And Alice Grant was the woman involved in the robberies. Alice Grant, with her diamonds and her lavish wardrobe, with her hardness and her essential cheapness. So that explained why she had stayed on in the village.

And Steve? Steve the gambler. Had he done it simply for the excitement? Surely he didn't need the money. Or had he done it for Alice herself? He had taken her away from Jed, danced with her again and again, always with that odd air of tension, of repressed excitement.

But Trooper Jackson had said five people were missing. Who were the other two? And Clay—Clay telling Julie that Steve would not be back. Clay being so sure about it, so grave. Was it possible that Clay was on a manhunt for Steve?

Which one had been shot? Her unregenerate heart prayed: Oh, don't let it be Steve!

There was a car ahead of her, pulled off the road. A shining new Chrysler. Elinor put her foot on the brake. There were no lights. No one in the car. She pulled up behind, reached for her flashlight and got out of the convertible.

She approached the car ahead of her cautiously, her knees shaking. All this was like something that had happened before. She looked in. The car was empty. Put her hand on the open window. Drew it back. There was something warm, sticky, on the palm of her hand. Turned on the flashlight. Saw the blood.

She took a long steadying breath and flashed the light inside. A man sprawled across the front seat, his face turned away. Blood trickled down his sleeve and dripped from the hand that rested on the floor.

She was running around the car. Stumbling. Tripping over a stone. The other door. The flashlight illuminated the quiet face. Her voice rose in a scream of surprise, of shock, of horror.

"Jed! Jed!"

She opened the door, fingers numb, slipping on the

handle. Touched his cheek. The skin was warm. He was unconscious but he was breathing. He was still alive.

She ran back to the Chevrolet, locked it, came back to the Chrysler. It seemed to take hours but it was actually minutes before she managed to shift Jed's heavy body away from the wheel, to prop him on the seat as securely as possible.

Thank heaven, the keys were in the car! Whoever had shot Jed had turned off the motor and the lights and left the keys in the new car of which he had been so proud, which he could so ill afford. Jed who acted as though he expected to have money before long. For diamonds? And instead he had been shot.

Why? And why had the keys been left in the car? She switched on the motor and the lights, moved slowly back onto the road, careful not to jolt the unconscious man on the seat beside her. Heard the clink of metal.

She stopped the car and peered down at the floor. There, within reach of Jed's hand, lay a revolver. Not attempted murder, then. Attempted suicide.

Elinor rested her head on her arms on the wheel. Too much had happened. She couldn't endure any more. Then she remembered Jed's wound and straightened up.

She drove carefully along the road, anxious not to disturb him or to make him fall on the floor and increase the bleeding. How badly had he been hurt?

Ahead of her a flashlight moved in an arc. She put her foot on the brake. Another flashlight. Car lights fell on one of the men moving toward her and she sighed in relief. A state trooper.

"Sorry, miss. We're stopping all cars. May I see your registration, please."

"Yes, of course, but don't bother about that now," she said breathlessly. "I've got a seriously wounded man in the car. I must take him to the hospital without a minute's delay. He's bleeding badly."

There was an exclamation. Another trooper came running. The car door was flung open, lights turned on

Jed's white, defenseless face, on the blood beside his hand, on the revolver.

Then the trooper questioned Elinor sharply. Her name and address. Car license. Driving license. The identity of the injured man. Where she had found him.

"All right. We'll let you take him to the hospital." He raised his voice. "Move your car, Fischer. Let the lady through. She'll need an escort, though."

He turned back to Elinor. "First, we'll go back to your car. Double-check. Have you touched anything here?"

She held out her hand, explained that the blood came from the window on which she had rested her hand while she looked in. She had moved Jed, touched the wheel, the emergency brake, the other door.

"The revolver?"

She shook her head,

"All right, come back with me."

She followed him to her car and gave him her keys. He unlocked it, looked in the back seat, searched the trunk.

"How did you happen to be on this road?" he took her aback by asking.

She was unprepared for the question. "I was just looking—" Her voice trailed off. Then she went on with more confidence. "Trooper Jackson asked us to help. My brother took his car and I took this one."

"Any special reason for taking this road?"

"Just a hunch."

He looked at her sharply.

"Have you found—any of the others?" she asked.

"The other what?"

"The bank robbers, of course."

"Oh, we'll get them in time. Were you thinking this guy you found was one of them?"

"I didn't know what to think. He's an old friend of mine. I hoped—but why else did he shoot himself?"

"He didn't put a bullet back of his left shoulder, lady, unless he's double-jointed. Looks to me as though something roused his suspicions and he was following someone when he got stopped—the hard way. The revolver was planted to make us think what you did think. Only—"

"Only you don't think so," Elinor said slowly.

"Well, you see we had an advantage. We know who they are. Makes a difference. Take your friend to the hospital. We'll have a man right behind you, driving your car. We want to go over that Chrysler when you get it there. And then you go home, miss." A grin played around the trooper's mouth. "Trooper Jackson will understand if you don't 'help' any more tonight. We've got it under control."

A magazine slipped from Elinor's lap to the floor and the sound awakened her. She sat upright with a jerk, surprised to realize that she had dozed off. The little waiting room in the hospital was quiet. Behind the desk an elderly woman in uniform sat before the switchboard working on papers. She was not a pretty woman but discipline and compassion had given her a quality of dignity and serenity. The hands of the clock above her moved on with their inexorable slowness. Four o'clock.

When Jed had been carried to the operating room on a stretcher, Elinor had asked permission to stay. Was she a relative? He had no family now, she explained. She was his oldest friend.

She had telephoned Ginny to report and heard the shocked cry of disbelief. She was staying, she said, until she knew Jed was out of danger. Was there—any news?

Nothing yet, Ginny had said.

At two o'clock Elinor had been told that the bullet had been removed. It had missed the lungs. Jed was out of danger. But still she waited. When he regained consciousness he would need someone.

At three, she gave up the pretense of reading the magazine the nurse had brought her and sat staring into space. There was time now for her own personal grief and it engulfed her.

The nurse had looked at her now and then without comment. At length she went out of the room on quiet feet and returned with a cup of scalding black coffee.

"Drink this," she said. "This is the low ebb of the twenty-four hours when courage begins to fail."

At five o'clock a house doctor, young and tired, came into the waiting room. Looked for her. Brightened.

"Are you Miss Elinor Parks?"

"Yes. Yes, I am."

"The patient is conscious and he's asking for you. Better to let him see you for a few minutes. Then we'll put him to sleep. But don't stay long. And don't excite him."

Elinor nodded and followed him out of the waiting room. Once in the white corridor she was assailed by the usual hospital smells and muted sounds.

Hastings had seemed to sleep all night, exhausted by its excitement. But here there was disciplined activity, nurses moving on quiet feet, doors opening and closing. The endless errands of mercy.

The doctor opened a door, looked in, nodded for Elinor to go in, and left her alone.

"Not more than fifteen minutes," he warned her in a low tone.

The room was dark except for a shaded light beside the bed. Jed lay still, his eyes closed, face colorless. The blanket was drawn up to his chin. A faint smell of ether was in the air.

He moved and one hand groped to explore his sore shoulder from which the bullet had been removed. Opened his eyes.

"Elinor?"

She came to kneel beside the bed, took the restless hand in both of hers.

"It's all right, Jed." Her voice was low but clear, infinitely reassuring. "It's all right. You're going to be well in no time."

"Who—shot me?"

She betrayed her surprise. "Don't you know? Didn't you see?"

He shook his head. For a moment, as his eyes closed, she thought he was falling asleep.

"The bank was robbed, wasn't it?" he said abruptly. She nodded.

"Have they—been caught?"

"Not yet. They will be."

"I was trying to—follow them. Then I heard the sirens and saw the lights at the bank. I knew—in a flash. But I was—too late. I—lost them."

"Who were they, Jed?"

"Alice. Alice and Sewell." He moved his head on the pillow, turning his face away from her.

"She ran down the stairs while the lights were out. I saw her take off that red jacket thing she wore and turn it inside out. It was black inside. Pulled a black cap over her pretty blond hair. Something—wrong. And Sewell was right behind her. I—followed."

Her hands tightened over his but she found no words with which to console him for his bitter disillusionment.

"When I saw the lights at the bank," he went on, his voice muffled, "I knew what had happened. All of a sudden, I saw what Alice—really was. A car shot away from the bank, and then a second one. I went—after. I don't know what I thought would happen. Only I didn't want Alice—hurt. She was—I thought she was so sweet, Elinor! The way she smiled at me. Her pretty voice. The things she said. I thought she—liked me. I wanted to be—something big, something important, for her. To have a fine car, and buy her diamonds. To . . ."

He was silent now. Slowly his fingers tightened over hers. "Elinor?"

"Yes."

"I've been—an awful fool."

"So have I, Jed," she said sorrowfully.

"You? Never you, Elinor. So stanch—so loyal."

"So blind," she concluded. To forestall questions she asked hurriedly, "How did you happen to take that road?"

"I followed the two getaway cars. The first one disappeared. At last the second one stopped, so I stopped, too. The other must have got away. I don't—know." He made a bewildered gesture.

"Don't worry about it now, Jed."

"Someone came back to my car. All in black. Elinor, which one of them shot me? Was it Alice or Sewell? I can't bear it if it was Alice."

I can't bear it—Elinor thought—if it was Steve. Which one? Which one?

The doctor opened the door. "Time's up," he said cheerfully.

The sky was light by the time Elinor got home. She let herself in quietly.

"Clay?" Ginny called eagerly from upstairs.

"No, it's Elinor."

Ginny came running downstairs in blue silk pajamas, a narrow blue ribbon tied around her hair. She looked at Elinor and screamed, "What happened to you?"

Looking down, Elinor saw the streaks of blood on her dress from her hand. She explained dully.

"Any word from Clay?"

"Yes," Ginny said, "he called twice. He sounded quite cheerful. Said everything was under control. Not to wait up for him."

"Have they—been caught yet?"

"No."

"Did they steal much?"

"The bank officials aren't sure yet. Still working. But there was a lot of currency that had been dropped down the night slot from the fair. And cash for the supermarket and the factory payrolls tomorrow."

"Have they found the money?"

"The police are still hunting and searching all cars." Ginny looked at Elinor. "I'm going to heat you some milk and put you to bed." She overrode her sister-in-law's protests and brought her the glass of milk. "Drink that. You look like death. How's Jed?"

"He'll—be all right," Elinor said drearily.

A car stopped. A door slammed. A key turned in the lock. Clay came into the hall and saw the two girls.

"Elinor! What happened to you? Are you hurt?" She explained vaguely.

"Jed was hurt?" Clay said explosively.

"He was shot. He's in the hospital. He'll be all right."

"But what was he doing on that road?"

"Following Mrs. Grant—and—" Elinor forced numb lips to frame the words, "Steve Sewell. One of them shot him. Left the revolver and his car keys so it would look like suicide."

Clay's face hardened.

"Any more news about the robbery?" Ginny asked.

Clay leaned back in his chair. "The troopers have a general plan of action. The bank officials are checking their vaults. Everyone is doing an essential job. And what kind of part did I draw? Doing an exhibition dance so the lights would be dimmed."

"You did that on purpose?" Ginny asked in surprise.

"Sure. All timed."

"But why?"

"To allow our playful little friends to slip away from the dance, where they had already established alibis, and make an inconspicuous departure for the bank."

"They were at the dance, then?"

"Well, two of them were," Clay said.

XVIII

When she had bathed and scrubbed the blood from her hands, Elinor tossed her discarded clothing into a hamper and dressed in blue sport skirt and matching silk blouse. She picked up a heavy white sweater and slipped into it. Spring mornings are apt to be raw. In sneakers she crept noiselessly past the room where Clay and Ginny slept deeply after the strain and turmoil of the night.

Once out of doors, cool air, fatigue, and a realization of what she intended to do made her shiver. Her teeth were chattering as she let the convertible coast down to the road. The second time within a few hours that she had made this escape from the house . . . She did not need lights now.

As she drove, she tried to foresee what might lie ahead, to plan her course of action. Last night, she had set off to find Steve Sewell and persuade him to surrender. She had been sidetracked, then, by the unexpected discovery of Jed and the necessity for taking him to the hospital. Now she was going to try again.

The fact that Jed had followed the getaway car to that deserted road, that he had been shot there, convinced her that her hunch had been correct. The Cape Cod cottage was involved in the bank robbery, and Steve had driven there with Alice Grant.

She remembered that the State Police had set up a blockade at the other end of the road. She must be careful to leave her car at some distance from the cottage, to approach it on foot.

How much did the State Police know? "We know

197

who they are," the trooper who had searched her car
had told her. And Clay's exhibition dance had been part
of a preconceived plan. That was why she had been
aware of an unspoken understanding between her brother and Bert Jackson. The police had deliberately lured
the robbers into a trap. And then, after all, they had
managed to escape with the money, as they had done in
the past.

There was an old ramshackle barn some way off
the road. Elinor turned the convertible onto the stubbled
field and jolted across to the barn, parking the car behind it, out of sight of the road.

No one on the road. No cars. No troopers. A bird's
song rose, thin and sweet in the morning air. "Phoebe!
Phoebe! Phoebe!"

She walked briskly down the road, feet light and
firm, heart heavy and unsteady. Surely, Steve would listen to her. He loved her. Or—or he had said that he
loved her. What was there left to believe?

Around a bend in the road she could see the Cape
Cod cottage. Her heart plummeted to her feet. There
was no car in sight. Steve hadn't come here, after all.
She had miscalculated. She stood on the road, staring at
the cottage. And yet she had been so sure she was right.

What was she going to do now? She couldn't stand
here indefinitely. But where was Steve? The roads were
blockaded. His car had to be somewhere. All night long,
the troopers had been searching. People don't just van-
ish.

Against an upper window something moved. A
shadow? A trick of light? Elinor's heart was leaping.
Someone inside. Steve! Perhaps he had hidden his car
as she had hidden hers. Of course, that was what must
have happened.

She looked at the window again but this time nothing moved. More confidently, she went up the driveway
to the house, put her key in the lock, turned it.

When the door had closed behind her, she leaned
against it, looking around. The place looked just as she
had left it, the dainty curtains giving the main room a

live-in air. Nothing had changed. No one could have been here. It was all just—

She moved forward to the window seat in the living room, walking on tiptoe. Looked again. The hammer was gone. She had left it on the window seat so she could finish putting up the hardware in the other rooms on a later day.

She stood motionless, holding her breath, listening. The house was empty. But someone had been there. Someone had taken the hammer.

She lifted her head alertly. What was that? Had something moved in the house? Did a stair creak under someone's weight? If she stood here any longer like a— like a zombie, she told herself angrily, trying to hold panic at bay, she would end by running out of the cottage like a scalded cat and there would be no one to stop Steve.

She took a long steadying breath and started slowly up the stairs to the second floor. There are no ghosts, she told herself. If there's anything—anyone—here, I'd rather meet it face to face.

On the second floor now. Surely that was a creak of floor boards. She turned her head swiftly, opened a bedroom door. Across the room the door of the adjoining bathroom moved slightly. Just the draft, she told herself. Opened a closet door. The bathroom door, next. No one there, of course. Opened the door of the bedroom on the other side.

Was that a shadow in the hall? Was there a rustling sound? Probably a mouse. Not that the thought of a mouse was particularly reassuring, but it was better than the idea of someone stalking through the house on soundless feet, always just ahead of her. She went quickly past the half-open double doors of the huge linen closet on the second floor.

Looked out the hall window. Was that a shadow on the lawn? Someone moving? No, a man had just darted out of sight around the house. Could it be Steve?

A clink of metal, faint and far away. Outside or inside? It sounded as though it came from the basement.

The basement, where the strange plumber had paid his mysterious visit. Elinor wished now that she had the hammer. Who could have taken it? Or even a flashlight. Anything that would serve as a weapon, that would protect her.

Whatever—whoever—was in the basement, she intended to see for herself. It would be Steve. It had to be Steve. She went downstairs to the first floor. The hall closet stood open! It had been shut when she went upstairs. She took a step forward. Looked—

There was someone behind her. She felt rather than heard it. Started to turn, said "Steve!" in a soft cry, and plunged forward on her knees. A blinding flash of light. She fell into darkness.

In the dim light behind the oil furnace in the basement a man shifted his position carefully. "What time is it?" He asked, his voice a bare whisper.

The man in black—slacks, sweater and cap—held up his watch. "After eight."

"We've been here eight mortal hours and it feels like eighty. I begin to think I've lived my whole life here," the other man said in exasperation.

"Quiet! Sounds carry."

The man in black stood motionless, relaxed but alert. There was a timeless sort of patience about him, the other man thought enviously, as though he could keep his vigil, this endless vigil, forever. A man who would never give up. . . . Daring, bold, reckless—but controlled.

"You missed out this time, Sewell. Your gamble isn't going to pay off."

"Yes, it is."

The man in black stiffened, raised his hand in warning. Someone was coming up the driveway, walking quietly. But the ears of the two men were attuned to the country silence. They were alert to the slightest sound.

There was a pause. Nothing happened.

"What's going on?" the first man asked impatiently. Steve shook his head. "Just being careful, I guess."

The first man eased his revolver in his holster and Steve shook his head.

"You aren't going to need that."

"I'm not taking chances. Someone is coming in." The first man was mouthing his words now—not even whispering them.

Steve nodded. Someone had entered the house. Was standing, listening as he was listening. Waiting. But waiting for what? Had anything happened to cause the suspicions of the person for whom he had waited all night?

Someone was coming down the stairs. The two men tensed. No, going up! They exchanged puzzled stares. The plan wasn't working out as they had anticipated.

"I hope Nelson keeps out of sight," the first man whispered. "Might spoil everything."

Steve, straining for every sound, made no reply. So far as he could tell, someone was walking aimlessly from room to room.

"Casing the joint," the first man suggested.

Steve shrugged. No use guessing. They could only wait. And he was prepared to wait.

The steps were coming down again. So quietly. So —there was a loud crash. The two men started. What was that? What had happened?

"Something scared him," the first man said. "Ran for it."

"Can't get away," Steve reminded him.

"But what difference would that make?" the first man moved so the morning light struck him. Bert Jackson. "Without proof," he said bitterly, "without the bank money as evidence, we'd be right where we were before. Sunk! Suspicions aren't enough to take to court."

Steve's hand tightened on the trooper's sleeve. At last the steps were coming down on the basement stairs. The men stood motionless behind the oil furnace. Someone had come into the basement now. Walked briskly toward the electric washing machine. Opened it. Began lifting packages out of it, packing them neatly into a suitbox and a large hatbox. Working quickly, efficiently.

The washing machine was empty now; the two boxes were tied with heavy cord, the cord cunningly concealed by flimsy-looking ribbon. The two boxes were picked up.

"Now!" Trooper Jackson emerged swiftly between the woman and the stairs.

"Going anywhere, Mrs. Grant?" he asked pleasantly.

Elinor woke in darkness, her head hurting intolerably. Her pillow was cold. Hard. Pillow? Her fingers touched the hard floor. Where was she?

She remembered then. Someone in the house. Someone behind her. The vicious blow that had thrown her to her knees, made her strike her head on the wall, knocked her out. The closet door shut behind her.

The closet door! She sat up and realized that the swift movement had made her breathless. There wasn't much air in the closet. The first day she had examined the house she had been impressed by the way it was built, the solid, well-fitting doors, the—

She pressed against the door, found the knob, turned it. Shook it, threw her weight against it. She had been locked in!

She fought back a moment of panic. She must not lose her head. She sat on the floor, bent over, feeling for a crack. The air should be better down here. But the door fitted without a crack.

To die like this! Alone in the dark. Shut out of the sweet, reviving air, forever. Oh, no! No. There must be someone to hear her, someone to set her free. But suppose she shouted for help, banged on the door, and— the person—who had locked her in was still in the house? What would happen to her, then?

There was no sound at all. The place was empty. Empty. And then—somewhere in the cottage a woman screamed. There were shouts from outside, doors slammed, feet pounded. The woman screamed again, and a man cursed loudly and then the woman was yelling in a horrible coarse voice and people were struggling.

There were voices outside the closet door now.

"Got the stuff?"

"Sure."

"See it's safe before you do anything else."

"Gladly. Prefer that to the woman you've got to handle. She's a wildcat."

"Wildcat! I'd rather tackle a panther bare-handed. She bit Jackson's thumb almost to the bone, and kicked Nelson and—here she comes! Be seeing you."

They were coming through the kitchen, dragging something that snarled and threatened. The front door opened. A scuffle. A shout.

"There she goes! Cut her off! Around to the left! Stop or I'll fire."

A shot. Running steps. More voices. Farther away.

Only then did Elinor realize that they were going away, that she was being left alone. She flung herself against the door, hammering on it in a fury.

She beat at the door again, but she wasn't so strong now, the sounds were feeble. It was hard to draw air into her lungs.

A key turned in the lock. The door was flung open on blinding sunlight, on air that was sweet and cool and filled her grateful lungs. Shadowy against the bright light stood a man in black.

"Elinor! Good God! Elinor! You here!" Steve drew her up off the floor and into his arms. Kissed her cheeks, her eyes, her lips. "Elinor? Are you all right?"

Her arms were tight around him. She pressed her face against his shoulder, sobbing.

She moved her head from side to side.

"What is it? What happened? Don't shake so. You're safe now."

Her sobs redoubled.

From outside came the snarling sounds again.

"Don't look," Steve whispered, holding the slim girl close in his arms. "Don't look. It's too ugly. Come away with me now, darling, this minute. Away from all this. I love you so terribly."

"I love you," she said, steadying her voice. As he tipped up her chin she put away his hand, looking deeply into his eyes.

"I love you, Steve. But we can't—just go away. We've got to—"

"Got to what?"

"Go to the police," she said. She freed herself from his arms. "We must go to the police, Steve. There's no choice." She took his hand. "I'll go with you. Now."

They walked in silence to the door. Men were struggling beside a police car, the door slammed and it moved off, siren rising and falling ominously.

Steve's car was behind the garage and he helped her in, drove quietly to the place where the road had been blockaded that night. No, the night before. Time had become meaningless as day had melted into night and night into day.

He turned right.

"Where are you going?" she asked.

"The State Police. That's what you wanted, isn't it?

He parked, helped her out of the car. Elinor, lifting her eyes, saw in bewilderment that he was smiling.

"Come on, my darling," he said. "It's nearly over. They'll ask you a few questions and then you can go home and sleep. Forget all this."

"Ask *me* questions?"

"Of course." The smile broadened. "Or do you make a habit of spending your time in locked closets?"

Before she could gather together her scattered wits, they were inside the building. The room was not small, but it was thronged with people. Troopers in uniform, the president of the bank and several tellers whom she recognized; young, keen-eyed men who were obviously reporters. Photographers.

A big man with thick shoulders. The plumber! He was sitting close to a trooper. He moved and Elinor heard the clink of the handcuffs that bound him to the trooper.

Mrs. Alice Grant in a smart black suit and silver fox cape her tiny hat pushed over one eye, her brassy hair disheveled. On a table a suitcase and a hatbox.

Harold Brown, looking exhausted from the night's strain, a gauze bandage around his head; and, beside him, Doctor Dick, looking grave and worried.

Elinor waited. Now. This was the moment. They would arrest Steve. Bert Jackson, beaming, laughing, was having his hand pumped by other troopers, his picture taken.

A car stopped and two men came in. A trooper walking respectfully behind a tall man with broad shoulders and a military bearing.

The other troopers snapped to attention. The reporters moved forward. Elinor waited, confused. No one seemed to pay any attention to Steve.

"Captain Relnox," one of the reporters called, "as head of the State Police will you permit us to take your picture with Trooper Jackson?"

The captain grinned. "My privilege," he declared. He shook hands with Bert. "A nice job. Very nice thinking and nice planning, Sergeant."

"Sergeant!" Bert said. A grin spread across his face like the Cheshire Cat's. "Wow!" He sobered. "Thank you, sir. But I have to admit that most of the credit goes to Mr. Stephen Sewell here. Without him I'm not sure we'd have caught these birds this time."

Elinor leaned limply against the wall. Without Steve's help!

Steve laughed. "Don't be misled by Jackson's modesty, Captain! My part was very small."

"What exactly was your contribution to these arrests?" the captain asked curiously.

"He made sure that the Hastings bank would be robbed," Jackson explained proudly.

There was a moment's silence and then a shout of amused laughter from the reporters, in which even the bank president joined. Only Harold Brown was not caught up in the contagion of laughter. His closely set eyes shifted to the right, to the left, like a rat in a cage, seeking a way out.

"I figured," Steve said, "that it would be a cinch to catch this gang if we knew which bank they'd tackle next. So I baited a trap for them. Seventy-five thousand dollars in bearer bonds. I knew they couldn't resist it. Then we prepared to close the trap."

"But how did you expect them to find out about the bonds?" the captain asked. He looked questioningly at the president.

"Mr. Sewell was willing to gamble that much money," he said. "After a lot of discussion we accepted."

"How many people knew about this bait?"

"Trooper Jackson, Mr. Sewell, Mr. Clay Parks"— Elinor started—"myself, of course—and . . ." The bank president's eyes were cold as ice. "And Harold Brown."

He leaned forward, his voice contemptuous. "Your friends weren't very grateful, were they, Harold? You open the bank and the vaults for them and then end with a bullet through your scalp."

"It was Harold," Elinor whispered aghast, "Harold —the gang leader?"

Harold did not look at her. He did not look at anyone.

"Oh, no," Trooper Jackson said. "He was just the local guy. The fall guy. This gang always uses the— used," he corrected himself with a triumphant grin, "the same pattern."

"Then . . ." Elinor's eyes traveled to the heavy man shackled to the trooper.

"This is Herbert Calloway," the trooper said. "A strongarm guy, and a gangster. That," he indicated Alice Grant, handcuffed to the trooper named Nelson, "is Mrs. Herbert Calloway. Leader of the gang; brains of the outfit. She's the one who shot poor Jed Gordon. And she shot Harold Brown when she saw he was getting scared, saw he might talk. As he has. And how!"

"I've got to get my patient to bed," Doctor Dick

said quietly. "Criminal or no criminal, Harold is a sick man. He needs my care."

"We've got an ambulance waiting, Doctor Dick." Jackson looked from Alice to Harold. "You're lucky she didn't kill you."

"Lucky!" It was the only word Harold spoke. It was more like a sob. He stumbled out of the barracks, between Doctor Dick and a watchful trooper.

XIX

"Go on," Merry demanded. "Go on, Elinor!"

"Don't talk now. I'm working on your mouth."

"Please finish the story!"

Elinor dragged her mind back from the courtroom in which the preliminary hearings were being held in the Hastings bank robbery case. She had given her testimony briefly, early in the morning. She could still see the defendants: Alice Grant (Mrs. Herbert Calloway), looking defiant; the thick man who was her husband, looking surly; Harold Brown, without the bandage but still pale, deathly pale, looking defeated and frightened and ashamed. She could not bear to watch him.

Jed, in a wheelchair with a watchful nurse beside him, had been there for a short appearance. Then he had been taken back to the hospital. He had sat staring at the woman he had adored, watching her with a kind of baffled surprise. He saw her now as others had seen her all along, and he wondered at himself. But he was cured. Completely cured.

Steve Sewell had arrived just as Elinor was leaving, eager to escape from the place, from the presence of the trapped prisoners. It was the first time she had seen Steve since the morning, two weeks before, when he had brought her home from the barracks. As his name was called, he walked with easy confidence to the witness stand, took the oath and sat down.

Julie had plucked at Elinor's sleeve. "Let's get out of here. Come home with me. Ginny won't be back from New York until the 4:10 train. There's nothing for you to do at home."

Elinor had hesitated and then yielded. After all, it was what she wanted to do.

"Fine. And I can finish Merry's portrait."

She had painted all afternoon, her attention divided between the story she was telling to keep Merry quiet and the scene being played in the courtroom. And under all this was the awareness that she had twice been bitterly unjust to Steve. For untrue reasons she had refused his love when he offered it; she had believed him guilty of theft and dishonor. How could she? How could she? And she had lost him by her own actions. No man as proud as Steve could ever forgive her, ever love her again.

"Go on, Elinor," Merry insisted. "Hum jumped off the truck of the man who stole him, but he's lost and—"

"And who," Elinor went on automatically, her attention in the courtroom—*What was happening there?* —"who was in the little Ford close behind the truck? Guess."

Merry hopped up and down on one foot. "Mr. Blanchard," she squealed.

"Mr. Blanchard. He'd seen the man steal Hum, and he followed all the way. So Hum got in his master's car and was driven home; and—"

"And they all lived happily ever after," Steve said in his deep voice.

Julie was beside him. "Heavens, Elinor, you've been working for hours."

"I've just finished. No, don't look now. Wait until I put on the frame I brought. I think it will be just right."

"All right. But I can hardly wait. Merry, up you go

for your supper. Elinor, we've got guests: Clay and Ginny and Dick. I tried to get Trooper—Sergeant—Jackson and Betty Martin, but they are celebrating their engagement tonight. Ginny brought you a dress if you want to change. I'll show you."

She swept Elinor down a corridor, opened a door. "In here. Bathroom is that door. Oh, hello, Ginny!"

Ginny looked up from the box she was opening on the bed. She lifted out tissue paper, carefully removed a white evening dress, with a full skirt over crinoline, the material so delicate and shimmering it seemed to dissolve at a touch.

She turned, half defiant, half smiling. "I bought it for you in New York. My last extravagance. But, oh, Elinor, it will be a dream on you." She refused to listen to Elinor's stunned thanks. "Got to run. I'll dress in the next room. Planned it this morning with Julie. Clay is dressing at home. He'll pick up Doctor Dick on the way here."

Elinor bathed and dressed, slipped the exquisite gown over her head.

A tap on the door. A smiling maid came in. "Madam thought you might need help."

She drew the dress down carefully, fastened it. Stood back.

"Beautiful," she breathed. "Oh, it's beautiful. And you are beautiful. Like a bride."

Elinor stood before the brilliantly lighted full-length mirror. Burnished dark curls. Larkspur eyes. Mouth warm and red and sweetly curved. Creamy shoulders above a frock like gossamer, slim waist and full skirt.

Julie tapped. Came in. Caught her breath. "Elinor, you—you're exquisite. The loveliest thing I ever saw." She held an ivory box in her hand. "These—will you please wear them tonight?"

Elinor opened the box. "Oh," she said softly.

"My mother's emeralds. They'd be perfect with your dress and coloring."

"Julie, they're magnificent, but so valuable that I'd be terrified for fear I'd lose them."

"Please. You'd give so much pleasure." Julie fastened the necklace and earrings and clasped the bracelet on the slim wrist. Stood back to admire her handiwork. "There!"

She made a laughing curtsy. "Will the princess graciously go downstairs?"

"I'm afraid I'll wake up. Pinch me. . . . Ouch! I'm really awake."

Side by side, they went down the wide flight of stairs and into the library.

"It's just family tonight," Julie explained. "The drawing room is too formal for a family party. It cramps my style."

They had all gathered by the time Elinor went in: Ginny and Clay, Doctor Dick and Steve. The three men looked at the radiant girl in the doorway.

"My God!" Clay exclaimed. "Where did you get those emeralds?"

"You're the most beautiful woman I've ever seen," Doctor Dick told her.

Steve took her hand lightly. Looked deep into her eyes, breathing as though he had been running. He said nothing at all.

During dinner, Julie, supported by Doctor Dick, resolutely kept the conversation away from the robbery and the day's court proceedings. They talked of the fair and of the money that had been raised to supply beds for children.

"But that's not all," Doctor Dick declared. "Do you know what Steve plans to do?"

Julie nodded, smiling.

"What's that?" Clay asked. "That man is capable of anything."

"He's going to endow a children's hospital that not only will provide for all sick children in the whole country but will have a completely equipped laboratory for research in children's diseases."

Clay lifted his glass in tribute. "I knew you were

going to be a fine citizen here. Let mine be the first word of thanks, the first expression of gratitude on behalf of all the people of the community."

"Oh, it's wonderful!" Ginny exclaimed. "But how on earth, Doctor Dick, can you handle any more work?"

He grinned. "I've taken on a permanent assistant."

"A new doctor?"

"Well, I'm planning to take on a young man to handle some of the work for me. But that's not what I meant. A lifetime assistant. Julie has promised to be my wife!"

There were exclamations and congratulations and laughter. Doctor Dick turned adoring eyes on the vivid woman who glowed with happiness. He shook his head.

"I still can't believe my luck."

"Neither can Merry," Julie exclaimed in delight. "She's crazy about Dick. She asked this morning, 'Can we really truly keep him all to ourselves?' I had to explain that we must share him, that other people needed him, too."

After a while, Julie, with her usual grace, turned the conversation away from herself and her future happiness to the children's hospital.

"When will work actually begin on it?" Clay asked.

"As soon as Jed Gordon is able to work again," Steve said, "and according to the report from the doctors, that won't be very long."

"Oh, Steve," Elinor exclaimed radiantly, "you're going to give him another chance! And such a magnificent opportunity."

"He deserves it," Steve said quietly. "He has proved that he can handle responsibility, that he is a competent architect. Right now, with his faith shattered, he needs to know that people believe in him. He's the kind of man who grows with opportunity, who doesn't shirk it. Watch him and see."

"I always believed in Jed," Clay said. "He was a fool about that woman, of course, but that's something that could happen to any young man. But he is honest in his very bones. Always was. People don't change fundamentally."

"But Harold—" Elinor began. And stopped. Julie hadn't wanted the robbery discussed. But it was too late now. Everyone wanted to talk about it, to understand it.

"Harold was never honest," Clay pointed out. "Not from the time he was a little boy. Ask Mrs. Groom. She'll tell you how often Jed and I took the punishment for the cookies he stole, the lies he told. And later—Jed told me yesterday in the hospital. It was Harold who was responsible for the trouble that sent Jed to the reformatory years ago. Jed wouldn't throw the blame on him. He'd never told tales in his life. He thought Harold would come forward and confess, but he never did. Jed took the punishment, but he has loathed and distrusted Harold ever since. At least, the truth about that will come out now. I'll see that it does. Any lingering doubts about Jed's integrity and reliability will be ended forever. Though why people ever doubted him . . . ! There's something about honesty that speaks for itself."

"Not always." Steve was laughing. "I've had a strong suspicion all along—look here, aren't you the man who checked up on my dark past?"

Elinor watched incredulously as color darkened her brother's face.

"Clay! You didn't!"

"Yes, I did," he admitted.

"But why?"

"I'll tell you later," he promised.

"Steve," she exclaimed in distress. "I'm so sorry. I'm really ashamed of Clay."

His lips twitched with amusement. "You needn't be. He had a sound reason. I like him the better for doing it." He raised his glass to Clay.

Men! Were they all crazy? Elinor looked in bewilderment from one smiling man to the other. They seemed to understand each other, to be the best of friends.

"But why?" she repeated.

Steve's smile deepened as he echoed Clay's phrase. "I'll tell you later."

Coffee had been served in the library, cups passed. Then Julie clasped her hands and leaned forward eagerly.

"Now!" she pleaded. "Tell us now. There's so much I don't know and so much I know but don't understand."

"It's Steve's story," Clay said.

"It's really Bert Jackson's story," Steve explained. "You know about his theory. All the bank robberies took place in April. They took place when the bank vaults had a lot of negotiable bonds and payroll money on hand. They were the work of three people, two men and a woman. In each case, the bank was not broken into, the vaults were opened without leaving any marks.

"So far, it seemed obvious that they were all the work of one gang, following the same effective pattern of procedure. In each case, though the roads were blocked, cars searched, trains and buses checked, the robbers got away. And the money got away. Not a trace. And yet so fine a net was drawn that it seemed as though a goldfish could not have slipped through it undetected.

"The one hitch was that the description of the three people differed widely. Jackson went over and over those eyewitness accounts until he saw that, with such superficial differences as hair coloring, dark glasses, etc., one of the men fitted all the descriptions and so did the woman. But the third—once he was short, once tall, once unusually heavy. Basic changes that can't be faked. Different every time. That's when Jackson hit on the idea of a man and woman working together but using a different person each time as an assistant. A local person. Most obviously, someone in the bank. They had to be careful, of course, to select someone who loved money and wasn't too scrupulous.

"Jackson's idea is that they were working on employees in three or four banks in the general vicinity,

prepared to tackle the one that would be the most rewarding. He's a sound man, you know. One of these
days he'll be among the top men in his entire field."

"More coffee?" Julie asked.

They shook their heads, watching Steve breathlessly. He got up and walked to the fieplace, looked
down for a moment into the empty grate—it was too
warm for a fire—and leaned against the mantel.

"Jackson believed that the money was not taken
out of the community at the time of the robbery. One
person left it. A second retrieved it. He hit on the idea
of empty houses.

"Well, the time approached for another big *coup*.
One person appeared on the scene who was out of place.
Mrs. Alice Grant, a wealthy widow, who put up at the
Hastings Inn for no obvious reason. A very queer operator, Mrs. Grant. Because, while she was ostensibly making a big play for Jed Gordon, she was seen on several
occasions talking in a furtive way to Harold Brown from
the bank. Yet Brown claimed that he did not know her.
They met at the factory building I later bought for the
fair and to establish a small industry."

Elinor's sudden exclamation made them look at her
in surprise.

"Oh," she said, enlightened. "That note I found
about an appointment 'at the usual place.' She must
have dropped it for Harold; I picked it up and he never
saw it. That's why she was so angry the next day."

She explained what had happened.

"But why," Clay asked, puzzled, "didn't you ever
mention it?"

"Well—" Color burned in Elinor's cheeks. "Steve
and Julie took the same table after Mrs. Grant—Calloway—left, and Steve was fumbling in his pockets as
though he'd lost something, and I—"

Steve shouted with laughter. "I'd forgotten my wal-
let," he explained, "and it just dawned on me I'd been
driving without any license. Left it at home." He looked
at Elinor with dancing eyes and shook his head at her.

"My, my. What a wild past you must have credited me with."

Julie looked at Elinor's scarlet face. "Go on," she insisted, trying to distract attention from the embarrassed girl, "tell us the rest."

"Well, here was someone who didn't belong in the Hastings picture at all. So Jackson began backtracking. The safety of these people rested on the fact that no one suspected them. He got a maid at the inn to look at the label in that mink coat and traced it. Sold it to Mrs. Herbert Calloway of Brookland, Connecticut."

"Speaking about that mink coat," Clay put in, suddenly—"Harold spilled all he knew about that. Mrs. Calloway went out to the Cape Cod cottage to find the right spot for the money to be cached, and Ho jumped her. She was wild with anger. Like a fool, in her desire to make money out of the trouble, she called attention to herself and tried to start a lawsuit. That is why Harold gave her that blow on the face that marked her. He was scared silly that she would do just what she did—make people wonder about her, attract attention."

"So it was Harold who struck her," Ginny said. She shivered.

"Well, Calloway," Steve went on, "was said to be an invalid. No one ever saw him. Kept completely out of sight. Mrs. Calloway was a red-headed woman whom people rarely saw. Those two certainly didn't want to attract attention to themselves. But a picture of Mrs. Grant was identified in Brookland as that of Mrs. Calloway.

"Every year the Calloways went away for the months of March and April, while he was supposed to get special treatments somewhere.

"Jackson was pretty sure that Alice Grant was Alice Calloway. He figured Harold Brown was the guy she planned to use to open the bank and the vaults—if they decided on the Hastings bank for their next big operation. But still no trace of Calloway himself. Then a strange man cropped up near one of my houses and frightened Elinor.

"It looked like the old pattern. But was the strange man Calloway or someone who had nothing to do with the robberies? No one knew what Calloway looked like.

"The worst problem, of course, was that the next robbery might take place anywhere. That's why I came up with the idea of depositing bearer bonds in the Hastings bank. Bait for the trap. We talked the bank president into it, made our arrangements, and then figured the obvious time would be during the fair, when the whole town would be milling around, and that the night of the dance would be a natural."

"That," Ginny exclaimed, "is why you provided a dance band."

Steve grinned. "I wanted to make it nice and easy for them. Clay arranged to do that exhibition dance, and we had the roads blocked, the bank was staked out— and we were all set.

"As soon as the lights dimmed, I saw Harold slip away and then Mrs. Calloway. I was right behind her, though she didn't see me. Poor Jed was at our heels, because he was jealous.

"We watched the whole thing. Harold and the man Calloway entered the bank with Mrs. Calloway. Calloway had some big shopping bags to carry the loot away in. They looked harmless enough. Mrs. Calloway shot Harold, and they got out. Moved like lightning. The whole thing took only a matter of minutes.

"Calloway threw the shopping bags into the back of a truck with the sign of some heating and plumbing concern on the side, and set off for my Cape Cod cottage. He left the stuff in the electric washing machine, and left town in the truck. No evidence on him to show he had anything to do with the robbery. He was one surprised hombre when he was picked up. Very indignant and virtuous. Demanded a lawyer. Said he was innocent. But they hauled him over to the barracks.

"Mrs. Calloway gave him time to get started and then followed him in another car, to make sure he was in the clear and had not been trailed. I was curled up in the trunk of her car. And behind the procession came poor Jed. By that time, of course, the alarm was out, the bank lighted up like New Years's Eve, and Jed knew the score.

"Well, Mrs. Calloway spotted Jed, of course. Pulled off the road. Went back and shot him. I was helpless.

"Then she drove to the cottage, saw the truck pull away and knew that everything was clear, and she went straight back to the inn. She sailed calmly in and went up to her room as though she had just returned from the dance.

"I went back to the cottage with Bert Jackson. We had Trooper Nelson upstairs and two more men outside. And then, just before Alice came in the morning, with that suitbox and hatbox, so she could go calmly back to the inn as though she had been shopping—what a smooth operation the whole thing was! No wonder they got away with it, time after time!"

"Don't digress," Julie said. "Keep talking."

Steve laughed. "Well, just at this exciting moment, what should happen but Elinor turned up at the cottage and nearly succeeded in getting herself killed."

"What were you doing there?" Ginny demanded. "I never understood it."

"I—" Elinor fell silent.

"She thought I was in on the robbery," Steve said smoothly. "She came to persuade me to see the error of my ways and turn myself in."

A gasp was followed by silence as the others looked at Elinor and she looked at the hands clasped on her lap.

"Well," Steve concluded, "Mrs. Calloway came to collect the loot, and we caught her with it in her possession, so everything was lovely. Harold talked, and the three of them are going out of circulation for a good long time. End of the chapter."

Ginny got up with a sigh. "It's the most excitement we've ever had it Hastings. But I'm glad it's over. Clay?"

"Yes, we must be getting home. Ready, Elinor? Doctor Dick?"

"I'll drive Elinor home," Steve said.

"Elinor," Julie suggested quickly, before she could protest, "why don't you give Steve that portrait of Merry now? Tomorrow is his birthday."

Elinor led the way up to Julie's sitting room and threw the light on the canvas. Steve looked at it for a long time.

"A child in Wonderland," he said at last. "I will always treasure this."

"Steve, can you forgive Clay and me? Neither of us trusted you enough. I didn't know that he had checked on you. Why did he?"

"I suspect," Steve said, his eyes intent on hers, "because a blind man could tell at a hundred yards that I was deeply in love with you, and he wanted to know just what kind of guy I was."

"You mean—you still love me?" she said huskily. "Even after I thought—"

His hands were on her shoulders, drawing her toward him. "I love you more than I can possibly say. Once before I tried to tell you. That time you wouldn't listen."

"Oh!" she cried, and he saw that one of the emerald earrings had caught on his sleeve. He detached it gently. "Julie's emeralds. Suppose I had lost them."

"Not Julie's. Our mother's. Julie has the diamonds. She turned the emeralds over to me today—for my wife. These have been waiting for you for such a long time, Elinor."

She was silent.

His hands dropped. "I'll get your coat," he said courteously, "and thank you again for the portrait. It's a magnificent present."

Her hands groped for him, caught at his coat. Her face was flushed, half-laughing, half-crying.

"But, Steve, that's Julie's present to you! Not mine. Mine is—"

She was in his arms now.

"Yourself?" he asked, his mouth against the soft dark curls.

"All myself. Oh, Steve, I do love you so much! All the time, I've loved you."

This time there was no doubt. Her lips, warm and ardent, answered his kiss.

He crushed her to him. "I feel as though I'd waited forever for you."

"We've got forever," she said. It was a promise.